Devices Of Man

S.M Fox

S.M Fox

Contents

Chapter 1

CHERRY BLOSSOMS DANCED IN the frozen slurries outside their window. Pulled in one direction to another as if by an invisible dance partner to a silent song. Tugged upward by the winds only to fall like stones. Petals rarely fell so much as they drifted. It must have been a precursor to the Ghost King's arrival. Minor gusts of his blight had been drifting into the village all morning, warning the villagers to prepare for the evening.

Throwing on her shawl, Kate stepped outside the door. Tiny flowers and solitaire snowflakes blurred around her and tangled in her black hair like adornments she sometimes saw the other village girls wearing.

Kate reached upward and grasped a handful of velvety petals. They did not crush in her hand, remaining sharp and defiant. Like blades, they left tiny cuts in her hand. So sharp she felt nothing but the sting of cold air. When she opened her fist, the blood-stained shards blew away.

There were new voices, harsh and peculiar, and they diverted her interest. Across the dirt street, between the blacksmith and the grocery, were a trio of riders with brown and gray horses with woolly feet. They were not like the working horses Jasper had. These horses were for riding, not pulling a plow. Their legs were long and lean, and their coats were sleek and glossed in the sunlight.

Staggering back from the strangers, Kate steadied her breath. Their thick coats were not uniform, but they were heavily armored with swords strapped to their belts. The strangers were not soldiers but something else entirely.

Warm hands stabilized her shoulders. "They're mercenaries," Baxter explained. "Either looking for a criminal from their lands or…"

The Ghost King.

Silver and fame were enough to feed a family or drink for the rest of their days. But if they killed the beast, she would never get the chance to study him. If the mercs got their way, her province would be defenseless and ripe for invasion. An unpicked Lemonberry bush or the first cinnamon sip of mulled wine in the peak of winter.

If they killed the Ghost King, her home would be a battleground for distant kings, and everyone would suffer the way she had once suffered. Loved ones would be lost. Famine and illness would spread across the lands as more people took up residence.

She struggled to remember much of the village she once knew, but what she did recall was that it was big. There were beggars on the dirt roads and too many unfamiliar faces.

"I hope he makes an example out of them."

Tearing away from the safety of her father's arms, Kate stormed into the shop. Her shawl fell from her shoulders, and she shook off the biting cold. Less than five minutes outside and her nose and ears were burning cold.

"Kate," Frank said softly.

Whatever he was about to say, she didn't want to hear it. The worktable was a massive pine table in the middle of the shop, and it resembled a war zone. Headless toy soldiers with appendages strewn about. To Kate and her parents, these were merely toys, but to the distant king of Sundersong, they were tools of war.

Grabbing a soldier, she jammed his arm into the socket too hard, and in doing so, the arm broke from the ball joint. Closing her eyes, Kate inhaled and exhaled.

Anger is a useless emotion. There is no purpose or reason for it other than to ruin what should be a wonderful day.

"We understand why you're upset," Baxter said, holding Frank's hand.

So, it was to be a combined effort?

"What your father is trying to say is that for all we know, it could have been an accident."

Kate threw the toy down and choked on a sob before running upstairs to her bedroom. There she sat at her writing desk and cried for no other reason than sheer rage and frustration. She cried so much that her sleeves were damp and smelled of salt.

Her fathers were right. For all they knew, someone's hearth burned out of control in the night, and somehow, everyone was unable to flee their homes. Wiping the snot from her face, Kate savored the bitter sarcasm of her thoughts.

Yes. Everyone just screamed in agony, thinking the flames were simply nightmares. Her mother's fingernails...

Opening her hand, Kate counted all the little cuts as thin as spider silk. She flexed and watched red seams glisten in the light, now icy white with cold.

From her window, she heard the mercs talking to the grocer. They must have bought provisions from him.

"Once that abomination is gone, your people will finally be able to join the rest of the continent. Dominion has held this province in his grip for far too long."

Kate scoffed. If their home was so bad, why was everyone so desperate to claim it?

Theirs was the province of the longest river and the tallest wheat. The greenest pastures and the fullest orchards. Their people were the wealthiest, for they did not pay taxes, but they were the most humble and honest. Was it so wrong to live a life unruled?

So what if they did not have cobbled roads and tall buildings like in Flosses or Taus? According to their beliefs, the people of her province were living in the way the Waters wanted. Simple agricultural industry and little invention apart from toy soldiers for murderous kings. There was no need for mercenaries in a nameless village.

They did not belong here.

The strain in her chest threatened to crack her ribs. Kate stretched and inhaled several steady breaths. A scientist who cannot control their emotions is not much of a scientist. Her fathers were right. She could not hate everyone who disagreed with her. Those men probably had families of their own. While her heart did not agree with their trespassing, her mind understood there was never a reason to hate.

She stood, shaking off the tension. Crying was not something she wanted to be seen doing, but the euphoric relief afterward always made her feel better. A lot was happening, and anxiety had been running amok downstairs all week. The bloods in her mind were clearly at work for all the emotions she had been experiencing.

The frustration in the little shop had reached critical mass. Her turmoil was also her fathers' as they battled over the great worktable, trying to find a solution. With nowhere to escape, the tension had seeped from the wide gaps in the attic floorboards. Strain and labor accumulated in Kate's room like a toxic gas. She pressed her lips together to keep from laughing, but her smirk went unchecked.

If the inventor's block was flammable, a single spark would have blown her tiny village into oblivion.

Kate sighed as she pressed her thumbs into the worn book. If the petals were any indication, the Ghost King would come that night. This was her chance to see him and complete the theory that would all but assure her entrance into the university in Taus.

The key indicators... Would they reveal themselves in his garb or manor? Her research in the library and the surveying of the ruins gave her only hints. Expositions stretched thin over scraps of clothing and architecture of unknown origin. Anything of real value was locked away in the university, all except for the Ghost King, of course.

If she could just prove her theory correct...

"You know that won't work!" Frank's voice rose from the shop below.

This would no doubt send Baxter into a huff. By her estimate, it would be five minutes before her parents marched outside and argued by the woodshed, where they assumed she could not hear. She could. But all families had their secrets.

As funny as it was, the tug of sympathy prompted Kate to place her bookmarker. Her theory would have to wait.

If she couldn't help, at the very least, she could open a window.

Creaks and groans from the stairs sounded Kate's descent. Her fathers froze on opposing sides of the worktable in positions that confirmed her timing was precise. A war would have broken out between them had she delayed a moment.

"Hi, Lemonberry," Frank said, his voice straining with pleasantries.

Folding her arms over her book, Kate regarded the state of the shop.

The workbench centered in the room had a legion of half-composed toy soldiers, their arms and legs strewn about. A decapitated head stared at her with unblinking eyes. The sink and oven that served as a kitchen were laden with pots and pans and burned porridge that had congealed on the cast-iron stovetop.

Her fathers lowered their heads in unison. "It's the arms," Baxter relented. "We can't get a proper fitting over the ball joint."

No matter how small their troubles were, they always tried to shield her from them. It had been years since she wore ribbons in her hair and stuffed her pockets with odds and ends she found in the forest, but they were still her fathers. Kate's eyes watered, and not from the odor of the two men working diligently through the night. Every child deserved parents like these. She was so fortunate they had found her when they did.

"Let's see what we have," she said, moving to her own small workstation by the window. She placed her book on the tidy surface—the last safe place for a book in the shop—and pulled on her leather apron.

The heat from the oven had risen in her attic bedroom, and yet Kate bristled with an unusual chill for a spring morning. Smoothing the goose bumps that prickled on her arms, she approached the battle-worn workbench and assessed the situation.

"The problem is that we're using wood," Frank said. "The arm joints can't pop in because the material is too rigid, but if we make them smaller, we will need something to keep the joints from falling out."

Baxter's red cheeks jiggled as he shook his head. "If we had used a pivot joint—"

"We don't have enough time to make thousands of pivot joints!" Frank's glasses had slid down his long, crooked nose and were threatening to end it all on the workbench.

Baxter threw his arms up and stepped away from the table, signaling his defeat. Sweat had stained his tunic in large wet spots under his arms and along his chest. Even in summer, her papa always wore long sleeves, but on this morning, it was a logical choice.

Kate winced. The truth of their desperation was apparent in the dwindling pantry and their threadbare clothes. They needed the commission. It kept them up at night and stole their sleep. They should have shared their burden with her.

It hurt her heart to see them so distressed. She resisted the tinges of anger that threatened to take hold. There was no one to be angry at. Kate supposed it was a reaction to an intangible threat. It was a desire to protect her parents in the same way they had always protected her. Anger was such a useless emotion.

Both parents were correct.

The commission was for eight hundred toy soldiers. That would be sixteen hundred pivot joints too small for Frank's failing eyesight. Baxter had his reasons for not wanting to go that route. The ball joints were an appropriate size. However, they would need to be capped.

Instead of studying for the landmark return of the Ghost King, the most exciting thing to happen in her village, and the bane of all scientific reason, Kate was attempting to fix toys. Only they couldn't be called toys to the envoys' faces; they were war tools for a mighty empire! Even in her mind, she mocked the voice of the distant king's envoy.

If the soldiers were merely placeholders on a map, why did they need posable arms? The only reason she could merit was the need to be a colossal waste of their time.

That was why there would never be a king in her nameless province. Not a living, breathing one, at least.

Clutching an armless soldier in her hand, Kate stared at it with disgust. How many people would die on the continent because of these toys? War was a distant thing for them. The Ghost King and his blight had a way of deterring invasions, but she had a taste of war as a child, and it was enough for a thousand lifetimes.

Her eyes stayed fixed on the vacant stare of the mindless soldier, but her mind traveled elsewhere. Echoes of agonized screams came from the toy. Hundreds of people crying out all at once. Frantic and pain-stricken. Her throat dried and ached, and for a moment, she feared the smoke from that day was still trapped somewhere inside.

"Kate?"

Jarred from the memory, she shook her head and looked up. Her fathers stared at her. If she didn't answer soon, Frank would begin fussing.

"You have plenty of wood scraps," she said, placing the toy on the workbench.

She grabbed the nearest parchment and pencil and drew out a sketch. Two C-shaped doors over the socket would be quick and effective. It would utilize the scraps that currently littered the floor.

"These should be easier to carve, and you can simply glue them in place."

Her fathers' stunned expressions indicated success, but to meet the deadline, Kate would need to set her books aside for the time being.

The three of them created a manufacturing chain. While Frank worked the wood, Kate painted, and Baxter assembled.

"How has the studying been going?" Frank asked.

Kate eyed Baxter, carefully gauging his expression as she spoke. "In all the history on Paradise Lost, I see no mention of the Ghost King."

"So, he didn't exist in that fallen civilization?"

"Precisely," she said, dotting another set of eyes on a toy soldier. "They were an advanced civilization. It's possible they created him."

Baxter's cheeks were so red they were reaching a purplish hue. "He's not immortal; he's dead. More monster than man."

"Monsters do not keep entire provinces safe from invasions," Kate reminded him. "He uses strategy and reason. If I can prove that he is a result of some experiment from Paradise Lost, just imagine the renewed interest. We could learn so much from our past if only people would care to look."

Frank pushed up his glasses, then resumed his carvings. "It's not that people are disinterested. They're afraid."

Dad spoke the truth. People feared the heights achieved in Paradise Lost because men in robes told them to. Without a factual reason for the civilization's decline, myth and superstition took its place. Resentment settled in her belly and snuffed out any interest in the watery porridge awaiting in a rust-speckled pot.

By late afternoon, the workbench no longer resembled a war zone. Soldiers were lined up in neat formations in rows of five. Despite their symbolism, the progress and the orderly appearance were pleasing. It was so satisfying when a project came together.

"Baxter, be a dear and stack the wood by the fire," Frank said as he carved the last of the joint caps.

Kate had just finished painting all the parts and was washing the paintbrushes in the sink. She was about to hang up her apron and put on a heavier shawl. Her breath made faint clouds in the air, and her fingers ached with cold. Was it time?

Excitement raced in her veins, keeping her chilled blood warm. Papa was a man of few words to begin with, but he said nothing when he began stacking the wood. Soon, he had piled so much wood that it towered over the oven.

Pretending to read her books on Paradise Lost, Kate watched with fascination as Papa built a second stack of wood. Did they truly need so much? Her fathers had experienced the Ghost King's visits several times. Kate did not doubt their precautions, but she was drowning on the inside with excitement.

Was the Ghost King a remnant of Paradise Lost? She had studied every book she could find on the lost civilization. Her own people were born from the remains of their existence but had yet to live up to their full potential. How did they make aqueducts that manipulated the flow of water or cut a child from a womb without killing the mother?

These innovative, lifesaving technologies were not entirely out of reach. Rather than educate others, the university locked away such knowledge from anyone they deemed unworthy. Countless forms were returned in the mail, all for one reason or another.

Her village didn't have a name, so she needed to fill out an additional form. The lack of formal education meant that Kate had to take a series of tests, but the expense of traveling back and forth from one side of the continent to the other made it impossible. Had she been under the age of sixteen, they would have permitted her as a student, but she wasn't. So, based on undue hardship, the university would only allow her admittance based on a strong, working theory.

While lost in her thoughts, Frank was making his own observations. "He…may not be what you expect."

"I just need to see him," she said. "Once I study his clothing and any other factual information, I can compare it to what we know of Paradise Lost and send my findings to Taus."

"There's a reason people fear him, why they fear the past."

A chill strummed up her spine. She noted the third stack of wood, fully grown. It was more wood than they used all spring for just one brief encounter. Already the ice fractures glimmered in the corners of their windows.

It occurred to Kate that she had never seen Baxter afraid of anything before. Sure, he fretted and blustered. It was his favorite pastime. This was different. Her papa was not the sort of man who frantically paced around the room, securing locks on the barred windows. As a sailor from Flosses, Baxter had fought high seas and even fish with teeth. If he was this nervous, the Ghost King must have been a terror to behold. His worries were becoming her worries. Anxiety was a contagion.

"The bars on the windows were never for robbers, were they?"

Frank shook his head and got up to make some thistle tea.

A low feeling sunk into her gut. In all the excitement of something new, of things she thought she wanted, Kate was oblivious to the reality the people in her village faced. There were no wars nor acolytes preaching the atrocities of Dominion in the shadow of the Ghost King's castle.

But perhaps that was because he was something far more dangerous.

"What do the acolytes think he is?" Kate asked.

Not turning from his kettle, Frank said, "You know we don't care about what they think."

It was a scabby wound she rubbed at, but she wanted all the current theories. "I'm not saying I agree with them, but how can I disprove a myth with science if I don't know the myth?"

She must have phrased her query appropriately. Dad sighed and joined her at her worktable. His suspenders drooped on his thin frame as he sat. "You know they worship the Waters, the essence of life as we know it."

Kate straightened in her chair, nodding.

"And Dominion is the source of evil in the world."

She knew this already. "Born from the devices of man."

"Okay, so, someone once said the Waters would bring about a messiah and a new dawn would rise. Dominion supposedly responded to this prophecy by making an anti-messiah, if you will."

Kate had read many things in her lifetime. Snake venom might have the potential to stave off hypothermia, and some species of bugs burrow into the skulls of the dead and use the carcasses as puppets. She had found sweet berries in the summer and could pinpoint the precise hour at which the cherry blossoms would fall...but she had heard nothing so stupid in her life.

"These are the same people that want to make it illegal for you and Papa to be married?"

Frank's face scrunched into a grimace. "And the ones who propose we throw water into the sea to make the ocean crossable."

Water did not make it possible to cross the oceans. Large boats like the ones depicted in the books did. But people feared inventions and lacked the know-how to make them. Kate shook her head and massaged the bridge of her nose.

Her father laughed and said, "Yeah, religion has that effect on us too. That's why we love this village so much."

Indeed. Subscribing to a myth would likely mean foregoing questions and simply accepting what couldn't be understood. She didn't think it was in her nature to yield so blindly. Imagine merely accepting the season's change or why the fuzzy bees could fly, yet chickens couldn't. It would make life much easier but far more boring.

"Move!" Baxter barked.

Forced from their spot, Kate and Frank watched as Baxter pulled on the iron bars along the windows. "They're as secure as the day I first installed them."

"But he's never attacked anyone unless they attack his people."

"That doesn't mean he won't change his mind."

Papa said he was a monster, but monsters didn't ride on horses or make calculated circles around villages to protect the inhabitants from the blight. Kate suspected Papa's reaction to the Ghost King was more akin to throwing water into the ocean than sound logic.

"We still have a few more hours of daylight," Frank said. "The soldiers are dry. We should finish them."

Working would take their minds off the coming events.

They glued and assembled the soldiers. Kate noted how cold and hard they were in her hands. As if their hearts were born hard and frozen in order to complete their missions. They were not the soldiers that burned down her village; these were just a rich king's toys. Perhaps he would be pleased enough with the miniature army that he'd forget warring with other kings and keep his men in the fields where they belonged.

As if he were unhappy with the first count, Baxter counted a second time. Papa was always the numbers guy. He could see measurements in his head and draft blueprints with a precision she could only hope to achieve after multiple rewrites.

Dad set a steaming hot cup of tea before her. Its muted, green scent hinted at flavor but would leave her tongue disappointed. Thistle tea was not her favorite. It was so bland and weak. Though it grew in abundance around the village and was better than drinking plain hot water. Sometimes in the summer, they would have slices of orange. When the peels dried, they made for a citrusy tea. Frank's tea creations never lasted through the fall, and by winter, they were back to the tried-and-true thistle tea until late spring.

Shortly after she managed that last gulp, a fog tumbled through the street like a lost herd of sheep in an unknown pasture. The sun hadn't set, but the sky was a gloomy shade of gray. Her breath caught in her throat. Fragments of ice were crystalline along the edges of the window. The noise from Baxter's throat signaled disapproval, but why? She rushed to the window and gasped with delight. The iron bars were frigid to the touch, as if they consumed the cold.

It was beautiful! The windows sparkled like the crystal punch bowl she saw sitting in a shop window in Flosses.

Her fathers paled and backed away from the window. It was as if they feared the cold. She understood the blight was dangerous, but iced windows and frozen pink petals were hardly things two grown men should panic over.

Kate secretly wondered if there was any real danger or if it was like the time Baxter came home drunk screaming about the wereshrew. Sometimes monsters grew in the absence of men. It had been so long since anyone had seen the Ghost King; perhaps they made him bigger in his absence?

Somewhere in her musings, Kate was only somewhat aware that the ice had grown entirely over the windows. She frowned and peered out the window to find the distorted village had closed. Her neighbors had shut their drapes tight, and she watched as one neighbor herded their chickens into the house instead of the coop. That would be a mess by morning.

Her parents were now huddled in the corner by the oven. This wasn't the wereshrew-type panic. They were seriously scared. About that time, the temperature bottomed out. Even in the coldest of winters, she had never felt such a chill. It was seeping into her bones, and her sinuses threatened to buckle from the sudden change in the air.

Baxter's bushy eyebrow furrowed as he resigned. "It's time."

Chapter 2

THE STREETS WERE VOID of life, as if instinct had driven all mortals to their homes. With the setting sun, their village had transformed into an eerie sight. Vacant streets without use and shuttered windows. The worn buildings took on a morbid appearance suggesting decay and ruin rather than lived-in and supported. This instilled a premonition of sorts. Of what their home could become should things change.

A breath of viscous fog splashed against the wooden homes of their village. When the tides were pulled back by unseen forces, heavy ice remained where the fog had touched.

So, this was the Ghost King's blight. Anyone caught in it was said to perish within minutes, but according to Kate's survey, no one in the village had ever seen it happen.

Jasper's father said he once saw the bodies of an enemy province frozen in place, but the farmer only assumed it was the Ghost King's doing. Roy claimed he helped pile the frozen corpses into a cart before returning them to their province. Some soldiers thought to claim the precious wheat mills for their own, only to meet a grisly demise.

One of the few towns in their province that was named, but she forgot to write it down. Somewhere on the border. Only lands with kings had names, but there were a few exceptions. The largest producer of wheat and grain needed a name for the sake of commerce.

Roy's tale was a harrowing one. An army from another province had invaded. He worked there for a brief period when his father, the old farmer outside town, had kicked him out. When the ice and fog rolled in, the villagers knew what it meant, and they fled to their homes. The next morning, the workers left their homes and found the soldiers frozen solid.

But no one had actually seen the blight kill a person. For all they knew, it could have been a natural phenomenon. The fog was so thick, she doubted anyone could walk in it. It could have been superstition or propaganda delivered by their merc acquaintances. Any number of things could have contributed to the legend. Impressive as the display outside was, she wasn't quite convinced.

"It's freezing," Frank said, shivering from under the wool blankets. "Do you remember it being this cold last time?"

Baxter only stared at his partner. Attempting to make light of the situation was an indignation the gruff old man would not suffer while cowering in a corner with a blanket over his head like a hood.

Kate suppressed a giggle and returned her gaze to the window. She focused on the lantern hanging on the doctor's porch across the dirt-paved street. It swung ever so slightly. Back and forth. Back and forth.

The urge to scream was sudden and overwhelming. Why was he taking so long?

Closing her eyes, Kate allowed herself to hear past what her eyes would allow. In the distance, there was a soft clopping sound. A horse was approaching.

Journal and lead pencil in hand, she sat atop her worktable with her face pressed to the iced window.

"Are you sure you don't want another blanket?" Frank called.

She had bundled herself up in two of them already and was still shivering. She doubted a third would do the trick. The fire from the oven was as hot as Papa could make it, but it only kept the shop from freezing over, just barely.

The hoofbeats grew louder, and so did the beating of her heart.

His horse had shoes?

She could tell by the metallic twang when they hit the occasional rock. Why would a ghost horse need shoes? She scrawled the question with a shaky hand. Questions for later. There was indeed a rider in the fog. How, she couldn't say, but it did indeed appear that a man was behind the blight.

A large plume of fog the size of a carriage was coming their way. It swirled with grays and ashy whites. One by one, the fire in the lanterns that hung along the porches died. Then, all at once, the cloud split down the seam and fell away, and a man riding a horse emerged.

Kate beheld his face. Her theories and questions fell away like the frozen cherry blossoms, and suddenly, the journal in her lap had lost all meaning. He was real. There was nothing in the natural order of the world that could explain this.

Her fathers' voices were distant when they called her name. They could not reach her any more than the cold. Her chest was engulfed with an unrelenting heat that surged with every thriving beat of her heart. She pressed both hands against the windows, only to find the separation between them unbearable.

The Ghost King was not a monster, yet he did not resemble a living, breathing man. His white hair jutted out in frozen chunks around his face and shoulders. An inky black glistened in the place of eyes. His skin was pale like hers, only his was hard and chiseled like the abandoned marble pillars outside the village. His jaw was marred by veiny, purple scars that coursed down his neck.

The Ghost King's clothing was different from anything she had ever seen. He wore a scaled silver plate of some kind. Once bright and pure but tarnished by age and negligence. Unique, individual scales made the armor light and flexible but stopped a few inches above the elbows. He wore a navy cape half draped over one shoulder and across his horse.

Kate thought she could make out white linen under the plate as well. He wore leather pants and shoes in line with the current style for men. Something he had taken from a fallen soldier, perhaps.

It was extraordinary. Every detail right down to his horse—a brown and tan mare. By all accounts, it appeared to be an ordinary horse. It did not fall in line with what she had expected. Wouldn't a mythical ghost man be riding on a stallion as black as the starless night?

But no. It was a comely little mare. Her mane was free and speckled with glimmering ice, but she otherwise appeared unbothered by the cold.

A bizarre thought came to her then. As though another part of her insisted when her mind knew better. If the horse was not affected by the blight, neither would she be.

Kate scrambled off the table, blankets and all. Like a moth drawn to the flame, she was compelled to reach him. Making for the door before her paper-thin logic could rip, she just wanted to get closer—no, she needed to get closer. To feel his black eyes locked on hers. A silent exchange, an understanding; They were going to change each other's lives.

"What are you doing?" Baxter hissed.

Numb fingers strained against the wooden beam Baxter used to bar the door. It was heavy, and she strained to lift it even with the cold and unyielding lever. Kate was lost in the surrealness of the moment, as if nothing could harm her.

Closer. I need to be closer to him.

Her hands clasped on the iron bars and the distant pan-icked voices of her fathers. She just wanted him to look at her. If he saw her, he would understand. He had to.

She had the door open. A wave of glacial cold pushed back as if to warn her, but Kate no longer cared.

A pair of burning hot hands gripped her from behind. "What is wrong with you?"

Kate reared and kicked as Papa pulled her back. "I'm here!" she shouted as Frank slammed the door.

She shoved them away and clawed her way to the window as fast as her icy legs would allow. He must have heard her. Even the slightest hesitation would give her one more moment with him.

I'm here. I'm right here waiting for you... Can you tell me why?

But the Ghost King did not look. He didn't so much as flinch. He marched onward as though she had said nothing at all. The dam broke inside her, and the disappointment went spilling out. She let go, allowing Frank to drag her back to warmth and safety.

Frank rubbed her hands to reheat them as her tears melted from her face. "What were you thinking?"

Papa was visibly shaken. So much so that his lips pursed, and his jaw quivered under his mustache. They deserved an answer, but she had none. Did the Ghost King make her do it? She let out a frustrated growl and paced the window.

The warmth came on all at once. The fire inhaled a deep breath and surged within the oven, but the lanterns outside remained unlit.

With the departure of the blight, the little shop was sweltering, and condensation was dripping from the windows. Frank closed the oven door and flue, but the heat from the stove would rage on well into the night.

"Do you want to sleep with us tonight?" Frank asked.

At this, she scowled. As much as she adored her fathers, she had stopped trying to share their bed at age twelve. "I'm too old for that."

Frank gave a helpless shrug that suggested he hadn't considered the practicality of the offer.

No, she barely fit on her own mattress as it was. And when she crawled on that mattress on the attic floor, she had no intention of sleeping. Not ever again. Whatever transpired, it was a departure from all logic. It was like her heart took possession of her mind and...

Howling into her pillow, she kicked off the blankets. It was too hot in the house!

She grabbed the journal by the mattress, the one she kept for dreams, and Kate jotted down a flurry of incomprehensible notes. Fleeting thoughts and irrationalities scrawled into a journal that she could examine once her mind returned to her once more.

More than anything, she wanted him to tell her why. Why had he invoked such a reaction from her? Why did her heart race and surge with such an unrelenting fever the moment she laid eyes on him? Perhaps it was an undisclosed power designed to lure victims to their deaths, but no one apart from her reacted so violently to the Ghost King.

She leaned her head over the side of the mattress, eavesdropping on her parents' conversation between the wide gaps in the floorboards. Did they know why she behaved in such a way? She couldn't imagine what she looked like to them in that moment.

"It's like she was bewitched!" Baxter said.

"Shh."

There was a noise of indignation from Papa. "How are you not frightened? What do you make of that?"

"I don't know," Frank answered.

"What about that monster and its blight made that girl forget all sense?"

"I don't know!"

She rolled on her back and stared at the attic's scaffolding. Perhaps she had been bewitched. It came on so suddenly. A bout of madness that could not be reasoned with. Like an irrational fear of spiders or a burst of anger. Like a fire that had lost control. It consumed her wholly, and if she didn't go to him in that moment, it would have devoured her from the inside.

Her thoughts were not of why or how it happened. The only question in her mind was how she was going to see him again.

Chapter 3

I F THERE WAS ONE person in the village who could understand her, it would be Lori. Sitting on an old sofa in the apartment above the library, Kate told her friend the events of the previous night. She fully anticipated her closest friend to sympathize or, at the very least, commiserate.

"You're in love with...*that?*"

Of all the overly simplistic assumptions, Lori had to go with that one! Kate was so jarred by the idea that her mouth hung slack as the words came stumbling out.

Lori laughed, the wrinkles around her eyes creasing as she did. "It's okay. I'm just surprised. You're so beautiful, and he's so...unconventional."

What she'd experienced wasn't like any kind of love she had ever seen. It wasn't the feeling she imagined her fathers experiencing for each other. Nor did it resemble anything she had seen in newlyweds or courtships. It was nothing like the quiet, longing glances Lori and Harvey exchanged when they thought no one was looking.

Kate had twisted her fingers together in her lap, and they were starting to ache. "I don't think that's exactly what's going on. It's not possible to be consumed by love with one glance."

"Love at first sight," Lori said with an exaggerated sigh. "Those books sell the most."

She didn't think it was possible to read too many books, but perhaps the librarian had proved her wrong.

"Not any books that I read."

"What do your parents think?"

She smiled at that. "Papa thinks I've been bewitched."

"And Frank?"

Kate imitated her dad by holding up her hands before waggling them about.

Lori cackled and imitated the motion. "Oh no! Not the dance hands! You've done it now, Kate."

Despite the lightness of the conversation, she felt as though she were wearing a heavy blanket over her head. All Kate had ever wanted was to study Paradise Lost and be a renowned scientist. The Ghost King was supposed to be an element of her theory. Not an obsession.

"I don't know that it's love," Kate said. "It feels compulsory somehow. I don't know anything about love, but I know it should not be an obstacle to my goals in life."

Lori's dance hands lowered. She observed Kate from her thin round spectacles and said, "Maybe it's not love. Maybe it's your heart's way of reminding you that it holds equal sway with your mind."

Kate groaned. "I think I'd prefer being bewitched."

If it were a spell, at least she could find a way to break it. She had yet to see proof that witches or their craft were anything more than herbal potions and a strong interest in crystals. The villagers all held varying beliefs on the topic. Some shrugged and mentioned an eccentric grandmother, and others swore they could turn people into rats.

Whatever the case, there were no witches in the village that anyone suspected, and she doubted they would waste such efforts on the inventors' daughter.

Shouts rang out from the street below. When they grew louder, the friends exchanged curious glances before descending the stairs and through the library. The children often played in the road, but these were adults making a fuss.

The front doorbell rang as they stepped out to find a dozen of the villagers circled around something at the edge of town. She craned her neck and stood on her toes, but Kate couldn't see past the crowd.

When they approached, several of the men tried to warn them off. "This is no place for women," the grocer said.

"Gauging by the amount of vomit I have to step around, I'd say this is not a man's place either," Lori said, lifting her skirts to avoid the bile.

Kate grinned. The expression of the grocer was one of abject humiliation, and he deserved every ounce of it. While some provinces might approve of men's and women's places, their people could never afford to make such a distinction.

Careful not to step on anything regrettable, Kate nudged through the crowd and emerged face-to-face with a corpse. Her stomach cramped, and the world sloshed around her. Fortunately, Lori held her hand and steadied her.

It was one of the mercs. While the blight vanished almost as quickly as the Ghost King had, the man remained frozen solid. All the exposed skin was blackened, and his lips were gone, giving him a macabre appearance. It looked as though he were reaching for the sword on his belt when the blight hit him. There was a milky substance around the eye sockets suggesting his eyeballs had burst at some point. Overall, one of the most horrid displays Kate had ever seen.

"The lumber mill workers found the other two," the blacksmith said. "They tried to beat him to his castle. Not that they stood a chance. Poor bastards."

Her mind went back to the day before when she had wished the mercs dead. She wished for it, and her parents were right to warn her against it. Not because it would happen but because it felt as though a stain had developed on her heart. One she could never wash off.

"We've seen enough," Lori said, attempting to pull her away.

Kate pulled her hand back. "Wait. Is there anything on him? Any way to identify him? The least we can do is notify his kin."

"No one here wants to touch him," the blacksmith warned.

She understood why. Not only for the practical reason of not wanting to touch a melting, ice-burnt corpse, but there were funeral rites to be acknowledged. If only they knew which one.

"I won't touch the body itself," she said. "I'm just going to check his pockets."

Wrenching away the heavy, frozen coat, she plucked an envelope that extended the depth of the pocket. It wasn't uncommon for travelers to carry personal items close to their heart. Everyone here knew that as well as she did; they were just too frightened to try.

Then again, Kate wouldn't have tried either if it were not for the guilt crushing her sternum. It was just a wish made in fear, and the only power fear had was what a person gave it. Her emotions, as wrong as they might have been, were not the man's actions. Had he left the Ghost King alone, he would not be dead.

"What if he can't burn?" the blacksmith muttered.

It was a good question, but it was a problem she would not touch. If he was a good man, like she hoped he wasn't, they would bury his body so that his evil could not pollute the harvests. If he was a good man—so help her—it was customary to burn the body so that the remains were scattered, sending goodness into the world once more.

"I don't know," Kate said, handing the letter to the grocer. "The women's work is done. The rest of it is up to you."

She left without looking back. Taking Lori by the hand to help navigate her and her flowing skirts to safety. Whatever they decided to do was up to them. Kate wanted nothing to do with funeral fires and refused to take part.

"You weren't curious about what was in the letter?" Lori asked.

Kate shook her head.

"Not even a little?"

Whatever was in the letter, it had nothing to do with Paradise Lost. Nor did it have any bearing on her theory. It was most likely a letter to a sweetheart back home. Several pages of boasting to some girl he was trying to woo with fame and fortune. Her stomach was too sour to think of it any longer. If she didn't get out of there, it would be her vomiting all over the village.

"We did the best we could for him," Kate said. "I have work to do."

Lori gave her a knowing smirk. "Research or survey?"

"What is your belief regarding the Waters?"

The librarian stopped walking. "What does that have anything to do with that?" she asked, gesturing to the corpse.

"The current theory on the Ghost King is that he is a creation of Dominion, an evil entity. Living in a home that strongly dislikes religion, I need to collect people's reasoning for believing this myth."

Lori tilted her head. "People don't believe things due to reason. They look for reasons to believe."

Kate needed her notebook. She would retrieve it after interviewing Lori, the librarian and the most learned person other than Baxter in the village. One of the two people in the village who had ever stepped foot in the university.

"So, people see the Ghost King, and their belief in Dominion is confirmed."

"Well, yes. Don't think about it, just put yourself in another person's position. What we saw last night was inexplicable, yet a somewhat frequent occurrence according to Harvey and anyone else who's lived here for more than fifteen years."

Fifteen years. An image of fire and screaming flashed in her mind. She was seven and holding her mother's hand. They walked the busy streets and slept on a quilted blanket with animals embroidered within the squares.

"Was that the last time he made an appearance?"

Lori nodded. "The last time was days before you were brought to the village."

He must have emerged from his castle the night her village burned. Maybe he tried to prevent it, or perhaps he killed the ones who did. The prospect of vengeance soothed her churning stomach, and she had to bite her lip to keep from smiling.

"I need my notebook."

"Just take it easy, will you? Not everyone enjoys debating religion."

Kate would make a note of that. She didn't understand how discussing a myth could be uncomfortable, but Lori always navigated social etiquette with effortless tact. If there was any lead to follow, it would be hers.

With the thrill of a lead, she rushed home to collect her things before screaming goodbye to her parents while they counted their silvers on the table. The commission must have been fulfilled while she was at Lori's and would occupy most of their afternoon.

She slammed the front door for the second time. It always got stuck in the warmer months. It was the third slam that summoned Bethany, the neighbor. "By the Waters, Kate! Quit slamming the door."

She froze, and the door creaked open once again.

The seamstress had a perpetual expression of disapproval on her face, but this time it appeared genuine and directed at Kate.

"Just the person I wanted to see," Kate said.

Bethany rolled her eyes. "Not another survey…"

If she hadn't stepped out and used a myth-based exclamation, Kate may not have bothered to seek out her opinion, but there they were. "I want to know your opinion on the Waters."

At this, the seamstress straightened. "I didn't think your fathers would approve, being as they are."

Too engrossed in her research, Kate didn't pick up the slight until later. "They don't, but it's for research. When did you first decide to believe in the Waters?"

"You don't decide to believe in things, Kate. You either do or you don't."

What sort of drivel was that? She wouldn't waste paper in her notebook for that. One word could summarize what Bethany said: indoctrination.

"There are a few theories about the Ghost King. Do you think he was created by Dominion?"

It was then that Bethany said something she did not expect. "I don't know." The expression on the seamstress's face was sad. She was staring in the direction of the castle. "He has moods, you know. Last time he was here, he was furious when he rode through the village. This time it was more like resignation. Those men gave him no choice."

Kate's pencil remained suspended in her hand.

Bethany had been raised to believe the words of the acolytes, yet she did not believe the Ghost King was evil. Her account of his last visit lined up with Lori's. Kate noted that while Lori was more cautious toward the Ghost King, Bethany practically revered him.

"Thank you, Bethany. That was incredibly helpful."

Bethany's expression did not suggest that she cared either way, but Kate noted her slight nod of approval.

It was a long walk to the farm, but she needed a varied sample. And if she were to take the shortcut through the forest, Kate would happen upon her favorite place in all the world. Not that she had seen the world outside her province, but she liked to think that it would always remain a best-kept secret.

The farm was at the far edge of the village. She walked along the dirt road that swerved around the tall hills armed with sharp boulders. Some of the hills had cracked and broken marble steps overgrown with weeds. The occasional pillar adorned the tops, usually half-broken, veering uncomfortably to one side. Rather than build on the foundation of past civilizations, her people preferred to avoid them. Paradise Lost was abandoned for a reason, according to their beliefs.

Except for when it was practical, of course.

Her people did not have the ingenuity to build bridges that lasted thousands of years like the one she was crossing. Solid, practical stonework that would remain well after she was gone. There was another bridge, identical to the one she crossed, deeper in the woods, but it was broken by time and the waterfall beside it. Few but Kate ventured that far into the forest, as if they feared the imagination of their ancestors was infectious.

The hills were seemingly abated by the longest river on the continent and gave way to a sprawling flat plain cropped by an old makeshift fence that outlined Roy's farm. There were many wheat farms, but their crops went northwest to the mills. The farmer had orchards, vegetables, and livestock.

Most people in the village had chickens and a vegetable garden, but this farm produced enough to keep the grocer well-stocked. The farm was alive with the sounds of so many animals. Pigs rooted in the mud, and she heard goats or sheep in the field behind the old farmhouse. Manure was not the sweetest scent, but when mixed with the dirt, it smelled like prosperity.

"Oy!" Jasper waved at her. He was sitting on the fence as if he had been waiting for her arrival.

"You knew I was coming?"

"No," the farmer's son said, hopping off the fence. "But I could see you coming all the way from the bridge. You need eggs?"

It was the most logical assumption. Rather than pay for the convenience of the grocer, Kate was often sent to the farm itself. "No, I am doing a survey."

Jasper's dark eyes smiled. "What is it this time?"

He led her to a barn twice the size of their home. Her questions were more for Roy, who was known to be a devout follower of the Waters.

"Must be nice," Jasper said as he led her past the cows. "No chores, just walking around asking questions all day."

Kate's upper lip curled into a sneer. "I'll have you know that we just finished a large commission. My parents didn't sleep for days. An inventor's work is just as laborious, though not as consistent as a farmer's."

The farmer's son rolled his eyes. "Right. Well, it beats feeding pigs and slaughtering chickens. Did you know their feet still kick after you chop their heads off?"

That was a visual she did not need. But Kate could empathize; she wouldn't enjoy killing animals either.

"Your family is the sole reason our village thrives," she reminded him. "Without the important work you do, we'd all starve. Besides, Baxter says that your animals are the healthiest and happiest he has ever seen—and he's seen a lot."

Jasper nodded thoughtfully before patting the top of a cow's head. Her eyes followed his hand as if she were expecting a treat or a good scratch. Kate also noted that the animals tended to wander toward them. If allowed, she imagined they would follow the farmers everywhere. Jasper smiled at the cow nuzzling his hand.

"Yeah, the animals are all right, I guess."

Inside the barn, she was pelted with the odor of hay and excrement. The two smells converged and were somehow more pleasant than the smell of her outhouse.

Roy was carving a workhorse's hoof.

Kate gasped as a large, sharp iron sliced off the poor horse's foot like a bit of cheese.

Jasper noted her distress and explained. "It doesn't hurt them. It's the same as cutting a toenail. If we don't do it, they can become overgrown and hurt the animal."

It looked painful. The way Roy gouged out chunks, sending debris scattering to the ground. The horse did appear unbothered. It rested its foot on the smoothed stump and chewed on the straw in the bag hanging on a nail.

If anything, the animal seemed to enjoy the process. Fascinating.

Understandably, Roy didn't look up from his work, but he did greet her. "Hello, Kate. What will it be?"

Her intent was to ask about religion, but another question brimmed at her edges. Why would a dead horse need shoes?

"I wanted to ask about horseshoes."

At this, Roy stayed his chisel and regarded her. Jasper had the same deep brown eyes and dark, curly hair as his father. They could have been copies, like the notes she rewrote when the pages of her book faded until illegible.

Roy had a lot to say about horseshoes. So much. The information overwhelmed Kate. As if the farmer had plunged her into a sea of unfamiliar words, her mind flailed and kicked, grasping for understanding. She opened her mouth to speak, but there was no space.

"Slow down, Da," Jasper said. "She has no idea what you're talking about."

If Roy could blush, he would have. "Sorry, it's just that I've never had anyone ask."

After a few pointed questions and some sketches, it became clear that horseshoes required no further innovation. They could be custom-made if a horse was lame or had bad hooves. "The only horses that need to be shod on a regular basis are the ones that are ridden on hard, rocky ground."

"Or if they're off to war or something," Jasper added.

So, the Ghost King's horse required shoes due to extensive use and varied terrain. To her limited knowledge, the dead did not require maintenance. This suggested that the animal and the rider were alive. The chill of the blight haunted her still. An involuntary shiver came over Kate then. How could a living, breathing animal withstand the blight?

The love and care Roy gave to the horse warmed her. She liked to imagine the Ghost King somewhere in his castle doing the same for his steed. If he went to the trouble of putting shoes on his immortal horse, he couldn't be some unthinking monster.

"Do you order the shoes, or do you make them yourself?"

"We can't afford to have someone come out and do it," Roy said. "The blacksmith makes them, and I shod the horses myself."

She doubted the Ghost King had a blacksmith on hand. He certainly didn't buy anything when he rode through town. This meant he either scavenged horseshoes from his victims or he made them himself. Kate liked to think he did the latter. She imagined the benefit of immortality was that one had time to learn many useful things.

On second thought, it was unlikely that the Ghost King worked a forge. It would have been impossible to work a forge when his blight smothered any warmth within reach.

This information only wound the enigma that was the Ghost King all the tighter. Like the wooden puzzle box her parents gave her as a child. Every time she moved one piece, another was blocked. Opening one door inevitably meant that another would be revealed. It was maddening, and yet every minor success endeared her to the source.

Voices from outside the barn sent the chickens scattering. Roy paused and turned in the road's direction. The sound of many horses beating along the road was foreign to her ears, but the farmers were equally perturbed.

"Jasper, go see what's out there."

Kate accompanied the farmer's boy around the side of the barn. Her legs went to lead at the sight. A dozen men on horseback were casually encroaching on their lands. Jasper's nostrils flared as if he, too, disliked the scene.

"Last time folks like that came through, they never left."

But these men were not the same.

They wore long, velvet robes that were uniform apart from the apparent leader at the front. His black robe had ornate gold embroidery at the edges. She was only slightly relieved that they were unarmed. "They're not mercenaries," she said. "These men are something else entirely."

In the last few days, they had more visitors from the other provinces than they had in the last several years. Sure, merchants came and went, but they were known to the village. They only had the one merchant, Harvey, but he often traveled with them.

No, these men were different. They were something she had never seen before, and in her heart, she knew they were there for the Ghost King.

Chapter 4

Most of the village had already packed themselves in the grocery by the time Kate and her fathers stepped in. The scent of sweat and mud threatened to stew throughout the village meeting. They wedged themselves into the back corner and waited for whatever announcement that took precious time away from her research.

"This better be good," Baxter huffed as he sucked in his belly to allow the tanner to squeeze past.

Sweat was already shining around the bit of Frank's head not covered by his cap. Much like Baxter's long sleeves, Frank never took off his cap. He began losing his hair some years ago and wasn't prepared for the whole village to know it yet.

"I hate crowds," Frank said.

She knew her papa didn't mind the overly populated confines. He was only grumping because Frank was uncomfortable.

It was sweet the way they defended each other without any awareness of doing so.

The crowd had Lori pinned at the front of the room with Harvey by her side. They exchanged waves as the grocer stood on a stool from the other side of his counter. He was a slight man, nearly as pale as Kate, with a mustache that rivaled her papa's. After three attempts to quiet the crowd, Baxter cupped his hands around his mouth and boomed, "Quiet!"

The room went silent.

"Thank you," the grocer said after a moment. "It's unusual times that force a united decision. One that can drastically alter life in our little village."

He produced a dirtied letter and held it up for all to see. "As we all know, the Ghost King passed through our village some days ago. There were three casualties. We initially thought them to be nothing more than mercenaries, but that is not the case."

A hard lump formed in Kate's throat. The heat in the room had reached a muggy, uncomfortable height. She wanted nothing more than to run from the room, but she had to know. She should have read the letter when she had a chance.

"One mercenary was a prince of Noranger."

Discontent erupted from the crowd. Although her feet were fixed to the ground, her body felt as though it were floating. Of all the people to come to the village and get themselves killed, why a prince?

A son to a distant king. Everyone knew the kings were searching for any and every excuse to claim their province. It was likely the reason her village was burned and why Roy saw what he did at the wheat mills.

The only thing that safeguarded their village was the Ghost King, but even he may not be enough this time.

"We must decide what to do," the grocer yelled over the mutters. "If we send word to the king of Noranger that his son died at the hands of the Ghost King, he may view it as an act of war, but who are we to deny funeral rites?"

Debates splintered throughout the village. Guilt still lingered in Kate's heart. It was wrong to deny the man funeral rites. It was the final judgment by the person who saw them off. There was little mention of what came after death, but the importance of performing funeral rites was sacred above all else in the province.

If he was a good man, to not spread his ashes across the lands was a waste. If he was evil, leaving his body unburied would let his evil go unchecked.

They did not know if the prince was good or evil, so they could not perform these rites. To treat the prince as one of their own and just burn his body was risky, as their custom might offend Noranger. To bury the remains of a good man was a sin. Sending word to the father was the best option, but all those scenarios were as good as sending a declaration of war.

Up until now, having soldiers in their province was about as useful as having a town hall. Both were things Kate never thought she'd wish for, but there she was. They had no defense other than the Ghost King.

Lori's voice rose above the clamor. "What about the visitors?"

She smiled with approval. They had been there for a day or so and had scattered around the village for lodgings like mice. Bethany was delighted to take in three of them, the brown-noser. Dad said they'd leave once they used up the village's hospitality; she hoped he was right.

"They are called the Ever Faithful," the grocer confirmed. "They are here for the Ghost King."

"Let them have him!" a man shouted.

She jerked her head in the direction of the voice. Who would want such a thing? Her face felt hot, and her ears burned. Removing their one source of protection was a death sentence for everyone.

"And what?" another shouted. "Invite the distant kings to invade?"

"I don't know about you," Roy said, "but no taxes are good taxes!"

It was good to see some in the village possessed common sense. At that, Kate cheered with approximately half the villagers. She glanced back at her fathers and noted they did not speak either way. Her reaction to the Ghost King had frightened them, she knew that.

Apart from her own disturbing reaction, there was an uneasiness in her heart. If he could provoke such a wild reaction from a scientist, Kate could only imagine what the Ghost King invoked in others. It was like she was possessed by her own heart in a moment of total folly. She couldn't define it, but she and the Ghost King were connected. Convincing her parents of that wasn't going to happen.

But their current debacle had nothing to do with her infatuation with him; this was an issue of security. He was their only salvation as she saw it. Someone needed to warn him, but that was difficult to do. One didn't send a postman to the crumbling, blighted castle.

"The body is still frozen solid." The grocer said it as though he had a nasty taste in his mouth. "But we must decide before he defrosts."

How long did it take for a body to thaw from the blight?

It was a question she instantly regretted thinking. Of all the grotesque things to ponder about, and she was turning it into a science experiment. She wanted to slap herself in the face, but it would have looked weird. Her fathers had been watching her like an owl in the night since the Ghost King's visit. Maybe they were right to do so.

As the crowd lessened, the more prominent certain figures became. Cloaked in all black, the Ever Faithful at least pushed back their hoods to reveal their faces. They were scattered all around the room, but she couldn't help but notice each of them held conversations with women.

Must have been lonely, traveling in a pack of gloomy-looking men around the continent. Perhaps they all naturally gravitated toward women because it had been a while? For some reason, Kate didn't think so.

The farmer's wife left, and the two acolytes chatting with her were drifting their way toward Kate. *Nope, don't think so.* Whatever they had to say, she didn't want to hear it.

"Time to go!" she told her fathers as she rushed to the door.

She couldn't escape the grocery store fast enough. The cool spring air freshened her skin and soothed her discontent. She was free of being bludgeoned by village opinions. Whatever they decided to do, they at least had some time to decide it.

It was a temporary relief. Kate found herself face-to-face with some of the Ever Faithful. It was a pompous name for a group. Were all religious cults so self-important, or were they an exception? She'd have to ask Papa later.

"Waters preserve you," one of the cloaked men said as though he bestowed some sort of gift on her.

"Hello." She tried to walk away before the conversation evolved, but the man stepped in her way.

"We haven't had the pleasure of meeting you yet. My name is Faustus. This is Emanual and Bob."

Kate choked back a laugh. You'd think Bob would have gone with a name with more grandeur. "Nice to meet you."

Before they could ask her name, two figures emerged from the crowd and stood behind her. She knew instinctively that they were her fathers, and Kate made no attempt to hide her smile as they sized up Baxter and took a step back.

"Waters preserve you, friends. We hope you'll come to our open discussion tomorrow."

There was nothing but silence from her parents. Kate hoped that would be the end of it. Something about these men irked her. Not in the way the mercs offended her. These men made the tiny hairs on the back of her neck stand on end. What did they want from them, and why wouldn't they just leave? Their village was facing a crisis and did not need religion butting in.

"What discussion is this?" Frank asked.

"We will be talking about the Ghost King's bride."

The confusion on her face must have been visible in the dark because Faustus chuckled.

"It's a lesser-known story, but no less important. You're the inventors, are you not?"

"What of it?" Baxter said with a reserved gruffness.

"No reason," Faustus said. "I realize some acolytes preach against same-sex marriage, but I'd like you to know that our order welcomes all unions."

It had been a point of contention for her parents and a large part of why they came to live in the village. If the Ever Faithful could move past bigotry, perhaps the rest of the religion would follow. Not that she was all that eager to spend more time with Faustus, Emanual, and especially not Bob.

"I'll let you go." Faustus stepped back, hands clasped in front of him. "We hope to see you tomorrow."

They said nothing as they crossed the street. She glanced over her shoulder to find them still standing there, staring. It was so weird. How was Bethany not creeped out by them?

Once the front door was locked, Kate spun around and asked, "the Ghost King has a wife?"

Frank looked to Baxter as if he, too, wanted to know.

Papa made a disgruntled noise and shrugged. "Apparently."

"You grew up in a religious city," Frank said, "and you've never heard of this?"

His mustache twitched while he thought long and hard about it. "In the stories I learned back in Flosses, the Waters promised a messiah, and Dominion is said to have created the Ghost King to mock her promise. No one ever said anything about him making a second one."

"Yeah, I've lived here for most of my life, and if he had a wife, I'm pretty sure we'd know it by now," Frank agreed. He went and put the kettle on, but the last thing Kate wanted was thistle tea.

There was a pinch of anger or resentment. It rubbed at her in a way she didn't expect. Something about him being married was upsetting. She cursed Lori for putting the notion of love in her mind. How could she love a thing she did not know? It made no sense.

Maybe this group, the Ever Faithful, had it wrong. After all, they did not live here; they knew nothing about the Ghost King. "I surveyed many in the town in regard to the Waters," Kate said. "Some aspects of the story are different, or people find more meaning in one part than the other. Maybe religion is like that on a large scale as well."

"That's probably what's going on here," Frank agreed. "It's like that game we used to play as kids; Messenger."

She and Jasper used to play it as children. One person would whisper something into another's ear, and they would pass the message on. By the time all the children heard the message, it was nothing remotely like what the first person said.

The province the Ever Faithful came from had an additional story. Their own local myths and lore worked their way into the story. She suspected it was to further instill the belief that the Ghost King was Dominion's creation. Once Kate disproved that myth with fact, everyone would know that science was their salvation and not superstition.

"What do you think the village will decide?" Kate asked.

Frank's dance hands signified that he had no idea. "I don't see how we can tell the king. Not without endangering ourselves."

Baxter huffed with agreement.

Kate lowered her eyes to the table. It was the most logical decision. The entire province was at stake. To risk tens of thousands of lives over funeral rites was far worse than not admitting to someone's death. People die all the time without their loved one's knowing. There were provinces strewn with nameless corpses.

Thousands of families would never have proper funeral rites, so why should one man get them when he denied the same courtesy to so many?

Still, it felt wrong.

It was the sort of wrong that was handed down from another. The kind that made thieves out of beggars and illegal hunting when the winters ran on too long. Not the sort that caused harm to any person, but the kind that ate someone from the inside. If they made this choice, other less savory choices would follow.

"What do you think, Kate?" Baxter asked, joining them at the table, his mug dwarfed in his massive hands.

In truth, she didn't have an answer. Being unable to find the right answer left her feeling messy inside. All tangled up and without a definitive right or wrong. Both had consequences that went beyond just her. She hated it, but Kate did not know what to do.

"We can't bet so many lives on doing the right thing," Kate said. "But what would it make us if we didn't?"

It wasn't as though they could deny what had happened. Only one creature on the continent had the ability to freeze a man solid in the early days of spring. Even if they left the body somewhere else, the frostbite on his skin would tell the tale. Not only that, but the king clearly kept correspondence with his son. He must have known where he was going.

"I suppose it depends on the contents of the letter. If we can learn what sort of man this distant king is or what he knew... Maybe he is the understanding sort—"

Baxter grunted. "I doubt it. His province has been at Taus's throats for the last decade."

"Noranger, that's pretty far away," Frank suggested. "It's one thing to fight nearby territories, but he'd need to send troops through those provinces to get to ours."

The bulk of their people lived up north, that was true, but in the wars, they had gained more southern lands. The borders swelled and contracted with so many skirmishes that Noranger was on the verge of being neighbors with their province.

"That's true," Baxter's eyebrows raised and sunk low on his forehead once more. "His son did not wear any sigils for a reason."

Kate rested her head in her hands. What a waste of energy. Here she was, fretting about something she had no control over when she should have been studying armor styles from Paradise Lost. The Ghost King's armor wasn't like anything she had ever seen before, but that did not mean the fallen civilization had created him. She needed more information. Anything to sift the truth from the myths, but that sort of information was probably locked away in the university.

Unclenching her jaw, Kate forced her strained body into a more relaxed position. Stressing over what she couldn't have did nothing to solve her dilemma.

"Times like these make me wish we had a king," Baxter said. "They have those envoys they send all about. Without a leader, we have no way of navigating this mess."

Kate peeked through her palms. "But we do have a king. Only, he does not know the situation."

Her fathers stared at her like she was slurping snails from their shells, but she was right.

If the Ghost King knew about the prince, he might be able to act. She could also ask him about this so-called bride. Confirming that the Ghost King did not have a wife might be enough to send the Ever Faithful away. Not only that, but if she asked him about his origins, it would confirm her theory.

Even if the university didn't want to hear of it, they had an obligation to respond to a theory submission. They barred her way to the library using bureaucracy, so she would do the same in turn.

It solved everything.

She went to her worktable and withdrew several books from her shelf.

"Kate..." Frank warned.

Baxter looked as though he were about to whistle like the kettle. "If I can find a way to survive the blight, I can warn him."

"After last time?"

She hesitated. There was no denying her reaction last time. Was her heart so hungry for love that it possessed her? The image of the prince was forever burned into her mind. It looked like a terrible way to go.

Frowning, she set her books down. All but one. "Perhaps you're right."

Kate swore she could see the steam release from Baxter's ears as he eased into his chair.

They were right. It would be a suicide mission. No amount of clothing could prevent the blight from freezing her solid. And even if she did get close enough to speak to him, that did not guarantee he would or could answer. She was assuming too much.

While Kate wanted him to be a man, the frozen prince at the fork in the road served as a reminder that the Ghost King was not to be trifled with.

She said goodnight and went upstairs. Try as she might, Kate could not surrender the tonics and remedies book. It was a small chance the book held a solution, but if she looked, she could say she exhausted every option.

The next morning, Kate woke to the smell of bacon.

Scrambling out of bed still in her nightgown, she followed the sound of crackling pork fat. It was a rare treat in their household, but after a large commission, her parents splurged a little. She sat at the worktable, where she found a bowl of steaming hot porridge topped with two slices of bacon.

Frank moved in, still holding the cast-iron skillet, and placed several more slices of bacon on everyone's porridge. "I heard a butcher is coming from Flosses next year," Frank's breakfast conversation fell on deaf ears.

Sitting across from her, Papa's eyes glazed over. Clearly, he was experiencing some kind of pork-induced euphoria, and she joined him without hesitation. "We will single-handedly keep him employed," Kate said with her mouth half-full.

"He's a she."

Kate raised her brows, exaggerating her surprise. "A woman-owned business!"

"The scandal!" Frank feigned shock.

"Our own butcher," Baxter said, joining them at the table. "We had one when I was a kid, but once Roy's father learned the butchers in Flosses paid more for the pigs, he never sold to our butcher again."

In the lull of bacon, it was hard to be angry by the story, unkind as it was. She had met Jasper's grandfather only once. It was hard to recall over the salty goodness, but he complained often and loudly. Usually about Roy. "I'm glad Roy isn't like his father."

"Yeah, the butcher was where the empty building is now, beside the library. That was once a midwife's home, but she married and moved to another town."

"It must be strange," she said. "Watching your village change so much."

Frank leaned against her worktable and stared at the ceiling, considering her statement. "Sort of. It happens so fast but so slow at the same time. That probably doesn't make sense."

Not out loud, but her heart resonated with the statement. Buildings came up in a matter of months, but empty lots remained for years. All of a sudden, a new shop would be up and running as though it had always been there.

"That, and it sort of comes and goes," Frank said. "The village was larger when I was a boy. Shrunk over the years. Now it's expanding."

"People go where the work is," Baxter said between bites of his bacon.

He made a valiant point.

"What's on your agenda today, Kate?" Frank asked.

To be free of the bacon grease that clung to every strand of hair and apron she owned? As much as she enjoyed it, Kate feared she would forever smell of pig rendering. Frank would use the fat to season all their pots and pans, and that was always stinky business.

Jasper's pigs were so fat, she almost felt sorry for the new butcher. They were more like the seals in the stories Baxter told when he was in a rare mood to say more than a few words. She had never seen a seal before, but Papa said their blubber was how they endured the freezing depths of the ocean.

She broke the bacon into chunks and chewed it bit by bit. The wheels in her mind were turning. Seal blubber could withstand glacial cold water...

Kate looked up and realized Frank was staring at her as if he expected something. "I'm sorry," she said. "I didn't hear you over the taste of the bacon."

Frank smirked, and Baxter laughed. "I was asking what you had planned today."

"I'm going to Lori's," she said, taking some bacon for the road. "I might go to the forest if I have time."

"Be safe," Baxter said, more to his bacon than to her.

Marching across the street, she waved to the blacksmith at his forge before reaching the library. The bell sounded, and she was just about to close the door with her greasy fingers when someone came in behind her.

"Sorry," she said absently, only to turn around and come face-to-face with Faustus's waxen face. It was strange in the daylight, like he was made of clay rather than skin.

"You decided to join us!"

She'd rather pick Botflies out of the frozen prince than spend a moment longer with Faustus. He was standing in front of the door, barring her exit with a placid smile. There was no way to slip out, and Kate suddenly felt like a rabbit caught in a snare.

There were a few people waiting in the library. Bethany was one of them. She was chatting with either Emmanuel or Bob. The tanner and his wife were also there with Lane, Roy's wife.

"Please," Faustus said. "Come join us."

"Actually, I need to borrow Kate, if you don't mind," a saintly voice called from the apartment above the library. "But don't worry, she will still be able to listen in."

Kate mouthed, "Thank you," as she rushed up the stairs to join her friend.

"Why are they here?" she whispered once she was in the loft.

"They asked to use the library for discussions," Lori said. "I couldn't say no. Besides, I could use a few more book sales."

"I don't think you're going to get them from this lot."

"Shh."

Rather than sprawl across the furniture like they usually did, Kate and Lori huddled together on the loveseat on the farthest end of the loft and eavesdropped on the Ever Faithful's discussion below.

"Thank you all for coming," Faustus said. "Waters preserve you."

The crowd repeated the phrase dutifully, if not cautiously. Kate and Lori raised their brows at the same time. She had to admit that she was curious about what they believed since there was no possible way the Ghost King could have a wife.

"Our sect shares much in common with the acolytes you've come to know. We worship the Waters and wage an endless war on Dominion. However, our chapter does not hold the same views on many things traditionally held by the acolytes."

This was something they told her the other night. She imagined that was why the villagers didn't send them away after a day or two. No one likes a judgmental wart for too long, even Bethany. Not that Kate had ever met acolytes from other chapters, it was just the assumption she had based on her fathers' experiences. According to them, if her family lived anywhere else, religion would have advocated for her to go to an orphanage rather than live with her fathers.

Imagining being ripped away from them was utterly nauseating. Losing her mother was devastating enough. To lose them... Kate shook her head.

"Our late leader and prophet foresaw that the Ghost King would take a wife. It is of the utmost importance that we end this unholy union, and that is why we are here."

"But he has no wife," Lane said. She looked around the room as if she were somehow left out of the letter everyone else got.

Kate was thankful she spoke out. Otherwise, Kate would have run to the railing and shouted it.

It was the equivalent of going to Roy's farm and telling the farmers that their crops were planted incorrectly. Did these cultists really think they could show up and tell the village all about the Ghost King?

"Yes," Faustus admitted. "It appears that way, but none of you have any idea what goes on in that castle, do you?"

The silence was admission to that fact. No one could get near the castle without being turned into a human icicle. From her hilltop, Kate could see the courtyard of the castle, but she never saw movement. If the Ghost King was able to remain out of sight, it was possible that he wasn't alone.

Kate's hand pressed against her heart. It couldn't be. How could one feel this way about someone that was already married? If it were true, she couldn't bear to face him for any reason. On second thought, if she went to the castle and confirmed her theory, she would have her ticket to the university in Taus. She could be far away from him and his wife.

The rest of the Ever Faithful's discussion was a blur, and it wasn't until the bell rang for the last time that Kate could think straight once more.

"Well," Lori said, "that was enlightening."

"Do you think they're right?" Kate asked.

Lori's eyes softened with what was probably pity. "I couldn't say. This is all new to me."

Her parents had said much of the same. "They have no basis for their logic other than a person's dream. How can they devote their lives to such a thing?"

Lori raised her brows and took a sip of her tea. "It certainly demonstrates a new level of zealotry."

"You don't think they will try to go to the castle, do you?"

"I can't imagine *anyone* would do something so dangerous." Lori stood over her, arms folded as if she were a scolding mother.

Kate squirmed under her friend's gaze. She was walking a fine line. One wrong word and Lori may find it necessary to tell her fathers. "It's currently impossible to do without grievous harm," Kate said.

Satisfied with her answer, Lori moved on. They spoke no further about the Ghost King's wife or the Ever Faithful, but when she left the library, Kate took several books with her.

"Just be sure to return these," Lori reminded as she escorted her out. "I loan books out to villagers at any time, but with the summer coming, remedy books are always the first to sell."

"I will," Kate promised. They would probably be useless anyhow. It's not like one had the cure for the blight contained within its pages.

Leaving the library meant passing the frozen prince. It was unavoidable, as he was at the fork. One direction was the route

Harvey took to Flosses, and the other led to the Ghost King's castle. Though he did not have eyes, the prince stared at her all the same.

She shivered and clutched her books all the tighter to her chest. It was as if he were blaming her for his death. It was her wish, after all. They all might pay the price for that wish, and then the frozen prince would have his revenge.

A single drip of water fell from the tip of the prince's frostbitten nose. She wiped the moisture from the corners of her own eyes. They didn't have long before he thawed, and a decision would need to be made.

Chapter 5

THE TANNER'S MOTHER DIED peacefully in her sleep. Everyone thought the cough would take her, but it had been steadily improving over the last few months. Her family believed she still had a few more years in her, but death came as it pleased. The villagers were all in agreement that dying painlessly in their beds at seventy-six was a proper way to go, but Kate wasn't so sure.

Old age was something she couldn't comprehend. It was a lifetime away, and there were still so many questions to be answered. The idea that she would just cease to exist one day made her feel gross all over. That and being burned on a pyre were her biggest fears. She still had nightmares of being trapped inside a burning building, of flames and unyielding smoke choking her until she woke drenched in sweat.

Sitting on a wooden bench, wrapped in a woolen blanket, she observed villagers go about their business. They passed here and there, carrying bundles of kindling and buckets of pitch to prepare for the old woman's funeral. The notion of what came next coiled her nerves so tightly that she struggled to breathe.

Pushing the heavy blanket off her chest, she stretched and turned her attention to her fathers hunched over their worktable.

"We may be doing another funeral pyre soon," Baxter huffed through puffed cheeks. "The prince is melting more and more."

Dread intensified in her mind. She wished Papa hadn't brought it up. The villagers had been inspecting the body daily, herself included. She took great care not to touch the skin, but the furs of the coat had softened, as had the dirt under the prince's foot.

"Why did you have to come here?" she asked him one day. "Everything was fine until you came to the village."

She couldn't deny her curiosity when it came to the effects of the blight on the human body. If Kate intended to find a way to warn the Ghost King, she had to know what she was getting into. The prince instilled a harsh warning to anyone who thought they could withstand the blight, and Kate was no exception.

Frank shook his head as he unrolled the scroll. It bore a wax seal of two lions fighting. The seal of Sundersong. It was the formal request for a new commission. The little prince of Sundersong saw his father's toy soldiers. He was so impressed that the king ordered several child-sized soldiers for his son.

No doubt, the family tradition of mass murder for the sake of territory would live on.

It was a fantastic job for her family that promised a lot of silver. Since the mechanical drawings were already done, they simply had to increase the scale to a size that Frank could see far better than their miniature counterparts.

"The village is entirely divided on what to do," Frank muttered. "We should just make him a pyre and be done with it."

Papa scowled at the back of Dad's head. "Oh yes, let's pollute our crops with a merc's ashes because daddy is the king of Noranger!"

Being a merc did not make the prince evil, but Kate had no intention of wadding into an argument between her fathers. Especially since she had yet to come to a decision of her own in the matter.

She was old enough to understand that this was their way. It wasn't about a ball bearing or how long to steep the tea. It had nothing to do with the matter at hand and everything to do with the fact that neither man could admit when he was wrong.

"Oh well, what's a few villages?" Frank said. "A few more days and there will be bugs, Baxter."

Papa snapped his eyes shut, not wanting the visual. "Don't bring them into this!"

"Maggots," Frank said slowly.

It was enough to make Kate's skin crawl. She shared Papa's hatred for the little crawlers. They were an important part of decomposition, but the idea of them wriggling underneath the skin—Kate gagged.

Her fathers regarded her, and the conversation ended. "Sorry, Lemonberry," Frank said.

Baxter was eager to change the subject as well. Hovering over the commission letter, he shook his head. "The cost of wood alone for this project is going to be enormous."

"I know," Frank said absently. "That's why I made him pay half in advance."

At that, Baxter laughed. "I knew I married you for a reason."

Despite their differences, the two men faced each other with a common goal and desire to make it work. Kate admired them greatly, even if they sometimes made her gag. She grew up believing she could overcome any and every obstacle with ingenuity and hard work because the two men squaring off at the worktable proved it was possible.

"All right, I'm off," she said, straightening her new work dress. It was a soft pink that Bethany insisted would bring warmth to her pale skin. It could have been mustard yellow for all Kate cared. What was important was the hem was shorter than most dresses. It stopped just above the ankle, which made for easier walks through the forest. "Do me a favor. No more bug talk."

"Deal," Baxter said.

"Off to the forest?" Frank asked.

She had no intention of being in the village when the funeral happened. "I have some books on loan that Lori will need back soon. Besides, I can't stand the stench. It gives me a headache."

"It's about time we head out as well," Frank said. Sympathy lined his voice as his eyes met hers. "We can stand in the far back. It's only fire, Kate."

"The villagers will take offense if you don't come," Baxter warned.

"I know that!" Kate chewed on a calloused fingertip and turned away. The villagers wanted so much of her. She carried their requests to and from the farm, and she was a dutiful daughter to her fathers. Did it really matter if she attended the funeral?

The scowling seamstress next door was probably to blame. No one else ever seemed concerned with Kate's social standing.

Lost in her own mind, she didn't notice that Frank was behind her. Her father pulled her close and kissed her temple. "If you don't want to go, we won't make you."

"Hmph," Baxter grunted in agreement. "Never mind what they think."

Relief broke at the notion of reprieve. "Thank you," she said. Her throat was hot and threatening to give way to sobs. "I just can't."

"You have every right to be afraid," Frank said. "If any of them could even fathom what you endured, they would understand."

Fire was not some animal that could be tamed. It was a devourer of life. The destruction of homes. It laid waste to dreams and left nothing but desolation if not kept in check. She knew this all too well and could not be expected to revere its chaos.

It was only in the charred aftermath did people develop proper respect for it. They didn't know, and how could they? She winced and shook her head. It didn't matter. The villagers could think whatever they wanted of her because it was in their rights to do so. Their opinions were not her responsibility nor her obligation.

At least, that is what she told herself. But in the small hours of the night, Kate woke to overanalyze every exchange, no matter how small, hoping she had made the right impression. She hated that. Why did she care what they thought of her? It wasn't like they woke in the night to have the same worries. But there she would be, tossing and turning on her mattress, attempting to recall if Bethany's nod was of approval or dismissal. Did her eyebrows arch in a good way or a bad way? If the villagers knew her mind, they'd find her anxieties as obnoxious as she did.

Without another word, Kate slipped out the door and made her way to the sanctuary of the forests. Away from the spaces people occupied. The forest didn't judge her. The forest didn't care. Cutting through the gap between the grocer's and the soon-to-be butcher's, she hurried out of sight before anyone could question where she was going.

She waded through ferns, ducking under sagging tree limbs and fallen branches. Leaving her fears behind, she used the remains of a building from Paradise Lost as a platform in which to launch over a fallen log. There was a quality of the air in the forest that was unlike the village or even the farm.

It was as though her very spirit was purified by the thriving wilderness. The natural cycle of the world could be observed within the forests. The way the lands reclaimed the remains of Paradise Lost served as a promise. Should anything befall man, life would go on. It was comforting in a strange way.

The lumber mill was on the other side of town. Not wanting to touch the relics of the past, they carved their way north. This part of the woods had been untouched by man for thousands of years. All except for Kate, of course, but she kept her footprints light and only took what the forest would not miss.

Cold mists from the waterfall glistened on her skin as she crossed the broken bridge. Careful to not disturb the vines and weeds that sprouted from the fractured stone and followed the overgrown trail to the tallest hillside this side of the mountains.

Kate huffed and puffed as she climbed the steep hill. She seemed to recall it being much easier when she was younger. These days, her back twinged, and sharp pains went up her side as if she were being ripped at the seams. Approximately two-thirds of the way up the hill, she vowed to get more exercise and spend less time eating crackers while reading.

It was well worth it when she reached the top. Few would understand why; there was nothing there other than a single cherry blossom tree and an upright slab of marble. The writing was long gone, and the edges were smoothed by time. Whatever it was, it made for wonderful back support as she plopped to the ground and opened her books.

As she suspected, none had a solution for the blight, but there were multiple references to a certain snake venom that could cause a long-lasting fever. There was also a root that was thought to delay hypothermia. Both were promising leads.

Kate was not a doctor, but she knew that having a fever for an extended time was dangerous. The last thing she wanted to do was sauté her brain in its own bloods. Her intelligence was her greatest asset, and without it, she would no doubt be insufferable.

She wasn't sold on the snake venom either.

Logistically, acquiring venom meant finding a snake and capturing it without getting bit. She was an inventor, not a snake charmer. How did the people of Paradise Lost even come up with such an idea?

There was another problem with using snake venom. It was a neurotoxin that her body would develop an immunity to over time. That would mean she would need to continue increasing the dose to be effective. To her, that felt like a slow death in exchange for a sudden one.

It wasn't like there were long-term studies on what happened to people who regularly ingested venom, but if she met the Ghost King, it would be just the one time, wouldn't it? Just to get her answers, warn him of the dead prince, then be on her way to the university.

In the eyes of certain death, arming herself with an untested tonic was like sliding her bare ass down a splintered wooden slide because she rubbed a little ointment on her backside. Only this time, it wouldn't result in Dad plucking splinters from her bottom, and instead, she'd be a frozen, eyeless corpse.

An involuntary shudder went through her then. No. If she was going to go to the castle, Kate would need to take every precaution. She would need an external protective layer. The tonics would only be a safeguard and a last resort, allowing her the ability to flee before the blight could penetrate her coverings.

Or she could set aside years of research and develop a new theory. One less dangerous and provocative in order to enter the university. She could continue her studies on Paradise Lost once she was allowed into the university. But that felt like lying, and if she knew one thing about herself, it was that she was a terrible liar.

She could not lie to herself either.

All at once she was brought back to the shop, pressing against the icy windows. Her bones ached from the very thought of the blight. He was so close, but she couldn't reach him. The urge to scream, but she had nothing to say. Nothing that made sense anyway. The way her emotions swept her to her feet was frightening but also exciting. As if her heart knew something her mind did not.

Her thoughts were interrupted by the smoke that rose from the village. It rose in a single stream that polluted the otherwise white fluffy clouds and tainted the skies. Tar gave way to a sickly-sweet odor, and the back of Kate's throat lurched. Even from the hilltop, she could smell the body. It dragged her, kicking and screaming, to the memories of her childhood. No one forgot the smell of their own mother burning alive. The smoldering embrace of charred skin and burnt hair. Mama had attempted to claw a hole in the dirt floor large enough for her to escape, but the flames came on too quickly.

Pressing her head between her knees, Kate whined and nuzzled the fabric of her dress. It was soft and fine, not like Mama's burlap dress. And when the wood splintered from above, the frantic voices got so loud. She was lifted out of the burning building before the fires could devour her, but not before they scorched her soul.

Wiping the tears from her face, Kate took a deep breath, using her dress as a filter. If the villagers had memories such as these, they would find a better way to celebrate the lives of those who passed on.

Focusing on her books was like attempting to decipher the lost language of Paradise Lost without a guide. The words bled and went fuzzy when she squinted. The smoke burned her eyes even at a distance. Kate even tried pushing the book closer to her face, only to realize the words were blurry up close as well.

Nothing helped. Every time she read three sentences, a gust of cold wind would pelt her face. She longed for the shawl hanging on an iron nail inside the shop, but Kate would not go home until the fires were smothered by dirt and water.

The forest would be warmer than the tall hill exposed to the winds. Besides, the sun was setting, and she was quickly losing the light. She rubbed the bridge of her nose and stretched her legs.

Many would never understand why the hillside drew her to its top, but then again, they didn't want to see. The peak she stood on was the best vantage point for the castle. From there, she could practically see inside the windows of the high tower.

There, she could see the scaffolding pressed against the walls of the fortress. There was even a courtyard of sorts. Nothing grew, of course, the blight saw to that, but at one point, it may have been a garden. A long-dead tree sat in the center as if it were a counterpart to the living one she stood beside.

If the Ghost King did indeed have a wife, what harm could she possibly do? He only ever left the castle when the sunset bled red and the smell of iron filled the air. A sad thought occurred to her then. What if he had a wife before he was turned into the Ghost King?

A heartbreaking notion. She imagined him coming home to a grand, lush home and a beautiful wife, only to have the blight destroy it all before his very eyes. Everyone always assumed the blight was something he could control, but what if it wasn't? It was more likely that the Ghost King's power was also his curse.

Kate hoped she was wrong, for that would be a terrible fate.

The smoke was thinning. It sputtered and waivered like water leaving the well pump. By the time she made her way through the forests, it would be over.

Frank and Baxter were waiting for her when Kate came home. Among the scattered blueprints and carving tools, there was a third mug of thistle tea on the worktable. They didn't say a word as she joined them, which suggested they had something important to discuss.

She took a few sips and warmed her hands with the mug. "The village has come to a decision, haven't they?"

"With almost everyone there, it seemed like the right time," Frank said. "The prince is melting. We had to make a choice."

Baxter remained silent. She didn't know if that meant he approved of the decision or if he was too angry to speak of it.

"Well?"

"The village has decided to send word to the king of Noranger."

Out of the turmoil of emotions, relief was at the forefront. Not because she felt the right choice was made but simply because it had been made. There was no good answer or outcome. Perhaps that was why she was paralyzed when it came to voting. It was a choice of doing harm or causing harm, and Kate was unwilling to do either.

The king of Noranger could take the body and do whatever customs they saw fit, allowing their conscience to be free of it.

Provided that the king didn't send a battalion. That remained to be seen.

"Whatever happens next will be on the Ghost King's head," Baxter said.

She pressed her lips closed to keep from reacting. That wasn't fair. The prince attacked the Ghost King on his own lands, not the other way around. The prince's hand was on his hilt, suggesting he intended to use it. Self-defense was one of the few natural laws among men that couldn't be denied.

Scowling at her papa, she pressed her thumb into her index finger from under the table. He feared the Ghost King the way she feared fire, but that did not mean they should be dictated by ignorance. He, of all people, should have known that.

"It was in defense. Besides, we assume the Ghost King can actually control the blight. For all we know, he can't."

Papa returned her scowl, but it quickly softened. "I had never thought about that. Maybe he can't control it. But I doubt the king of Noranger will see it that way."

The anger that swelled in her chest wouldn't allow her satisfaction. Why did her heart betray her with such useless emotions? "What's done is done," she said as she climbed from the bench, abandoning her tea. "The three of us will focus on the new commission and do what we can to shore up the village's defenses."

"Solid plan," Frank agreed. "We're certainly going to need your help."

They weren't the only ones.

With the threat of war and the Ever Faithful running amok, the village would need weapons and locks on its doors. They would need many things, but more than anything, they would need a king ready to fight.

The villagers were content to sacrifice their only salvation on the basis of superstition, but she was not. His blight could kill legions. Instead of waiting for the bloodshed to summon him from his castle, Kate would call upon him.

Chapter 6

KATE STOOD BESIDE LORI outside the library. She took the librarian's hand and squeezed it while her friend cried as Harvey rode away. Rather than take his cart, the merchant would ride horseback, allowing him a quicker, safer travel through the war-torn continent.

"For the record, I voted against sending the letter," Lori said as she wiped her face with a handkerchief. She and Harvey both did, yet it was them who stood to lose the most.

Had she been at the voting, it wouldn't have mattered. The village voted overwhelmingly to send word to Noranger. Kate was happy she wasn't there because she still didn't know what she would have chosen. Though she suspected the Ever Faithful had influence over this decision. Who else would be so willing to upend the Ghost King?

"Envoys are never harmed. Harvey is our envoy." Not like that was going to be a source of comfort for Lori, but it was all she could think to say.

"Let's go have a drink."

It was the middle of the day and she had so much work to do. Between helping her fathers build their soldiers, designing a suit that could withstand the blight, and the tonics, she scarcely had time to spare.

But the smile that crept across her face could not be denied. "Let's do it."

They retired to Lori's apartment and opened a ceramic bottle of clear wine imported from Taus. Kate did not ask how Lori managed to acquire such an exotic drink. She already knew the answer. But despite their years of friendship, Lori was still too reluctant to talk about her relationship with Harvey.

"Did you know that the Taus have been using the same recipes for their wine for the last seven hundred years?" Lori asked.

She did not know! Kate peered into the cup with admiration. "Fascinating."

"We're big on tradition. Taus does love its ceremony and history."

Lori seldom talked about her life before coming to the village. Kate didn't want to pry, the librarian kept her secrets safely guarded, but she had never been anywhere but the village and the occasional family trip to Flosses. The wars made sure of that.

"What is it like there?"

The librarian considered the question while she sipped her wine. "It's like a neat curio cabinet. Everything has its place and is safeguarded behind glass."

Kate had hoped for a more literal description, but she feared she was treading on thinning ice. "I mean, what does it look like? What are the people like? How do they dress?"

"Oh. Well, the weather changes on a whim, so they dress in layers and always carry parasols. Their cities are busy, and everyone has half a dozen servants. Even servants have servants."

"Sounds like too many people in a household."

"Well, their houses are much bigger, and the servants have their own houses on the properties."

It was a romantic notion. Not chopping wood or sweeping the shop. Having someone else to fetch the groceries and other errands. Yet, given the servant-to-employer ratio, Kate imagined she would likely end up a servant's servant.

"Why did you leave?"

Lori eyed her for a moment as if she were deciding whether she'd had enough wine to say. "Like most in Taus, my marriage was an arranged one. A wealthy, noble family, but he was a total bastard. When my family refused to help, I left."

She didn't need to explain further. Kate was well aware of the atrocities many women faced in the other provinces. As her lips met the cup, molten-hot ceramic warned her that it wasn't safe to drink.

Frowning, she examined the cup to find nothing unusual otherwise. It wasn't that hot a moment ago. It was inexplicable.

As if her hands had reheated the mug itself, but that was ridiculous.

Setting the cup down, she said, "Good for you."

"Harvey found me walking the road to Flosses and offered me a ride, and I never looked back."

The merchant was another sticky topic for Lori, but with the information she had just learned, Kate could see why. Lori was technically married to someone of wealth and power with the means to retrieve her. Still, she had been in the village for over a decade without issue.

Everyone knew Lori and Harvey were a couple. They just pretended they didn't.

Even though he only stayed at the library while in town and kept most of his important belongings in Lori's loft...they were not together. He brought her gifts from faraway lands and various alcohols and expensive chocolates as a thank-you for allowing him to sleep on the couch. Or something like that.

They were three drinks in before the question came tumbling out of Kate's mouth. "Why do you hide your relationship with Harvey? He hasn't come for you, and no one here cares if you're married or not."

"But don't they?" Lori poured herself another. "This is certainly not Taus, but there are still expectations where women are concerned."

Kate's expression prompted a laugh from the librarian.

"You've never been asked about getting married? Having children?"

"Bethany sometimes makes comments, but she has opinions about everything."

"Like it or not, Bethany is the mouthpiece of this village," Lori explained. "What she says to you, the rest of the village would if they had the opportunity. Lucky for you, no one wants to answer to Baxter."

The oversimplified version of her life was like a knife twisting in her gut. The only reason people didn't push her to marry was because Baxter would be towering over them? The anger rose in her throat. Between the wine and the conversation, she reeled in the urge to say something regrettable.

"So, you are with Harvey but wish to keep it a secret to avoid scrutiny on your personal life. I can respect that."

"I know you can, dear," Lori said, rubbing her shoulder. The warmth in her voice soothed the malcontent. "I just don't want to make it your burden. You already have so much to contend with."

"About that..."

It turned out that Kate was going to say something regrettable after all. The damned wine was to blame. Her plan spilled from her mouth, and then Lori knew everything. It felt good to say it out loud, even if Lori was swaying in her seat.

"You're going to go to the castle."

"In a suit designed to protect me from the blight, as well as several tonics as a safeguard."

"I don't know, Kate—"

"He needs to know," she argued. A hiccup burst from her at precisely the wrong time. "The Ever Faithful, the threat of Noranger... We need his help."

Lori was up and pacing her living space. "You're not wrong. If the death of the prince leads to war, only the Ghost King can protect us."

She was relieved that Lori understood her logic. "We have no armies. No defenses other than him. If an army does come, he can be ready for them. Otherwise, we would have to wait until Noranger wipes out a village or two."

The buzz from the alcohol went flat at the thought.

No one deserved to experience what she went through as a child. If there was a chance to prevent a massacre, not taking it was cruel negligence. Her guilt over the prince was bad enough. A whole unarmed village would haunt her forever.

Plopping in an overstuffed chair, Lori said, "Okay, what kind of suit?"

They spent the next few hours sketching out a design. While Lori was not her fathers, she was well-read and her worldly knowledge proved effective. "Seal blubber is going to be costly, and you'll need to go to Flosses for it; tallow might serve just as well."

"I thought about sealing it with pitch," Kate said. "The blight doesn't affect the forest like it does people."

"How are you going to afford this?"

It was a notion that Kate had been reluctant to accept. The seamstress would have questions. Buying furs from the tanner was another problem. A fully enclosed suit made of fur, covered in tallow... The cost would be outrageous.

Kate had small savings from her share of commissions. She had wanted to use it for something like a new roof or for a doctor in an emergency, but this was important.

Short of hunting the animals herself, she didn't know how to acquire the things she needed.

"I can make the pitch," Kate said. "I'd like something thicker than deerskin, but unless another pack of wolves comes through, I don't have many options."

Lori was pacing again. Her fingers were pressed to her lips as she was deep in thought. "Harvey said that the people in Noranger have an abundance of buffalo furs. They sell them on every street corner for coppers."

Two furry buffalo hides would be enough to fully enclose her. She could order four hides and fill a layer with sheep's wool. The outside layer would be covered in pitch to seal out the blight. She was on her feet and embracing Lori. "You're a genius!"

"Well, yes—"

"I need to start the pitch production. Can you send word to Harvey? Ask him to pick up some furs while he's in Noranger?"

"I can send a letter with the next merchant that comes to town. I know which inns he frequents on his routes. If the price of pitch isn't too much, I'll see if he can fetch some of that as well."

With the development of the suit in motion, Kate would need to work on her tonics as well. She kissed Lori goodbye and took to the forest. Rather than cross through the town, she went behind the library, hoping to encounter some of the roots from her books.

Much was cut down from the nearby lumber mill, but that might make it easier for her to find what she needed.

The deforestation was...depressing. Grounds littered with stumps that bled the scent of pine. She did note that the lumber workers carved small holes in the center of the stumps where saplings emerged, green and hopeful.

The lumber mill was not a destructive force like many would assume. They were more like caretakers of the forest. Their cuts were strategic. They removed trees that threatened the others, allowing the younger trees sunlight and nutrients to grow. It wasn't beautiful like the untamed forest, but much thought and care went into the operation.

She set about foraging for the plants drawn in the remedy book. They were frilly things, much like ferns, but they shot upward and had far fewer leaves. Kate looked for what felt like hours. Moving steadily into the untouched forest, she noted a distinct line of where the lumber mill ended and the remains of Paradise Lost began.

Moss had grown over what was once a ground floor, but smooth white steps rose from the forest. There were two massive pillars at the top. Their broken arches suggested it was once the entrance to an outdoor arcade or perhaps a market. Nature had reclaimed much of the site, making it impossible to determine.

Kate theorized that this area was once a town. One day, she would need to come out here and set up markers around the perimeter to see if there was a definitive border. There were many theories on why Paradise Lost was, well, lost.

There was the myth that the Waters destroyed the civilization as punishment for creating Dominion. A standard belief throughout the continent, but scholars found little to confirm it. Farmers had a way of accidentally tilling up ancient battlefields, which suggested they fought themselves into extinction.

There were other, more random theories, but it felt like those scholars were simply tossing their hats into the ring just because they could. She never did see the importance of proving what ended Paradise Lost. To Kate, recovering their technology was far more relevant.

She once read they had a technique for taking a babe from a mother's womb without killing the mother. How useful could that be if all doctors knew it?

Imagine being able to funnel water from rivers directly to farmlands instead of using a well. How much time and effort it would save. The increase in production. All these things could make for a better world if people didn't shun them over an ending they couldn't verify.

A stagnant, ripe smell wafted in the air. Kate paused and focused on her surroundings once more.

Looking down, she realized that if she had taken a few more steps, she'd have slipped and fallen into a murky pond. A frog with big black eyes stared at her from the water's brackish surface as if he were preparing himself for the worst.

"Don't worry," she said. "I won't eat you."

She also noted that there were fewer birds, and the ground was clear of insects. What was more, the pond was not entirely responsible for the smell. There was a tang to it that was almost chemical. Kate followed the scent and found herself staring into a snake den.

Dozens of snakes were coiled around one another in a black-and-yellow-striped mass. She wished she had her book with her so she could identify the snakes. Kate had come for roots and was not prepared for an encounter with snakes.

But if they contained the venom she needed, it was important to make note of the den's location.

Kate walked east as straight as she could. It took far longer than she expected, but Kate had never been more grateful to find the back end of the abandoned home at the opposite end of the village.

She was hungry, and her head throbbed like it was stuck between squeezing clamps. The alcohol had long since subsided, which was good. Nothing like telling your fathers about how you stumbled around in the woods drunk and alone.

Her fathers were carving large wooden balls when she came in. Wordlessly, she carved off a slice of bread and cheese.

Frank was holding a ball in each hand, comparing them. "This one is bigger," he said.

"Then shave it down," Papa said.

"But it's so perfectly round!"

Oh, if she had heard that conversation drunk. Kate sat at her worktable and opened her book, flipping to the pages on snakes.

"Well, if it's not noticeably smaller, who cares. People have different size heads too," Papa offered. "Makes them more realistic."

Her dad was not satisfied with this answer, however. "Yeah, but this one will sit lower than the other."

"That's what balls do."

Kate turned to regard her fathers. Were they really making those kinds of jokes with their daughter in the same room? Baxter winked at her, but Frank was still fretting over his big balls.

"What did you do today, Kate?" Papa asked.

With a bit of cheese still in her mouth, she replied, "Got drunk with Lori."

Baxter grinned and made a grunt of approval. "What kind of alcohol? Beer?"

"Wine from Taus."

Papa pursed his lips together in a whistle of admiration. "I've heard that's good stuff. We should make beer! The village would love it."

"We tried." Dad looked up at his husband through his thick spectacles. "You drank faster than we could sell."

There was a gruff of disappointment, but the notion of beermaking was squashed.

According to her text, the snakes she saw were indeed the ones she needed for the tonic. If only she could find the roots. There was still so much to do. She would need to figure out a way to collect the venom without getting bit, and even after finding the roots, there was still formulating and testing.

What would take years had to be done as soon as possible. Who knew how long before Noranger sent word. Or what the Ever Faithful might try in the meantime. As far as she could tell, their presence had been only somewhat influential. The people who were already religious flocked to them, and the others only observed with interest. There hadn't been this much excitement in the village her entire life, and Kate feared that excitement would provoke people to find ways to create more.

"Have either of you spoken to the Ever Faithful more?"

"We don't have time!" Baxter said. "Even if we did, what would religious people have to say to gay inventors?

"They don't seem to care that we're gay," Frank said. "Or inventors. Usually acolytes dislike the former, but the latter sends them running for the hills."

The acolytes of the Waters never visited the village, so Kate had no idea what was different or what wasn't. She relied entirely on the reactions people gave, but even then, something about the Ever Faithful felt...off.

She couldn't say why, but they reminded her of the peddler that came to the village from time to time selling talismans and bottles of water sworn to be blessed by the Waters herself. They were selling something, and she was worried the village would buy it.

"I'm just surprised they're still here," Dad said.

Baxter made a grunt of agreement. "They're looking for this so-called bride, but even the village elders have told them there is none."

"Their former leader claimed to be a prophet," Kate explained. "He told them there was a wife, and now they're intent on finding one."

Papa shook his head. "We're still waiting on the last prophecy."

"Sounds to me like their prophet needed to stop eating the spotted mushrooms," Frank said.

Kate was inclined to agree.

"Have either of you seen this plant?" Kate asked, holding out her open book to a picture of the plant she needed.

Her fathers leaned in. Frank had to squint hard to see it, but Baxter's face lit with recognition. "I've seen those. When I worked summers at the lumber mill. You find them along cliff sides and exposed tree roots. Why?"

Kate didn't have a reason planned.

"Ah, I was just curious. For research." The lie was so forced and obvious that even she didn't believe it, and it was coming from her own mouth.

"You've been looking into medicinal plants a lot lately," Frank acknowledged. "Are you thinking of becoming a doctor?"

"No, not exactly. I've always wanted to develop inventions for medical reasons, though." That was not a lie. Part of her reason for researching Paradise Lost was for the medical advancements that it could bring to society.

"I'm trying to develop tonics that delay hypothermia," she explained, deciding that telling lies that paralleled the truth worked far better. "It kills so many each year. I imagine it would sell in the northern regions like Noranger or Taus."

Her fathers seemed to approve of the idea. Whether or not they believed her, she couldn't say.

"Interesting," Frank said, returning to his work.

"Yes, yes, that's fine and good," Baxter said, giving her a wooden arm. "But first, we need you to level the joints."

Kate sighed and did as she was told. It was getting dark, and she wouldn't be able to return to the forest. Anyhow, finishing the commission would provide her with a share of it. That was coin she would need to create her suite.

Chapter 7

THE FROZEN PRINCE WAS no longer frozen, more like the lukewarm prince.

As Frank predicted, the flies were taking an interest. While there was no smell, there was a puddle forming around his boots. She had never noticed before, and she should have, but his clothes were well-tailored. They should have known he wasn't an ordinary merc.

The villagers put the body in the water and tied it down to a rock to slow the decay. It would have been a terrifying sight for any who happened upon the body under the bridge, but they had no new arrivals other than the acolytes that swarmed the village in a way that reminded Kate of the flies on the prince's corpse.

Nearly the whole village surrounded the merchant's horse when he arrived. Poor Harvey was covered in dust, and he had bags under his eyes as if he hadn't slept in days. He must have ridden hard to get there as fast as possible.

Kate and Lori were among the crowd. She was just as eager to learn the fate of their village and possibly the whole providence. They wanted to know if they should prepare for the worst. There was talk in Bethany's household of fleeing to Flosses. Kate didn't imagine they were the only ones.

Not bothering to get off his horse, Harvey gave everyone the news right then and there. "The king of Noranger did not see me, but his envoy did. When I told him what had happened, he said he would come at once. I do not know what they intend to do."

Disappointment had stolen all the potential of the day. She rubbed the dust from her eyes as the crowd slinked away. One of the Ever Faithful rubbed the tanner's back as if he were consoling him. No one was happy about the news. More strangers in the village, just what they needed.

Noranger envoys were coming. It was better than Noranger troops, but it did nothing to alleviate the anxiety shared throughout the village.

As Harvey slipped off his horse, Kate saw the rolled bundles of what looked like brown fur. Yes! He'd gotten the message Lori had sent. Her savings would shrink, but Kate would begin constructing her suit as soon as possible.

Fighting through the remaining crowd, Kate made her way to the horse and the merchant. "You got the letter!"

"Hi, Kate!" Despite his long travel, Harvey was happy to see her.

She imagined he'd be happier to see Lori, who had gone back inside, so she'd keep it brief. "She missed you," Kate whispered.

Harvey's skin was the color of dried wheat, and his hair was a sunburnt brown that matched his eyes. He was somewhere in his forties, about Lori's age, but unlike Lori, Harvey had no gray hairs. Kate could see why the librarian was so taken with him. It probably helped that he was a man that traveled all over and was able to keep up with her.

"We both know she'd never admit it," he said with a grin. "Here's your furs."

"How much?" She asked, suddenly aware of the weight in her pocket.

"Nothing," he said. "They were gifted to me when I bought more mead than I should have at an inn."

She couldn't allow that to pass. Harvey had made this trip without compensation. Everyone in the village contributed to pay for his expenses, but Kate doubted it was enough to get him to Noranger and back. Pulling a round, smooth silver chip from her pocket, she said, "Please take it. I insist."

Kate had been saving her share of the commissions since she began working with her fathers at the age of thirteen. Since then, she had been able to trade most of her coppers into silver, and she had six.

Harvey eyed the coin as it glimmered in the sunlight. "If you insist."

She wove through the crowd, avoiding her fathers, who were talking to Faustus and the blacksmith. The last thing she wanted was to explain the bundle of buffalo furs in her arms.

So, she whisked them away to her bedroom.

Deciding it was a space for her and her alone, her fathers never went up there. Like any attic space, the room was dim, with only a single round window. She would need lots of candles, but with the commission nearly finished, her fathers would be too busy to notice the late-night candlelight.

At this point, she had a whole stockpile of materials—everything she would need—including wool, needle and thread and two round glass caps for eyes. They were tinted green since they came from canning jars. The Ghost King could ice over glass, but if the windows didn't break from the blight, neither would the thick glass of the bottles.

Assessing all her raw materials, sketch in hand, Kate took a deep breath and said, "Right."

Frank did a little sewing from time to time. Nothing on such a massive scale, usually just a button here or a hemline there. Anything to save a few coppers between commissions. The process wasn't a total mystery to her, but it wasn't until she unrolled the hides that Kate began to worry she was out of her depth.

She couldn't go running to Bethany for help on construction, so Kate laid on the hide and used her ink and quill to create an outline along the hide. When she finished flopping about the floor, she stood over the line. Her face crinkled with disgust.

Was she really so fat? It seemed like every few years, her dresses needed to be let out, but she hardly ate. With a string, Kate measured across her hips, then laid the length across the outline. She had left a bit of a gap in the outline for seam allowance, but perhaps there was too much.

So, she laid on the hide and did a second, more accurate outline. Careful not to stain her dress with ink, Kate got up and placed her hands on her hips. No, that wouldn't do either. She would need more room within the suit for the stuffing.

She let out a frustrated sigh and shook her head. Uncertainty was the undoing of progress, but with limited resources, it was best to measure many times and only cut once.

Nothing about the suit would be easy.

In the weeks after Harvey's return, Kate had spent much of her time on a night schedule. It was no easy task avoiding Frank's suspicions. If she could stop falling asleep while reading, it would have helped, but the long nights wore on her. When she was younger, she could stay up all hours with little repercussion. These days, it felt as though she were half a person when she didn't get a full night's sleep. When did she get so old?

But she had made a lot of progress. Unfortunately, she had also burned through two dozen candles and cringed at the thought of needing more. Whenever she entered the grocery store, the grocer would wordlessly collect a handful of beeswax candles and set them on the counter.

Her savings were fading faster than the summer days, but she was so close to finishing. Candles, of all things, cost nearly as much as the hides. She just hoped it would be worth it. And by worth it, she meant remaining alive long enough to tell the Ghost King that war was coming. It would be ideal if she survived the encounter altogether.

Kate stood back and regarded the suit. It was taking a slightly different shape than the one she originally pictured.

In her sketch, it was more like a rounded hood with a flat covering to shield her face, but she had severely overestimated the difficulty of sewing. Bethany did it every day like it was as easy as breathing. It was arrogant to assume she could pick up an occupation that the seamstress had dedicated her entire life to.

Working with such a thick material didn't help. The top puckered into a point, and when the pitch dried, the whole thing became too stiff to manipulate.

Two green eyes shimmered with every flicker of her candle-light.

Propped up on a wooden rack, it was like a Kate-sized fish monster. She wanted nothing more than to throw it into a fire and start over, but there was no time or coin to spend. The envoys from Noranger would be there any day, and she had yet to get the snake venom.

The possibility that she may not have time for testing kept her up at night. She'd toss and turn while the fish suit stared at her in the dark. She had no choice but to retrieve a snake the next morning while the pitch on the fish suit cured.

She woke the next morning groggy. Her eyes hurt from lack of sleep. Dragging her fatigued body down the stairs, she found her parents searching the room.

"What is that?" Frank asked himself as he sniffed around the room.

"What?" Kate tilted her head as her dad bent to look under the table.

"I keep smelling sap or something."

Baxter sat at the workbench, eating his porridge. "My nose doesn't work this time of year."

"Well, mine does, and the smell is overpowering. Kate, are you working on something upstairs? The grocer said you've been going through his candles."

Fully alert, Kate already had an explanation. "It might be my fault. I've been working on a combusting fire starter."

Frank's thin brows raised on his large forehead. "Really? That's quite clever. I'm just surprised since you hate fire."

Loathe was a better description, but even she had to accept its utility. Should she encounter the Ghost King and the suit failed, she would need something to start a fire even in the coldest conditions. It was more of an afterthought, having made far too much pitch; she just hoped the little fire abominations wouldn't be needed.

"I doubt I'll ever use them, but maybe the villagers will."

Her fathers approved, and Frank was seemingly resolved of his suspicions. "I'm off to forage for berries!" she said before they could ask any more questions.

The blacksmith begrudgingly allowed her to borrow his poll. It had a curved hook on the end. Ideal for catching snakes. Papa sometimes used it when he went fishing upriver.

"Just leave it on the porch when you're done."

With the poll slung over one shoulder and a burlap bag in the other, Kate retraced her steps to the far end of the village. She was just about to disappear into the tree line when one of the Ever Faithful stopped her. It may have been Bob or one of the others, but they had morphed into two people in her mind. Faustus or Bob.

"Fishing?" he asked.

"In a way."

"I hear you're quite the inventor."

"I'm surprised your people don't mind," she said. "Are inventions not the work of Dominion?"

The acolyte tilted his head from left to right as if debating himself on what to say. "They can be, but not all inventions are bad. Take a fishing rod, for example. Without it, people starve. Without medicines, people suffer. If we threw away all the devices of man, there would be great suffering indeed."

This was a level of sense that she didn't expect from a cultist. How was it he could see reason in some regards but not others? At what point did an intelligent, scrutinizing mind look at something completely far-fetched and decide it had to be true despite all evidence otherwise?

"I wholeheartedly agree. But I should go. I'm losing the morning."

"Good day," he said with a slight bow and made no attempt to follow.

She noticed he did not say the thing they usually said. Waters preserve you, or something like that. Perhaps he didn't want the Waters to preserve her.

It didn't take long to find the pond. Kate must have been drunker than she'd realized. It wasn't but a half mile from the village. She must have been circling around the same area for hours.

Her nose led the way. According to her book, the offensive smell was from secretions the snakes made while mating. She stood at the opening of the hole in the tree and shook out the nerves, suddenly wishing she had put more time into studying snake behavior.

Placing her bag on the end of the rod, Kate slowly maneuvered the curved hook around the opening of the snake den.

Adrenaline was spiking at the prospect of catching something new. She opened the bag a little more before hooking one strap through the rod. Taking a deep breath, Kate slipped the curved part of the rod farther into the den, and when she felt the weight of something bearing down. She pulled.

A massive black and yellow snake spilled out of the den and slithered into the bag. Kate used the hook to pull one strap through the other, securing the snake, and released a roar of victory.

She had caught a venomous snake! What came next was going to be harder. She swore she could hear Frank shrieking somewhere at the thought of what was about to happen.

In the warmer months, the door to the shop always swelled and stuck in the frame. If she weren't so excited and had two free hands, she would have pushed the door open. Instead, she bashed the door with her shoulder before walking into the house backward, extending the rod and bag as far away as she could.

The conversation between her fathers died. Their chairs skipped across the shop floor as they stood.

"Kate?" Baxter said, slowly coming to a stand. His eyes were on the movement within the bag.

"You both might want to leave."

"What's in the bag, Kate?" Frank asked slowly.

She turned around to face them. "I caught a venomous snake," she explained. "So, you might want to leave the room."

Despite the horror on his face, Dad shook his head. "Leave you alone with a poisonous snake? I don't think so."

"Venomous," she said. "There's a difference."

"Not when you're dead," Baxter scoffed.

Kate had to admit both had valid points. Especially since the realization that she would need to handle the snake was fast approaching. She hadn't considered how she would get the snake out of the bag without it biting her, and there was no plan as to how she would get the snake to bite the fabric lid of her jar.

Her eyes went from the bag to her fathers and back to the bag again.

She had come so far just to be defeated by ill planning. It wasn't like she had all that much time left. It took days forging for those damn roots. Between making soldiers and constructing the suit, there was scarcely time to breathe, let alone plan.

Frank sighed. "I'll get the work gloves."

Baxter thought it best to stay at the far end of the room. He was a large man, and the last thing they needed was to accidentally bump into him, drop the snake, and unleash lethal chaos in the shop. Frank went into the attic storage and returned with giant leather gloves.

"I used these for training hawks once," he explained. "They should do the trick."

The snake moved around in the bag as Frank helped put the gloves on her. They went clear up to her upper arms. "How do you want to do this?" he asked.

Kate's belly writhed and twisted. Not now; she couldn't afford to buckle now. "Grab it and try to get it to bite the lid."

"Use the rod," Baxter said from the corner. "Use the rod to take it out of the bag and to pin the head down."

"Are you kidding me?" Frank asked.

"The snake wranglers at the ports never used gloves, just a hook and one hand to support the tail."

Kate would have to take off her gloves to grab the head safely. She looked at Frank, whose forehead was glistening with sweat. She was scared, but Kate trusted her fathers. She took off the gloves while Frank held the bag. Inside, the snake was coiled into a figure eight.

"Move to the big worktable," she said.

While Frank maneuvered the bag, Kate retrieved the hook from the floor where she had dropped it. "Just lay the bag down," she instructed.

"You're both going to need to restrain it," Baxter warned. "Snakes are much stronger than they look."

Kate pinched the edge of the bag and lifted until the snake came sliding out, a tangled mass of scales, and hissing. For a moment, she was paralyzed, not by venom but by fear. Its beady glass eyes watched their every stilted breath. Its thick scales forged a heavy ridge on the top of the head, resembling an angry brow.

She didn't really look at the snake before it fell into her bag. It was no butter corn snake. It was a massive, deadly serpent that she had brought into the house. "Frank," she muttered. "I'm really sorry. I get it now."

"Press that rod just below its head," Baxter urged. "Before it slithers off the table."

"I'll be right behind you," Frank promised.

"I know."

She released the breath locked in her lungs. Rod in hand, Kate firmly pressed the head down. The snake whipped around violently, forcing her to press down on the body with her free hand.

In an instant, Dad was beside her, grabbing the belly and pointed tail of the snake. This freed up Kate's hand to wrap around the snake's head, and she was able to drop the rod. The sketches made it look so easy. It was not easy. It was like fighting with a creature ten times its size, and there was little way to grab and restrain it.

"Lift on the count of three," Kate instructed. "One, two, three."

Her heart bounced in her chest as they lifted the snake and brought it to her worktable. It tried to recoil, and it nearly succeeded. Baxter was right; snakes were strong! The snake threatened to knock her off-balance, but Frank had a vice grip on the thickest part of the body.

She showed the snake the jar, uncertain if it would open its mouth, but it did. Kate was not some fainting lady, but when the snake opened its mouth and exposed the two-inch fangs, her vision darkened. Even when it was restrained by two adults, the snake still had enough power in its neck and jaw to lunge.

The snake latched onto the lip of the jar. Its fangs punctured through the starched fabric like it was an autumn leaf. A neon green liquid splattered against the glass. Ignoring the cold sweat and wobbly knees, Kate waited until its fangs retracted before removing it from the jar.

Still holding its head with shaky hands, Kate nodded to Baxter. "Can you grab the bag?"

The snake slipped into the bag without a fight.

A collective sigh came from the family as the opening was secured.

Baxter slumped against the wall beside the door. Frank took off his cap and wiped his bald head. He looked much older and frailer without his hat on. It made her feel uneasy. Both men aged rapidly in the last few years. A vacation wasn't enough.

"I'm going to release this thing back to its nest."

Speechless, Baxter waved her off.

"Next time," Frank said, "please warn us."

She had woefully underestimated them, especially Frank. This wasn't a lesson she would ever forget. "Thank you," she said, pulling the door open. "I was in trouble back there."

Frank gave her a nod before turning to Baxter. "Adopt a daughter, you said. It will be fun, you said!"

"Hmph."

"You promised me bows and tiny dresses! Not dead guys and poisonous snakes."

"Venomous," she gently reminded him.

Her fathers jeered as she shut the door behind her.

Chapter 8

T HE DAY WAS MARKED in her journal, along with a list of things she needed to bring. Kate barely slept the night before. Once the dawn began to rise, she gave up on the pretense of sleep and dressed. Wearing her winter clothes, a long-sleeved dress with a knitted bodice, Kate double-checked her bag.

Letter; check. Untested tonics; check. Fire starters; check. Journal; check. Suit; sadly, a check. She hoped it didn't look as horrendous as she thought. People were often far more critical of their work than others were, but it looked like a sack of human flesh void of insides. There was no way it would fit in her bag, so Kate folded it in half and slung it over the bag.

She gave one final look at the shop before closing the door, knowing she might never see it again. In the wake of what would be a life-changing moment, Kate found herself in the mists of nostalgia. The ghosts of her childhood reenacted all her most cherished memories all at once, as if pleading with her to stay home. To linger in the past was tempting, but the future waited for no one.

If the suit did not work and the potions failed, Kate hoped the Ghost King could read the letter. It was the ninth version of the letter. It took that many drafts to pare down everything she needed to say, and even then, it took up three pages. Not that she wrote pages upon pages of things...

The first letter was a simple, itemized summary of events like, "War is coming," and, "The Ever Faithful want to kill your wife...if you even have one."

The other two pages were detailed accounts of what had transpired and why she was willing to risk life and limb to meet him. It wasn't just because her curiosity had gotten the better of her or because her fiery nightmares had been replaced by dreams of eternal ice.

She followed the road and turned right at the fork where the frozen prince had stood for so many weeks. Past the lumber mill, the road whittled to a trail, and Kate's breath quickened. Not only because of the tornado of emotions within her but also because there was a growing incline. *I'm going to be walking more and snacking much less. No more crackers while reading...*

The castle just had to be built on a hill. It occurred to Kate that she wouldn't be able to see so much of it from her hilltop otherwise, but she never considered it until she had to huff her way up the foot of the mountains. The heat of exertion and her winter dress kept her plenty warm, but the prickle of the ever-cooling air had grown so intense that her goose bumps were developing goose bumps.

Kate stopped and unfolded her suit. If her teeth were chattering so far from the castle, how cold would it truly get at the top? She had only done preliminary fittings, and that was enough to know walking in the suit was slow and cumbersome. The last thing she needed was more weight on an upward incline, so she trudged on, enduring the cold for as long as it was safe to do so.

If only she had a horse that was inexplicably unaffected by the blight. It would make this trip easier. How mad would he be if she borrowed his horse for the return home? If there was one. She had only seen him once, but the Ghost King did not strike her as the forgiving type.

The castle was a slate gray backdrop behind thin trees with barren limbs. Snow from the mountains drifted in flurries all around her. It would have been magical if it wasn't a precursor of a horrid death.

Kate set down her bag and jotted notes in her journal while waiting for her tonics to take effect.

She frowned at the looming heap of a building. It held no resemblance to the remains of Paradise Lost whatsoever. The base of the castle used the same granite as the bridges, but the rocks stacked on top of that were a darker, coarser material she didn't recognize. There were four types that she could differentiate, and the stuff strewn about the ground was yet another.

The loose stones piled on the ground were a familiar material. The dark, smooth stone with jagged peaks was flint. A common material used in larger cities like Flosses. It was a rock that was found in abundance and easy to mine because it lay in chalk.

The spike in body temperature hit Kate all at once. Her skin flushed as her stomach roiled. What was once freezing air washed over her like a light summer breeze. The tonic took effect much sooner than she anticipated, and there was no telling how long it would last.

Kate unfolded her suit and stepped inside.

Despite all her careful measurements, the suit was twice her size when all was said and done. Between the initial layer of buffalo skin, the layer of tallow sealed by pitch, a layer of sheep wool, and the sealed pitch layer, her arms were unable to touch her sides. And oh, was it heavy. She had anticipated that much, but expecting something was a lot different from experiencing it. Every move was like walking in water but with stones tied to her arms and legs.

She almost hoped he wasn't home...almost.

Approaching the wooden double doors braced with iron, Kate hesitated. Should she knock? It was the polite thing to do. If she barged in, he might think it was an attack. Kate raised her padded hand and struck the door with a balled fist.

The noise wasn't so much of a knock but more of a soft thumping, like a dog's paw beating the floor amid the throes of a good scratch. Well, that wouldn't do. She doubted anyone could hear that from within a massive castle.

So much for that.

Clapping her concealed hands on one of the handles, Kate pushed, but the door refused to give. It must have been barred from the inside. Of all things to consider, she did not anticipate a locked door. Perhaps there was another way in. Between the suit and the tonic, fluster gave way to frustration, urging her to just go home. She could send letters to all the villages warning them of imminent war and hide under her covers until the zealots decided they found his bride in some unfortunate girl and be done with it!

It was only when she peered at the hinges through her green-tinted glasses did she realize the doors needed to be pulled open.

Releasing an annoyed huff, Kate pulled the door, and it opened easily.

"Get it together, girl," echoed in her helmet like the inside of a barrel.

The door opened to a vacant hallway.

No carpets, furniture, or other adornments. It would have been rather creepy, but it wasn't like the Ghost King could shop for décor when he wasn't chasing the blood of his enemies. He wasn't exactly a welcome patron in any furniture store.

She traversed through the hallway, her steps muffled by her suit, and followed it down a series of uneven steps that opened into what was probably meant to be a hall. There was no furniture to signify the use of the space, but there was a grand fireplace on the opposite end of a second platform leading to a new set of stairs.

If this were a great hall, she imagined a king and maybe a queen would sit at a separate table on the platform overlooking the subjects dining by the fire. She couldn't quite explain it, but the room reeked of hope and unrealized intent. A faded dream long abandoned. Perhaps from a time when he thought such company would be possible.

How long had he been alone within these walls? Perhaps it was the fever, but she was nearly overcome by sorrow. He endured this all alone for so long. It made her wonder what kind of man could withstand such loneliness and what remained of his humanity. Perhaps nothing.

Before she could dwell on it further, Kate took the few steps up the platform and entered another hallway. This one was much narrower than the first, but it gave way to a series of rooms. Some had doors, and others were open, revealing more empty rooms.

It was a semicircle, she realized with an odd excitement. The two openings from the great hall led to a wider set of stairs. Why did it have to be more stairs?

The erratic beat of her heart was a reminder that the tonic was alive and well in her system. The fever hadn't increased since it hit its peak in the dining hall, which she was thankful for. Any higher, and Kate feared she'd begin to hallucinate.

Ghost Kings may not have needed railings, but fever-addled, fish-suit-wearing scientists did. Kate had to put a hand against the wall for support as she heaved her heavy legs up the stairway. No landing in sight, even halfway up. A stabbing pain started in her lower back, reminding Kate that her days of youth were a thing of the past.

By the time she reached the top of the stairs, she was unreservedly panting and bracing herself against the wall. If he could speak, they would discuss those steps. Perhaps there was another way to the tall tower she was unaware of.

Still breathless, Kate realized she was in a circular courtyard. Three doors were visible around the barren yard. The only focal point was the dead tree in the center. Looking up, she could see the great tower overlooking the rest of the castle.

There was a natural conclusion that within the highest peak on the tallest tower was the Ghost King. There was no logic to this, apart from it being the most difficult to reach, and thus, it had to be. There was no law that explained the phenomenon, but there should be since everyone knew it to be the truth.

She took the door closest to the tower and climbed even more steps that led to the rooftop. Standing in the shadow of the tower, Kate tried to look into the window through her green-glass goggles. She was close enough to the window to see inside.

And surprise! It was empty.

At least from what she could see.

Sitting on the ledge of the castle walls, Kate took a much-needed rest. The suit had grown so heavy that she dreaded taking another step. The fever wore on her energy and emotions so much that she was experiencing mild claustrophobia. Thoughts of facing the blight without it were becoming stronger by the moment. Even the visions of the frozen prince didn't seem like such a bad fate compared to remaining inside the suit. It was just the fever and fatigue talking. She needed to remain calm.

Where was he if not here?

All this effort and she couldn't find him. She still lived, so she supposed that was a positive, but this was her chance to unlock the secrets of the Ghost King. The only way to protect her village and province was missing in action, and the suit was unbearably hot. Would it be enough to leave the letter? It was an assumption that he could even read their writing. She should have translated it into the written language of Paradise Lost.

It would have confirmed her theory without ever having to risk her life to the blight, but she wrote it in the common language, and there was no telling if he even understood it.

Failure was something scientists experienced in abundance. There was no reason to be upset, but her heart ached, and her jaw stung from strain. Why must her emotions be such a hindrance? She knew failure was the path to success, but perhaps her heart was unable to understand her mind.

That, and deep down, Kate wanted to see him. It was a childish wish, but she couldn't help it. Just to speak with him and know that there was a connection. If the castle told her anything, it was that he was utterly alone. She had overcome every obstacle known to man, and it still wasn't enough to see him and tell him she was there.

Cool tears streaked across her heated face, and she couldn't wipe them away because of the damned suit. So, she sobbed and let the moisture drip down her neck, creating a sauna within her helmet.

She would go back to the village with nothing to show for herself other than her stupid suit. Her breath hitched as she stood. She pulled her arms free from the sleeves. Twisting and yanking at every corner, she found that getting out of it was far harder than getting in.

If she could just find the buttons...

A bracing cold pelted her suit. Ice crackled over her bottle cap goggles. She stumbled back against the wall, her heart pounding. There was a yelp from the white-haired figure stumbling back. It was hard to see just what was happening, but his arms were waving about before he disappeared off the wall altogether.

Had it been him? It felt impossible, but it was the logical conclusion. Kate peered over the edge. Amid the frost and ice now covering the ground, the Ghost King was lying flat on his back, staring straight up at her.

Chapter 9

"I MEAN NO HARM!" Kate shouted through the suit. Her excitement rose her voice to unheard heights. "I came to warn you."

The Ghost King stared at her as if he were in a daze. He may have very well been concussed by the fall, that is if undying creatures could have concussions.

It was him! She would have danced with joy if she could. "Are you all right?"

There was a long moment where he did not speak, and she feared for the worst. He was what Baxter suggested, an unthinking, unfeeling monster that blighted anyone who trespassed on his territory and nothing more. A wild animal she had stunned with fear. Would he gnash his sharp teeth and unleash the blight upon recovery?

The bare interior of the castle was nothing more than a place he occupied when he wasn't murdering princes. Ugh, she hated when Papa was right, but if he was right, at least he'd never be able to tell her so. There was no way she could outrun him in the suit.

The Ghost King's black brow furrowed. "Are...you a person?"

She gasped and laughed with delight. He could speak! And what a voice he had. It was soft and raspy, with a strong accent she did not recognize.

It was only then that she recalled just what she was doing when he happened by. She couldn't imagine how strange it must have looked as she tried to yank off her suit in a fit of rage. A hysterical laugh erupted from her chest. He was walking around the corner, minding his own business when he came upon a pitch-covered monstrosity flailing with utter abandon.

The Ghost King did not move; he only stared at what probably looked like a giant laughing fish with green-glass eyes.

"My name is Kate. I live in the village down the hill. This is a suit designed to combat your blight."

He was nodding, but it was the kind of nodding people did when they wanted it to look like they understood when really, they couldn't hear you. So, Kate repeated herself, this time more loudly.

"Yes," he said, holding out his hand as if to stop her. A gust of ice pelted her suit, nearly knocking her over. The Ghost King winced as though he hadn't meant to do that. "You should not be here."

His accent was much thicker than she had anticipated. It wasn't so much of an accent and more like he struggled to speak. He hadn't spoken to anyone in a long time. It made sense that speaking would be difficult after hundreds, maybe thousands of years of silence.

"I had to come," she said. "We're in trouble. I...I think you're in trouble."

Propped on his elbows, he regarded her with caution but said, "Can you feel the blight from up there?"

Not through her suit. It was as hideous as it was effective. She imagined he wanted to see the person inside. "I felt it when you were up here, but it feels as though it can't reach me when you're down there."

It was at least a twelve-foot drop. While the whole courtyard was an ice-laden death trap, the frost climbed two-thirds of the way up the walls. Perhaps the blight was unable to reach upward. "Ah," he said, sitting up and shaking his head.

"One moment."

With more deliberation and a lot less anger, Kate was able to maneuver within the suit. She worked the set of buttons that went down the back until the opening gave way. An air colder than the hardest day of winter greeted her.

Her tonics might have worn off, but the cold was most welcome after enduring the sweaty suit. Freedom was a frigid gust of air that tingled along her damp skin.

Kate was able to see him, and he was able to see her. There they were, closer than ever, but it wasn't enough. The ledge was all that kept her alive and what kept them apart. It would have to be enough. Everything in her went all fuzzy, and she couldn't stop herself from smiling. She came with grim news but was practically glowing.

All the while, he observed her face and her clothes as if he were absorbing every aspect of the rising dawn for the first time. That did not help the impulse to leap over the edge and embrace him before...

Get it together, girl!

"What is this danger, Kate from the village?"

She told him about the prince. About how envoys from his lands were coming, and they didn't know for what. The Ghost King sat on the ground with his arms wrapped around his knees and listened the way a child did during story time. He even closed his eyes at some point, as if savoring the sound of her voice. The empty rooms and echoing halls came back to her then. He was in torment, and her voice was a temporary reprieve.

"So, the villagers have decided that if the king of Noranger wants vengeance, they will lead him to you."

"As they should," he said. "I am the one who killed him."

She bit her lip. It wasn't his fault. He was attacked by them on his own lands. If anything, it was them who declared war on him. "And what of the villages they burn along the way?"

At this, he nodded. "You want me to patrol the borders to intercept an army if it comes."

"Precisely."

"This I can do."

He was strategic and logical, as a king should be. His only desire was to protect the inhabitants of his province, yet he barred no one from coming or going and asked for nothing in return. Why couldn't all kings be this way?

"There's another matter," she said, fearing this may evoke something other than nobility. "Do you have a wife?"

The Ghost King's eyes went wide, and his jaw dropped, revealing a mouth full of sharp, pointing teeth. It was unsettling and something that would go in her journal later. He struggled to speak as if it overwhelmed him before giving up and simply stating, "No."

The way she framed the conversation was awkward and was not how she intended. "Oh, I mean... A religious group came to the village. They seem to think you have a wife. They want to kill her. We told them you have no wife, but they won't believe us."

His eyes narrowed, and his claw-like nails gripped his legs. "What is the name of this group?"

"The Ever Faithful," she said. "If you could tell them, maybe they would leave—"

"I will do no such thing," he said briskly. "I will not risk the blight on anyone unless I must."

She supposed if there was no wife, the Ever Faithful could do no harm. Still, she did not like them. Things could go back to normal if they left. It was something Kate would need to concede.

"I understand," she said through chattering teeth.

Despite the safety of the heights, the cold was still working away at her soft, living tissue. Her lips were numb, and the tips of her fingers were turning a plum color. She looked up from her digits to find the Ghost King leaving the courtyard.

"Wait!" She still had so many questions.

Abandoning her suit and bag, Kate went down to the courtyard. She followed the path he took, but it was too late. Emerging from the other side of the wall, she found herself on a balcony. He must have jumped over, knowing she would be unable to follow.

Below the balcony was an empty stable and nothing more.

She returned to the courtyard. The ice was dispelling like a bad dream, leaving slush in the dips along the grounds. While he was gone, she would be free to search the castle for clues on Paradise Lost, but it felt wrong to dig around in his belongings—if he had any. There hadn't been anything to signal occupancy that she had seen thus far.

That was when she noticed a glimmer on the ground where he fell. The closer she got, the colder it became. On the ground lay a pile of white sand. She squatted down to investigate. A stinging sensation bit at her fingertips, forcing her to drop it. Whatever it was, it was freezing, and the ice remained steadfast around it.

Could this somehow be the source of the blight?

She collected her things from the wall and scooped some of the sand into her bag for further study at home.

The way home was a steady decline. As if the forces of nature itself were pushing her away from the castle. Her trip was the very definition of success, but Kate could not shake the feeling of rejection. What more could she have asked for? The Ghost King would patrol the border, keeping the province safe, and he did not have a wife. She could take the Ever Faithful to the castle for a look if they wanted. With no wife, they might still leave.

And she did not freeze. All her fingers were still intact, and her untested tonics did not kill her. There was much to celebrate, yet she felt as though she were draped in a wet blanket.

All the energy was zapped from her. Unable to muster the ability to pretend she was okay, she went to the library rather than home. Her friend would surely console her and maybe even explain to her why she felt so crestfallen.

Lori came when the bell sounded. Leaning on the railing, the expression on her face must have been enough. "Come on up."

An entire pot of tea and several sandwiches later, Kate had told Lori all about her encounter with the Ghost King.

"Yet, congratulations are not in order?" Lori didn't understand her melancholy any more than she did.

"I don't know," Kate struggled to form the thoughts. "I guess I wanted him to see me the way I see him."

"I see."

"When I first saw him," she started, "there was this connection. It was alive and thrumming. Positively electric. Yet it was like he couldn't wait to get away from me."

One side of Lori's mouth squished as if she were restraining words. "Well, you did show up in that." She motioned to the suit. "And there is that whole blight problem. If I wanted to see a pretty woman again, I'd make sure she lived long enough for another visit."

Lori was right, of course, but try explaining that to her heart.

Bowing her head, Kate stared at her empty teacup. Feelings of doubt and inadequacy surged. What if he did not want to see her again? She imagined herself trying to open the doors of the castle only to find them locked. The idea that she would never see him again struck her harder than any slap. She sniffed but made no effort to restrain the tears.

"What is wrong with me?" Kate sobbed.

Lori was at her side in an instant. "Oh, shh, shh. Nothing is wrong with you. You're just in love. It's unfortunate that it's an impossible love. But it makes sense!"

She failed to see how. "How does it make sense? The only one I've ever wanted is an untouchable, inarticulate beast."

"He is a mystery. A scientific anomaly. There is no one like him in the world; it only makes sense you're drawn to him. He must have so much knowledge, especially about Paradise Lost. There isn't a single man in this village who holds a candle to that." Lori embraced her then.

Kate leaned in and let the librarian stroke her hair, though she wished it was him.

"I fear this all came about because there are so few in this village for you to connect with."

Perhaps. She couldn't help but feel like there was more to it. Something that went beyond the bloods in her brain or the lack of prospects in the village. But she must have been wrong. Otherwise, he would have surely felt the same.

"Maybe his heart is too cold to love," Kate said at last. "I don't think people are supposed to live so long in isolation."

"Being alone for a long time can do that to a person. I swore I'd never fall in love, but Harvey never gave up on me."

"I'm glad he didn't," she said.

It was comforting to know that love was not always instant. Lori had gone through so much in Taus, but Harvey remained by her side. He was the light that guided her home. Maybe the Ghost King needed that as well. She would try to be that for him. To be patient and consistent, allowing him time to work through the years of silence.

The suit worked. They had also found a loophole in that the blight emitted horizontally and not quite vertically. She had the means and a reason to return to the castle seeing how she never got the opportunity to ask about Paradise Lost. Impossibility was only named as such until invention found a way. If she could continue to see him, perhaps she could thaw that frozen heart of his.

But what if he did confirm her theory?

What if there was no such thing as Dominion and he was a product of some medical procedure? If he confirmed her theory was correct, the doors of the university would open. She would need to leave if she wanted to review their archives and walk among their relics. It would only be a temporary visit. He would understand, wouldn't he?

"What do you intend to tell the villagers?" Lori asked.

"Everything, of course," Kate said, sitting up.

Lori's cautious gaze made her second-guess that plan. "Are you sure that's wise?"

She had always assumed they would be relieved and grateful to learn the Ghost King was on high alert and guarding the border. If Lori did not think it wise, it might mean she knew something Kate didn't.

"What is it?"

"Well, it's just that the Ever Faithful have continued their discussions here at the library. Many people had never seen the Ghost King until recently. It scared them, I think, seeing the way the prince died."

It should frighten them. It certainly scared the shit out of her. She imagined he would be even more terrible in the eyes of their enemies. But how did that pertain to her?

"I'm just saying. The villagers may not react to your news in the way you think they should."

She couldn't withhold the information and allow the anxiety in the village to continue to grow. What was the point of making discoveries if the knowledge wasn't shared?

"I'll do my best to be tactful about it."

"Good."

Full of tea and cheese sandwiches, Kate returned home. What Lori said may have been true, but her fathers were not fearful, superstitious men. Not in the slightest.

When she opened the door, Frank whirled around and asked, "Where have you been?"

She stepped back, surprised by the anger in his voice. "I was just about to tell you."

In the space between their silence, she could hear fierce whacks from the back door. Baxter was chopping wood as though winter had snuck up on them.

"One of the lumberyard workers saw you heading to the castle," Dad said. "Tell me you didn't."

But she had, and she had every intention of doing so again.

"I went to the Ghost King," she said, holding up the suit folded along her chilled bag. "I spoke to him, Dad."

Frank sat down as if his knees were threatening to buckle. He took a deep breath. "Do you have any idea, any idea at all, how scared we were?"

Wood splintered again and again out back. "She's back," Frank yelled at the back door. "She's fine."

He could have given her a few more minutes of peace before Papa busted in. She waited for him to come in, all red-faced and blustery, but the wood chopping resumed. He was so angry that he didn't want to face her. It hurt, scaring them so. She didn't mean to, but she also didn't exactly consider them when she left that morning.

"Well," Frank extended his hands outward, "are you going to tell us what happened?"

It wasn't the greatest reception, but she understood why. Kate spared many of the details and told him the important things. The Ghost King was, in fact, sentient. That he took the blame for what was happening and that he was going to patrol the borders.

The mood in the room did not budge. Her fathers were angry that she jeopardized her own safety. The rest of the village had children they currently believed were still at stake. Wouldn't knowing they were safe help people sleep easier at night?

"Okay," Frank said. "I can appreciate what you did. Your reasons are sound, but you're not fooling us, Kiddo. Ever since you first saw him, I don't know, it's like you're obsessed."

Kiddo was a nickname she hadn't heard in at least seven years. Dad was pulling the parent card as though she were not mostly sound of mind at twenty-seven.

"Perhaps I should have spoken to you both about it first," Kate said, her fists forming hard knots under the table. "But this is a huge achievement, and I won't have you guilting me out of it!"

Kate slammed her palms on the worktable. She was standing and yelling at her dad. She didn't realize she was doing it until the smell of burning wood singed her nostrils.

She lifted her hands and took a step back, revealing two handprints scorched into the worktable. What just happened? Had she actually conducted enough heat to scorch a table? Kate gasped and looked at her father, who was also staring wide-eyed at the table. Inspecting her hands, she saw no sign of fire. Her open palms appeared perfectly normal. Perhaps it was a residual side effect of the tonics or some kind of reaction to the blight. Nothing like that had ever happened before.

"All right," Frank yelled, his dance hands in fighting form. "House meeting!"

Chapter 10

They were somewhere near the coast.

Kate wasn't entirely sure as to where, but it was westward and heading toward Flosses. One of Papa's secret fishing spots. She set up the tent while her parents fussed over which fishing pole they preferred. Left to contend with the pop-up tents that did not, in fact, pop up. She didn't fish, so there wasn't much else for her to do.

They left me with the hard job. Figures.

The whole course of events that led to this fishing trip was still foggy to Kate. One minute, her hands burned into the table, and the next, her parents insisted on whisking her away in the middle of the night for a fishing trip.

It was not the best time for a family outing. If anything, they should have been trying to figure out what happened and why. People didn't just burn things with their hands, and yet her parents were avoiding the topic with a vengeance. She concluded that the impromptu fishing was a punishment of some kind.

Like the incident when the tanner arranged for his daughter to marry the much older grocer. When his wife found out, she and the daughter went home to her mother until the tanner relented. Perhaps her parents were going to make her go fishing until she conceded and agreed to never see the Ghost King again.

"We've been planning this for months, but we've just been so busy!" Frank said with a nervous pitch.

It was the only answer she was given when she asked why. They thought she couldn't see the silent exchange they kept giving each other. As if Frank were warning Baxter to say nothing more.

They may have planned the trip in theory, but it was more of a wish than a solid plan. It was something her parents had spoken of doing without her, yet here she was, fighting with Papa's not-so-pop-up tent. Just when she got one corner upright, another would collapse.

The only logical conclusion Kate could render out of the whole trip was that Lori was right. Her parents would never say as much, but as they were packing the wagon, Kate noted that Jasper was making a late-night delivery to the formerly abandoned building.

"Is the butcher finally here?" she asked.

Jasper rubbed the back of his neck as he glanced around the empty village. "Yeah. I should go. Da wants me home."

She didn't even say goodbye and he was already on his wagon, urging his horses to run. Kate stood there in the dust, confused by the exchange. Perhaps his father did want him home soon, it was the middle of the night, after all, and he was expected to wake early the next day.

Still, something about the encounter didn't sit right with her. Kate couldn't shake the feeling that the boy who used to follow her like a stray puppy was avoiding her.

The only real way to get answers was to pretend to sleep in the lopsided tent while her fathers talked freely. She wanted to remind them she was not a child and deserved to be included in the conversation. But that wasn't how it worked.

If Frank issued a gag order, Baxter would be forced to uphold it. Trying to persuade one or both to explain an uncomfortable truth often led to the lecture about how she was their daughter. No matter how old she was, that would always be the case, and as her parents, they reserved the right to protect her.

Kate arranged stones into a circle for the firepit. The wood was all ocean-breeze damp, but it was an opportunity to try out her fire starters at least.

She had just organized her area of the tent when Baxter approached with an armful of wood. "Here," she said, stretching out her hand to give her father a square cube with a cord on the end. "Pull the cord really hard and it should combust, lighting itself and the wood."

Papa's thick fingers struggled with the loop at the end of the cord, but he pulled with the casual ferocity a man of his size had, and the flame puffed to life.

He made a surprised grunt and said, "That's neat! How did you manage that?"

Kate beamed with pride as she explained it to him. Inside the pitch-covered sawdust case were two dried sticks. When he pulled the cord, Baxter created a high amount of friction between the two sticks, causing it to catch fire. If the cord failed, which it had half the time, some flint and steel would serve to light the box and allow it to perform its duty.

"You should sell these," he said.

"I'd like to, but sometimes they don't work."

Baxter shrugged. "So, skip the inner mechanism and just sell them as is."

Anyone who would use such an item already had flint and steel. The allure for most would be the fact that it burned consistently. Should someone be stuck in elements not conducive to a fire, it could save their lives.

"I'll need to make several dozen more," she said. "But it would go quicker without the inner mechanism...if anyone is willing to buy them from me."

She noted the shift in Baxter's eyes as he watched the flames. There was indeed a reason they insisted she come with, and it had everything to do with Jasper's reaction the other night.

Looking over his shoulder for Frank, Papa said, "Things will calm down in a few days. Rumors come fast and hard, but without further incidents, they tend to fade away."

Her parents weren't the only ones the lumberyard worker visited.

It wasn't fair to them, hearing it secondhand like that. Being forced to worry the entire time she was gone. Had he not seen her, Kate would have been able to break the news in a better fashion. She wasn't sure how she would have done that exactly, but anything had to be better than secondhand gossip.

"I know I scared you both," she said. "And I'm sorry. That was the last thing I wanted. I couldn't imagine being in your place. But the Ghost King is my life's work. He is my destiny. I don't know what the future will bring or how that will work, but I do know that he is my path forward."

Baxter let out an exasperated sigh. "Have a girl, he said. It will be fun, he said!"

Kate laughed. "Oh, but it is fun. Just admit it."

Papa reluctantly agreed. "Your birth parents would have been proud. Not as proud as we are, of course, but I'd like to think they were something like us to create a daughter such as you."

That made her sad, but she couldn't say why. A lost connection, she supposed. Kate had always felt her upbringing was responsible for molding her into the woman she was. What other family would encourage their daughter to work instead of marry? They taught her to read and write at an early age when other girls were learning how to darn socks for their future husbands.

Deep down, she had always assumed her birth parents would have been appalled by her ambitions and independence. Kate liked to think that one way or another, she would have found her way to Frank and Baxter.

"What was it like for you growing up?" Kate asked. He seldom ever spoke of it.

"There isn't much to know. I grew up on the ports of Flosses. My father was a fisher. My mother died of illness when I was twelve, so I worked with my father until the lumberyard recruited me."

"You don't have any siblings? Do you still write to your father?"

Papa shook his head. "No. He once told me that if he ever caught me with another boy that he'd beat me to death. Very religious man. I never even thought about romance at that time, but my father must have known something about me that I didn't."

It was a horrid thing to say, but Kate understood most parents resorted to violence. They bragged about beating their children and laughed about it. She never thought it was funny. Kate suspected the reason her parents never relied on corporal punishment was the same reason Roy never belted Jasper.

Both parents had experienced beatings far beyond what most considered punishment.

"Is that when you met Dad?"

Baxter grunted. "I was living in a shack no bigger than an outhouse at the lumber mill. Your father's family had left the village and he needed a roommate."

She knew Frank's history. When his father died, his mother and four other siblings went to Sundersong to live with her sister, but Frank was not invited to come. "Did they leave him because he's gay?"

"No, Sundersong doesn't care as much about that. Not like Flosses! Sundersong was conscripting soldiers at that time. His brothers were too young to be sent to the military, but he wasn't."

The very image of Frank as a soldier racked her body down to the last nerve. Her dad lost in a sea of uniforms. Faceless and stripped of everything that made him Frank. He'd be forced to engage in battle and deeds that would harden his heart until there was nothing left.

Before she could stop herself, Kate was trapped inside the burning house with no way out, and it was Frank who held that awful flame of fate.

The fire starter she held in her hand crackled and burst. Flames burst from the device. So hot it burned blue. Instinct and abject terror should have kicked in, but it didn't. She was panting from fear—no, something else—rage. She stared at Baxter, who was paralyzed.

Kate closed her fist on the fire starter, sending crumbles of flames falling to the ground.

"By the Waters." Papa gasped.

The fever pitch of anger subsided. Nothing remained but confusion. He wasn't afraid of her, Kate understood that. He feared for her, which was something far worse. Frank wasn't nearly as surprised as she was, and neither was Baxter. They knew something and were not telling her.

"Papa, what am I?"

Rubbing his arms through his long sleeves, Baxter shook his head. "We don't know. After word got out that you went to the castle, the Ever Faithful came knocking. They were asking all these questions..."

Setting her combusting hands aside for the moment, she focused on what prompted the sudden flight from their home. "What sort of questions?"

Baxter shook his head. "They wanted to know if you had ever made a pact with the Ghost King and other such nonsense."

She was more than capable of answering for herself, but her parents were afraid of religious sorts, and rightly so. Their reaction wasn't an effort to infantilize her; it was just their dire need to protect and survive. Just like her reaction to soldiers, it was not something easily controlled.

"Kate," Baxter said with a sad softness, "you can't hold on to that anger forever. What happened to your village was atrocious, but don't hold out for revenge. You may never learn who was responsible."

Papa always did have a way of seeing into the hearts of others. For him, glimpsing into hers was no more difficult than seeing pebbles at the bottom of a stream. Her thirst for knowledge in all things stemmed from not having answers about the day her village burned.

The inability to control her emotions in the direct sight of logic was the need for vengeance against some foe. Perhaps that was the true reason she risked so much to see the Ghost King. There was darkness in her heart, and it relished in the destructive power he unwillingly possessed.

Before she could dwell further on this, Frank came stumbling back to the camp with a line full of plump fish. He was so proud of himself, waving his line. "We're eating good tonight!"

Papa's eyes went wide. "That's why I wanted the long poll!"

And that was the end of the conversation.

Her parents carried on as if she hadn't developed a bizarre power to burn things with her hands. It was too much to come to terms with all at once, she decided. And she was grateful for the reprieve. Why fire, of all things? Why couldn't she be gifted with photographic memory or super strong eyesight? Another year or two and she'd need reading spectacles, but oh no, she developed the ability to accidentally burn down the shop instead.

Frank thrust his fish line at her with an all-too-pleased-with-himself grin.

"Excuse me?"

"I caught the fish. You have to clean."

That was hardly fair, considering she didn't come willingly. The trip was a punishment, after all. Planting her hands on her hips, she said, "Why not Papa?"

"Because I tried to fish," Baxter grumbled. "I would have caught something if I hadn't given your father the good pole."

Their logic was not rooted in gender roles. It was based on the fact that she refused to go fishing. Had she taken up a pole, the one who caught the least number of fish would be the one gutting them. Kate chewed on her lip and swiped the line. "Fine."

She was an inventor. The first person to encounter the Ghost King in thousands of years and come out unscathed. An expert on Paradise Lost, even without the help of the university. She could light a fucking fire with her hands!

None of this mattered to the fish, who stared at her with lidless, dead eyes.

Fine. She would clean the fish and eat her fair share of them, but tomorrow, Kate would catch so many fish that it would put her fathers to shame. They would be the ones relegated to cleaning the slimy guts and roe out of tomorrow night's dinner.

After the messy business was concluded, the three of them ate filets roasted over the fire. The fish were admittedly delicious. The only sound was the crackling of the fire as she flaked the filet with the turn of a fork. The fragrant scent of pinemary mingled with the smoke. It made for a peaceful end to a long, eventful day.

It was possible to catch fish in the river closer to home, but they were small and boney upstream. Most of the villagers ignored them in favor of easily available bread, cheese, and porridge. Sometimes the grocer would get beans, but Kate had a strong disliking for beans. The green ones that grew wild on vines were fine, but the brown ones tasted like dirty mush.

Frank beamed with far too much pride for her or Papa's liking. "I think that's a record."

Baxter made a neutral grunt and poked at the fire with a long stick.

"A fine catch," Kate agreed, with a slight grin as she sketched in her journal.

She knew it wasn't Frank's intent to rub salt in the wound. He wanted Baxter's praise was all. At some point, Papa would stop pouting about who had the longer rod and he would congratulate Dad.

Despite the daunting fatigue from the day, Kate waited. She waited until the yawns of her fathers came on with a frequency no one could deny. Baxter stood at long last and declared it was time for bed.

"Are you going to sleep in the tent?" Frank asked as they unbuttoned the flap.

Already wrapped in a blanket and properly settled by the fire, Kate shook her head. "Too comfortable to move."

"Fair enough," he said. "Just be sure to yell if you see a wereshrew."

Kate giggled. "I will."

There was no such thing, of course, and they both knew it.

"I saw it, I tell you!" Papa blustered from inside the tent.

It was all she could do to contain her laughter. The trip Baxter came home raging about a giant shrew the size of a wild dog was the last time Baxter was allowed to drink the discounted brew the grocer and blacksmith concocted using old wheat and rooted vegetables they found in the forest. A vegetable they swore was heart-shaped and so purple that it stained everything a peculiar shade of red. In all her time in the forest, she had never seen such a root, but who knew.

Papa muttered about the wereshrew until even he grew tired of it and snores replaced his banter. Kate was about to get up when a sudden snort jolted Frank awake.

"Roll over," Dad whined.

"What does she want with old frosty hands, anyway?"

"...What?"

She muffled her snicker in the blankets. Of all the names Papa could have given the Ghost King, Kate rather enjoyed that one. Baxter only responded with more snores. It wasn't until Dad's snores joined in symphony that she clambered out of her blanket. She lit a torch—the conventional way—and padded out to the river.

Fueled by a petty vengeance, Kate worked through the night. Her hands were chilled to the bone, and more than once, she slipped on the wet rocks and nearly fell into the water. But come sunrise, Kate had built a C-shaped dam with sticks and other debris in one corner of the river.

Fish had begun to trickle into the well before she finished. So many had become trapped that they were threatening to spill over the dam. Kate frowned at her work. She should have built it a bit taller.

Her fathers could wake at any moment, so there was no time to spare. She plopped on the flattest rock near her dam. There she netted out fish, multiple at a time, before slamming their heads on a rock. Once they stopped moving, she put them on a line full of hooks.

After she filled the first line, Kate moved on to a second and a third. Was it petty? Most certainly. Kate did not enjoy killing as a sport. She winced every time she killed a fish. No matter what she told herself, the guilt was unceasing.

Fish after fish, she tried not to think about it. The sole reason she was killing them was to get back at her fathers. Was it worth it? The three-dozen fish wouldn't have agreed. The wetness on her face was not river water or even fish blood. Gritting her teeth, Kate raged and kicked the dam. When it broke, so did she.

Vengeance was not so sweet after all.

Kate returned to the camp, soaked and red-eyed. Frank dropped the basket he held and ran to her. "Are you okay?"

She wanted to thrust the fish at him and tell him to clean them, but the need for reprisal fell away. "I don't like fishing!" she said before breaking into sobs all over again.

Frank embraced her. The weight of her lines had been lifted from her shoulder.

"There's enough to feed the whole village," Baxter said. "Let's clean them and return home to share."

That was an idea. Everyone could eat fish and be happy. "I don't want to sell them," she said.

"We don't have to," Frank assured her as he stroked her back. "Fish is really healthy, you know. It's a wonderful gift for those who can't catch them."

Kate sniffed back the tears and nodded. The lives of those fish would go to sustaining the lives of children. Not a scrap would go to waste. Bethany could put them in jars and cure the fish to make them last during the winter when food was limited at best.

Her fathers hurried to clean the fish while Kate packed up the tent and other belongings. Weary with exertion, emotional and otherwise, she fell asleep on the wagon ride home.

Chapter 11

"What is it?" Baxter asked. "We didn't place any orders."

Even if they had placed orders, her parents often forgot by the time it landed on their door. Half the time, they stood there scratching their heads, trying to recall just what it was they had ordered months prior. Only this time, the delivery was hers.

It had finally arrived! She was beginning to think it had gotten stolen or was too difficult for even a master blacksmith to make. Kate was so excited she could barely stand it. Rummaging around the house, she tried to remember where the crowbar was.

"Well, don't keep us in the dark!" Frank said.

Fumbling through the chest under the window, Kate pulled out a crowbar and said, "You guys are going to love this."

Wood creaked and groaned as it fought against the nails. Ignoring the accumulating crowd, who were all curious about the contents of the box, Kate leveraged all her weight onto the bar until, finally, the lid gave way, and straw came spilling out.

The three of them peered into the box and gasped.

They were beautiful! Just as she had wanted. The blacksmith did not have the ability or the amount of labor available, so she had to send her design to Flosses. Pulling one of the six devices from the box, she held it up for everyone to see.

"What is it?" someone asked.

"This is a projectile device," Kate said. It resembled a pipe with a handle and a combustion chamber. "It fires lead balls at a speed two times faster than an arrow."

She had made the design well before the prince of Noranger decided to get himself killed. It was for euthanizing animals in a painless manner. Something that she didn't deem a priority until recently. Roy's cow was only getting sicker. Besides, the devices might hasten their visitor's departures.

Hands were reaching into her box before she could stop them. All of those grabbing hands belonged to men.

"How does it work?" Baxter asked.

It was a process, to be sure. One would need to pack the explosive powder into the barrel before putting the ball in. Then, they would need to light the wick. Kate never considered it to be all that practical except to the farmer, perhaps. If anything, it could serve to frighten off coyotes who preyed on the chickens.

Men were fighting over holding the devices like children fighting over holding a kitten or the way women fought over new fabrics. They took turns posing with the projectile devices and pretending to use them on one another. It was most bizarre and even a little gross.

"What a horrid machine," Bethany said. A pack of women was with her. An invisible line was drawn between their porch and hers. In normal circumstances, Kate would have told Bethany to piss off, but she couldn't help but agree.

"It's only for self-defense or a painless end to an animal," Kate said. "It is not a toy but a farmer's tool."

If the men of the village heard her, they were deftly disregarding her words.

"You're not going to sell those, are you?" Lane asked as she stood to the right of Bethany.

"Absolutely not," Kate said loudly.

"But what if Noranger troops come!" the blacksmith's son asked.

"Under dire circumstances, we will loan them to people in the village," Kate answered.

She didn't like the way the projectile device had drawn the men's attention so. It was as if the thing was a beautiful woman, a lump of gold, and a job well done all rolled up into one. When she searched their eyes, Kate swore she could see flames illuminating back at her.

Snatching the projectile devices out of various hands, Kate marched back into the house. There, she went upstairs and hid them under a loose floorboard in her attic. The balls and the powder would remain on her worktable, but the devices themselves would be hidden.

What came next was even more disturbing.

Kate answered a knock at the door and found herself face-to-face with Faustus.

"Hello, Kate!" he said with a merriment that gave her chills.

"What can we do for you?"

"I wanted to congratulate you on your ingenuity. Those were quite a marvel!"

Kate ignored the sour taste in the back of her throat. "We have yet to test them. For all we know, they may not even work."

"Ah, that is why I've come," he said. "I am staying with the farmers, you know. Lane mentioned that Roy has a sickly cow."

She knew which cow he spoke of. It was the inspiration for the device in the first place. Roy had a milking cow with an open sore for some time. The farmer had dedicated so much time to the heifer that his wife complained the rest of his duties were falling to the wayside.

"Is he ready to put the poor thing down?" she asked. Last time they spoke of it, he clearly was not willing to consider it.

Putting down a cow was not like ending the life of a chicken or a sheep. Cows were large and intelligent creatures. In order to kill one, Roy would have to hit it in the head with a sledgehammer. If he wavered or if his aim was off, the poor beast would suffer. The farmer hated it, and Kate didn't fault him for that. After the fish incident, she doubted she would have had the fortitude to do such a thing.

"Eh, the sore is growing, I fear," Faustus said with genuine dismay. "I offered to put a dagger to her heart, but Roy refused. He said she's his animal and his responsibility."

"She was the first calf he pulled himself."

Faustus lowered his head. "I don't envy him. I pray your device works."

"You can tell them I will come soon."

"May the Waters preserve you."

The straw was still fresh on the porch, and already, men were looking for reasons to use the projectile device.

She had made it specifically for this reason, but her stomach knotted at the prospect of testing it. What was so fascinating about them anyhow? Its sole purpose was death. It was a chilling prospect, but perhaps that was exactly what compelled them.

***

The cow was worse off than she had imagined.

What had been a small cut that refused to heal was now a large chunk of exposed, infected flesh that went from the back leg to the flank. Roy was with the cow when she arrived. With the rest of the livestock safely locked in the barn, it was just the single cow in the pasture.

Out of all the men eager to get their hands on the device, Roy was not one of them.

Under the watchful eye of Faustus, Kate packed and prepared the device.

"You aim and squeeze the trigger," she said with a shaky voice.

Tears were welling in the farmer's eyes, but he nodded and took the device. Using the lantern, Roy lit the fuse. She instructed him to wait until the fuse was fully lit before pulling the trigger.

The farmer took in a deep breath and gave his cow one more gentle pat.

A loud pop was followed by the smell of explosive powder. Smoke filled the air.

She and Faustus both lowered their heads and allowed a moment of silence for the animal, who had fallen to the ground with a thud.

After several minutes, Roy held out the device for her to take, as if it were a noxious poison he couldn't stand so much as handle. Kate felt the same way.

"It was much kinder," he said. "She went down quickly."

Kate nodded. She couldn't quite bring herself to be glad, but at least the animal was no longer in any pain.

For better or for ill, the device worked as intended. Far more testing would be needed to gauge failure rates and accuracy with long-range, but they did work. Which was unfortunate because she had a strong desire to melt them down in the blacksmith's forge and be rid of them forever.

"If there's nothing else," Kate said.

Roy shook his head.

It was a sad walk home on an unbearably hot day. She tried to cheer herself with thoughts of the teas Frank was making. All the citrus fruits were ripe, and Dad was already drying the peels on the window ledges. She promised herself that this winter, she would ration out the tea and not drink it all within a month, but she made this promise every year and had yet to keep it.

Distant laughter interrupted her thoughts. Kate turned and noted something was moving through the wheat fields to the west. Shielding her eyes from the daylight with her hand, Kate could see three tall figures riding along the outside of the field.

They had to be soldiers because they were dressed in the same bright red uniforms that she had never seen before.

Kate packed the projectile device with no small amount of disdain and got closer.

They were tracking something in the field. Perhaps they were following a wanted criminal or a wolf. If that were the case, she'd leave and let them have at it. But as she got closer, Kate recognized one of the voices. It was Jasper.

"Just leave me alone!"

The soldiers were running down the farmer's son on horseback, shooting at him with arrows to encourage his flight. He had taken to hiding in the field to lose them, but they must have caught up to him again.

The closer she got, the more horrid the scene was. Three soldiers with bows and arrows were shooting into the wheat field. Occasionally Jasper would shout, and they'd laugh and adjust their aim. They really did not care if they hit him!

Device still in hand, Kate marched in their direction. Fury had her sights flashing red. She opened her mouth to shout at them and her words came so hotly that she scarcely recognized her own voice. "Hey!"

The horses stirred at her approach, one even tried to rear away as if it instinctively knew it was in trouble. "What are you doing?"

"Kate?" Jasper called from the field. "Just go away. I'm fine."

He was most certainly not fine. How dare they come to this land and treat her people like moving target practice? They had no right to be there.

"And just what are you going to do?" a soldier said, taking aim at her. They wore fur-lined uniforms with furry hats. All three were fully bearded. They must have been from Noranger.

It was as though her head had imploded. She was not some simple peasant girl they could frighten. And Jasper was far more important than they could ever hope to be. Their tacky costumes and fancy horses did not give them the right to attack villagers.

Her hands had gotten so hot that the scorching noise of a lit fuse sounded. Kate gave the attackers a grin, took aim, and pulled.

A cloud of smoke obstructed her sight. It stung her eyes. Horses screamed, and men shouted with panicked words before the thunder of their hoofbeats pounded into the distance. She had taken aim at the man, not caring if she shot him dead.

He deserved it for trying to kill Jasper. Those were the type of soldiers that burned villages. She would not let them.

When the smoke cleared, nothing remained but a hat. Kate picked it up and investigated the fibers recoiling from flames. There was a hole shot clean through the crown.

The aim wasn't as precise as she had expected, but she supposed she was grateful for that. With all the anger released at the pull of a trigger, she could have actually killed him in that moment. Something she would have most certainly regretted. It was a dangerous weapon indeed. One that took the heart's intent and made it a reality.

"What happened?" Jasper asked as he stumbled from the wheat field.

She swallowed the hard rock in her throat. "You're fine now. Go home."

He eyed the device wearily. "That's the thing everyone's been talking about."

Kate nodded, fearing what he would say next. Things hadn't been right between them since she saw the Ghost King.

Jasper shook his head. "It's evil, you know. Ma says you've taken Dominion into your heart. He whispers in your ear, Kate."

Her eyes welled with tears. Maybe he was right. The device was an abomination born from mercy. Yes, it could kill painlessly, but it provided her heart with means of instant retribution. Were her actions out of need to protect Jasper, or were they the need to get back at anyone who resembled the culprits of her childhood trauma?

She couldn't defend her actions or her creations. There was no point in even trying to. Kate turned and walked home without another word. She restored the device to its hiding place and spoke nothing more of it.

Pulling her black hair into a tie, she began working on defensive prototypes for the homes in the village. Her chest ached from woe as she sketched and measured ways to make rooftops more resistant to fire and functional locks for doors. Baxter already had the blacksmith creating bars for the windows like the kind the shop had.

She would need rope and wood slats for portable ladders if villagers needed to escape the second story of their homes. Rubbing the bridge of her nose, Kate closed her eyes to ease the ache. Only a half dozen homes would require them. They would need windows or doors on the upper stories if they didn't already have them. Frank could help with that.

The biggest problem would be keeping the homes from catching fire. Dry wood and thatching on a summer day would catch fire within minutes. The whole village would be up in flames within a half hour. How she would do that, Kate had no idea.

Crossing out a pulley system from the well with long, angry lines, Kate stared out the window. Down and raw from the day's events, she wanted nothing more than to crawl under the blankets and sleep for a month. Maybe two.

Chin propped on her fist; she watched the road go from casual traffic to people running toward Lori's end of the village. Frowning, she got up and slogged to the door. Suspecting the worst, Kate hoped it was not a group of soldiers, but no such luck.

Armed with fancy uniforms and beards like the men she nearly killed in the fields, Noranger had reared their lice-ridden heads at last.

She may have been done with the day, but it seemed it was not done with her.

Chapter 12

Not willing to be huddled with the frantic masses, Kate stood apart from the crowd just outside the tanner's home. Her eyes searched for Lori, but she must have been standing on her doorstep and out of sight.

There were twelve of them altogether. Collectively, the Noranger group had enough beard to put a sheep to shame. The one at the front had the most medals and a black sash that went over his uniform, signifying that he was an envoy and not a soldier of war. He was the mouthpiece of the king. An honorary title that few would harm. As the adage went: don't stab the messenger.

"Water's preserve you all," he said through his beard. "My name is Shawn. I am the envoy of his royal majesty, the king of Noranger."

Bethany took it upon herself to speak for the village. "What news from the north?"

"We have come to collect the remains of our departed prince."

Kate noted the air of the conversation lacked tension. It was as if they were there to pick up a package or a wayward goat and nothing more.

"We did not know he was a prince—" Bethany began.

Shawn raised his hand to silence her. "The prince defied the king's orders and acted entirely on his own. To think he could kill the Ghost King," he said with a forced laugh. "The king holds no ill will and hopes you and your king can forgive this intrusion."

He said *your king* like his collar had suddenly become too tight.

They were afraid of him. Even as far as Noranger, where people endured the harshest of winters, people feared the blight. Her village feared they would consider the prince's death an act of war, but Noranger feared the same. Being so close to the castle, Noranger must have assumed they were in contact with the Ghost King. If they had known he issued no order nor collected taxes, they might have approached the village with less formality.

"If that is the case, we welcome you to stay and rest your horses," Bethany said.

"Oh," he said, wiping the sweat from his brow. "That's very kind of you."

Kate spotted a soldier without his hat. It was none other than the one who tried to kill Jasper. There was no way she was going to let it go. She didn't want any of them there, but especially not the three that attacked Jasper.

"Not them!" she shouted loud enough that everyone turned. Kate made her way through the crowd and pointed out the three she had encountered earlier. "Not those three. I caught them shooting at Jasper, who was hiding in the fields. They nearly killed him."

Shawn the Envoy frowned and turned to regard the men. "Is that true?"

"No, sir!" the hatless man said.

To his credit, the envoy was having none of it.

"Where is your hat?"

"Back at my house," Kate said, folding her arms over her chest.

"Your quivers are nearly empty," Shawn said.

Outraged that her word was taken over theirs, the hatless soldier pointed a stubby finger at Kate. "She's a creature of Dominion," he said. "She shot fire from her hand and nearly killed me."

Mutters from the crowd broke out. She wanted to shrink under all the eyes upon her. The faces of the people she'd known her entire life were contorted. Ugly, mean strangers took the places of those she loved. They glared at her like she was the monster, staring with judgment that they had already come to their minds. The tolerance of the village was running dry. She blamed the Ever Faithful. She had no proof, but she was certain it was all their fault.

Kate took a step back, only to be braced by the arms of her parents. If she could have melted into them, she would have.

"Whatever she is," Shawn the Envoy boomed, "it does not detract from your actions. We are here to make peace, not terrify them. If you harmed the boy, this village might not have been as welcoming. You three are dismissed without pension. Leave now."

And just like that, they left. Pulling the reins of their horses, the rest of the group gave way in a trained fashion, allowing the disgraced soldiers to take the road to Flosses. Good. She hoped they would never return.

It was an impressive display of power. One that signified that the envoy was truly there to collect the prince's body and leave. It should have endeared her a little more to them, but apprehension was gnawing at her from the inside.

Where would they put those nine men? The Ever Faithful had a whole group spread out among the village. At this point, they might have to build an inn. Then again, she doubted the Ever Faithful had coin.

She had seen them out and about, feeding chickens in their long black robes. Floating around like wraiths carrying water pails to their master. They even chopped firewood in those robes. It was comical, really. That is until a girl walked by and they stopped what they were doing to stare.

With summer all but spent, the berries wilted, and the leaves were beginning to fall. Winter's approach was racing toward them like a pent-up stallion. The villagers might decide the additional mouths were not worth the effort when the snows came. She hoped so. It was more than a hope; she was practically frothing at the mouth with the prospect of all the newcomers leaving.

Her concern was overshadowed by the scowls of Bethany and her family as they passed by.

"Please move," the tanner said. "You're not welcome on my doorstep."

It was a slap to the face. She couldn't manage a response she was so hurt and surprised. The villagers really did hate her. All she did was try to help them.

"You'll always be welcome on ours," Frank said with a patronizing tone as he pulled Kate toward the shop. "Because we don't turn on our own."

Baxter's ears were purple with anger. Kate clapped a hand over her quivering lips. If they felt this way, she couldn't show how much it hurt her, or they would exploit it. "I'm not sorry I saved Jasper," she said when they got inside.

"And we're not sorry either," Frank said.

Baxter gave a nod of approval, and for a moment, she didn't care if everyone hated her, just so long as her parents never did. "I don't deserve you two."

The moment was cut short by a black-cloaked figure floating past the window.

Kate winced, hoping he would keep on floating. Wasn't there a child to scare or some housewives to frighten? But no, he knocked at their door. The horrid day just continued as though it wouldn't be satisfied until Kate spiraled into a full meltdown.

"Why don't you go for a stroll?" Frank said. "We got this."

The knocking became more insistent. Kate regarded her fathers. It was an offer she should have taken in an instant. A slip of paranoia brushed against her without consent. *What if you come back and your parents turn on you as well?*

She instantly dismissed the thought. That was absurd. She was just feeling insecure and afraid. And she wasn't about to make them clean up yet another one of her messes. "I can't leave you with that!" She gestured to the door. Kate didn't know if Faustus could hear her, but she hoped he could.

"Kate," Frank said, "I didn't live through six decades just to be afraid of a man wearing crushed velvet."

Baxter gave a stern nod of agreement.

There was nothing for it. She did them no good by remaining in the shop, pouting. Kate armed herself with her suit and bag, intentionally showing it to her parents as she walked down the stairs. Frank eyed the suit for a brief moment before nodding to the back door.

She didn't imagine the Ghost King was at the castle, but a good scientist prepared for multiple variables. Oftentimes the village would spread rumors of his sightings and whereabouts, but they weren't exactly talkative to her as of late.

Skirting around the back of the buildings, Kate glimpsed across the street to find Lori standing on her doorstep as if waiting for someone. Waiting for her, most likely. The librarian spotted Kate and moved to approach, but she stopped her with a gesture and shook her head.

I'm sorry, Lori. I don't want to drag you down with me.

Lori's business was barely getting by as it was. Kate noticed several sections of the library were empty. Too proud to ask Harvey for money, the librarian must have sold them off to another merchant when he was out of sight.

If Kate was seen with her, Lori would suffer for it. As if she understood the predicament, Lori turned around and kicked the building before going inside, slamming the door shut. Kate smiled a bitter smile. Lori was no doubt wishing it was someone's head she was kicking, but there wasn't any single individual to blame, except maybe Kate.

Kate made a wide trek around the village and up the path, taking care to avoid the lumberyard. The last thing she needed was more gossip. She wasn't entirely certain why she was going back to the castle. It would have been far more comfortable in the forest or even on her hilltop, but her heart was once again dictating her actions, damnable as they may be to the village.

The second time she beheld the castle up close was just as spectacular as the first. With the trees shedding their leaves, the rubble around the walls was hidden, and it appeared slightly taller than before. As if it had grown in the weeks she had been away.

Instead of walking through the front and up all the stairs, Kate went around the side to the stables. Her skin burned with the cold emanating from the horse that stared at her expectantly.

So, he was there after all.

Try as she might to smother her excitement, her hands fidgeted along the strap of her bag. Kate put the suit on while the horse watched. At least this way, she wouldn't terrify the poor thing. She giggled at the image of a giant fish monster coming around the corner. It would have killed even an undead horse.

The mare wasn't afraid of her at a distance, but that did not mean she appreciated the suit up close and personal. She ran around her expanded stall. Kate noted there was no hay but rather a floor of the white sand Kate sampled from her first visit.

Kate bent over to look through the green glass. Hard, metal platforms surrounded the mare's hooves. The animal was properly brushed, and its mane was braided back. The eyes were the same inky black as the Ghost King's eyes. As if the whites of their eyes died when they did. But she was a normal horse otherwise.

It explained why the horse didn't die from the blight, but it raised a lot more questions. Did her ancestors intentionally do this to a horse? She couldn't imagine a reason for it other than to give the Ghost King a faster means to travel or even as a companion.

Perhaps they tested on horses first. Kate could see the appeal of immortal horses. She doubted the mare ever tired. If the horse was the true aim of Paradise Lost, why make the Ghost King? It must have been for the sake of greed. Why stop at immortal horses when a single man can fell nations?

Religious myths suggested that Paradise Lost fell because of man's greed and horrid inventions. The Ghost King could have easily been a product of greed. There was no other reason to create a man with such uncontrollable power. Was it so far-fetched to assume the myths were true in a more roundabout way?

"You again."

Kate looked up to find a lean figure standing on the balcony. Her breath caught in her throat. In the place of his chain mail was a dusty but tight woolen jacket that buttoned along one side of his chest. There were no lapels. Rather, the collar stopped halfway up his neck like a cuff. The tapering of the garment showcased his broad shoulders. Had he worn it for her, or was he totally unaware of the effect he had on her?

"I didn't think you would be here."

"So, you came to rifle through my belongings?"

She wasn't aware he had any.

Kate was shaking her head only to realize her response was obscured by the suit. There was a moment when she didn't quite know what to say. Her village didn't want her around, and she left her fathers to be interrogated by the Ever Faithful. Neither were things she could say out loud without breaking into sobs.

In a bout of self-pity and raw vulnerability, she said, "I had nowhere else to go."

It was difficult to tell through the goggles, but she thought she saw his face soften as if he, too, knew what it was to be an eternal outsider. She supposed if anyone would understand, it would be him.

"I'll remain in the tower. You should be safe along the wall where we first met."

She waited as long as her heart would allow before following him, and even then, a blizzard pelted her suit. He was nowhere in sight, yet his blight remained trapped in the halls of the castle.

In the courtyard, Kate noted the ice that surrounded the narrow slit of a window in the tower. She worked the suit off, abandoning it, taking only her bag up the stairs to the wall.

This time, she also packed a blanket. It was one of the thinner ones, easily carried in the bag. When she made the suit, Kate hadn't factored space for her winter coat. That was before she learned the radiance of the blight. It made removing the suit even more complicated, but she was grateful for the patchwork of furs that covered nearly two-thirds of her body.

The blight echoed from within the stones of the tower, containing most of the curse.

He said nothing from his tower window. She supposed that was fine. It was enough to be near him and away from the villagers.

"Are you an invention of Paradise Lost?" she called.

The Ghost King didn't respond. Kate reasoned that he probably didn't know what she was referring to. It was likely he hadn't spoken to anyone since that era. He would have no idea what people today called the fallen civilization. She was lucky that he spoke the same language.

"It's what we call the people before us," Kate said. "My people fear it. They say the people of Paradise Lost were worshippers of Dominion—"

The king's scoff was clear from the tower. She grinned at the struck nerve and noted his response in her journal. So, Paradise Lost was not an ally to Dominion, if such a thing existed to begin with.

"I had hoped to study the relics that remain in the university, but they won't permit me unless I contribute a theory. I had hoped you would provide me with evidence that Dominion is a myth."

"And what if he's not?"

The admission knocked the wind from her chest. Everything she had been working toward, and he was telling her that the myth was real? She swallowed a gulp of humbling self-doubt and noted that response in her journal as well.

"My current theory doesn't need to be correct," she told herself as much as him. "I just need a viable theory to present."

"For what reason?" the Ghost King asked. "Why does Kate of the nameless village need access to such relics?"

"The inventions of Paradise Lost can be life-changing for our civilization," she explained. "Medical and agricultural advancements could benefit our lives if only people were not so afraid of the past."

He was silent then, as if contemplating her words. For all she knew, he could have grown bored and fallen asleep, but she liked to think he was considering her words. Closing his eyes and savoring each syllable as he did the last time. The urge to reach out and touch his face nearly brought her to her knees.

Don't get any ideas. Besides, he probably locked the door.

"If knowledge is all you truly desire, then you shall have it," he said. "The eastern door in the courtyard will take you to my library. Feel free to borrow whatever you wish."

Kate was on her feet. "You mean that?"

"Just be sure to return them," he said. "They are my only solace, and you don't want me to come to your village to ask for them back."

He was trying to be funny, she realized. It would be almost a joke if it weren't so terrifying.

"Thank you so much! You have no idea what that would mean for me."

Her excitement was shrouded in dismay then. Even if she unlocked the advancements of the past, who would want them? In the span of a few months, Kate had become the village pariah. Even if she could teach them safer ways to birth children and feed their crops, they wouldn't accept it.

Deflated like a ball mushroom, she slumped back to the ground. "Everyone in the village fears me. They think Dominion whispers in my ear," she said, wrapping her arms around her knees. "Maybe they're right."

"Dominion doesn't whisper in the ears of man," the Ghost King said. "He roars on battlefields and sits atop metal thrones."

"He doesn't urge men to create atrocity?"

The Ghost King was bracing the window, looking out at her from the slit, and an icy gust ricocheted against her face. "Men create atrocities all by themselves. It was they who created Dominion, or did your people forget that too?"

Myths were a relatively new concept to her, so Kate couldn't say for certain, but if the Ghost King spoke the truth, it would rock the world they knew. "You're saying that Dominion, the scourge of the Waters, was created by man's need for power and cruelty—not the other way around."

He nodded slowly.

She thought back to the projectile device. The way the men flocked to it. Her design was not inspired by any deity; it was out of need, nothing more. What men saw in the device was power over their perceived enemies. Dominion was man's need for power made flesh.

The revelation would be a whisper throughout the continent. A slow trickle of information she could impart bit by bit until all was revealed. But how? If only she had a way to reproduce the written word hundreds of times over without her hand cramping.

Information belonged to everyone, whether people chose to accept it or not. Kate would learn as much as she could and spread it to anyone willing to listen, not lock it away like the university did. Beyond that, it was man's choice to move their civilization forward.

She no longer had need of the university—not when she had a firsthand account of Paradise Lost. But the ramifications were startling. Kate had come to change the world with science but returned with myth instead.

"I can't imagine what the village would make of this," she said. "They would either bow down to my new understanding of myth or throw me in the river with stones in my numerous pockets."

He said nothing. The Ghost King only observed her pity party from afar.

Even with her winter coat and blanket, the cold was getting to her. Her core body temperature was fine; it was the exposed extremities that were suffering. The tip of her nose—as flat as it was—and her earlobes were burning from the cold.

Kate pulled a fire starter out of her bag. Holding it tight in her hand, she thought about it catching fire.

Come on, come on!

She had done it before. Maybe it didn't work when she was already cold or because the blight was currently filling up the nearby tower like a noxious fume. Giving up on her random power, she tried the intended way and pulled the cord.

The wood spun, and she could smell the smoke from the friction, but the device refused to catch. Picking up the fire starter, Kate inspected it for fault. Perhaps it had gotten wet somehow or...

With a sputter and a sudden pop, flames engulfed the fire starter in her hand. Her heart leaped into her throat, and Kate let out an unseemly cry as she dropped the thing and scurried several feet away, only to realize her folly.

She had dropped the fire starter far too close to her bag. There was no preventing what would happen next. Hiding by the curve of the tower, she watched as her fire starters erupted in a single, spectacular fire.

And as if that wasn't bad enough, the Ghost King had witnessed the entire thing.

"Are you all right?"

No. Not at all. Being thrown into the river by the villagers may have been a mercy at this point.

"I'm fine," she called.

"You don't seem fine," he argued. "You're terrified."

With the pounding in her throat and between her temples subsiding, Kate approached the fire and warmed her freezing fingers. "I have a fear of fire," she explained, unsure why she wanted to tell him. "My village burned down when I was seven. I was the only survivor."

His eyes narrowed as if she had said something wrong.

"Collect your books and go home, Kate of the nameless village."

And before she could ask what she had said wrong, he was gone from the window.

Chapter 13

BOOK IN ONE HAND, Kate used her free hand to shovel porridge into her mouth. It had been three days since she left the castle, and she wanted to absorb every detail his books had to offer. Taking every opportunity to read them meant that she could return to the castle that much sooner. She took notes on as much as she could, but there was just too much.

Her plan was to borrow a set, return them for a new set, then go back and reread the previously borrowed one. If it took the rest of her life, so help her, Kate would read them all.

"So, he has a library," Frank said.

It was another attempt to strike up a conversation. She wasn't trying to ignore them; she only wanted to finish reading and read them a second time, but with notes.

"A massive library," Kate corrected. "It puts Lori's to utter shame."

It was unlike anything she had ever seen before. When he told her he had a library, Kate expected a few books or maybe a few shelves. But when she stepped into the room, it was like walking into Paradise Lost itself.

Her mouth dropped as she slowly turned in the center of the room. It was the size of the dining hall, but instead of barren walls, it held floor-to-ceiling bookshelves. Smells of parchment and leather still lingered as if impervious to the blight. Her fingers twitched as she lunged at the nearest shelf. The books varied from poetry to study of the stars, from collections of bawdy songs to the philosophical lectures of Paradise Lost.

Everything she could have ever wanted was there, along with things she couldn't imagine. She was laughing and crying, unsure which emotion to go with. Even the university wouldn't have such an extensive library.

Well, maybe they did, but not pertaining specifically to Paradise Lost. No, this was how they thought, how they lived. There were cookbooks and mechanical drawings. Odds and ends the Ghost King must have collected through the centuries, and it was all there. Safely tucked away from any zealot who might think to burn them.

At the far end of the library, Kate spotted a furniture arrangement. A chaise sat under the only window in the room because even the Ghost King needed proper lighting. There was a writing desk with a chair. His quill and ink had seen better days. Then again, she imagined he didn't have many to write to. There was even a rug! The design on the rug was long faded, but it was a weak pulse of life in an otherwise dying castle.

Her hands grazed the cracked and worn reading couch. It sagged in the middle, suggesting that the Ghost King preferred this seat to the others in the room. She imagined him laying there, with his ankles crossed, reading all hours of his lonely days.

"And he said you could read them?" Frank asked, snapping her back into reality.

"Just so long as I bring them back."

"No late fees with that one," Baxter warned.

Kate smirked. If Papa had any idea he and the Ghost King made essentially the same joke, he would have stolen her away for another fishing trip.

Frank joined her at the table. "If this is to be an ongoing thing, we need to think of what to tell the villagers."

"Why not the truth?" Kate offered.

Baxter agreed. "She's not exactly the best liar."

Ignoring the jab, Kate said, "Information is the best defense against ignorance. The more they know, the less they fear."

That, and Papa had a point. She was a terrible liar. The bigger a lie was, the harder it was to get away with. Suppose she told the villagers that she had forsaken all her inventing and was going to dedicate her time to religion. She might be able to convince them for a time, but the truth would eventually trickle out, and then they'd never believe anything she said ever again.

"So, I tell them that the Ghost King is an enemy of Dominion and that they have no reason to fear him?"

"And that he has many books," Kate added. It humanized him and explained her motive for frequenting the castle. Everyone knew that she would do just about anything for a good book.

"This almost makes sense," Baxter said, scratching the top of his head. "I bet if we talk to Faustus about this, he could help us."

Kate halted her reading and stared at Baxter. "What?"

"The Ever Faithful are oddly sympathetic to our situation," Frank reasoned.

"The whole town turning on us the same time they came was not a coincidence," she said through gritted teeth. She wanted nothing to do with the Ever Faithful. All of this started because strangers occupied their village. Now they wanted to lean on them for support?

"You're probably right," Baxter said in earnest. "Who knows what they say about us when we're not there. They don't seem to be going anywhere either."

Frank stroked his chin. "They keep saying they're here to protect us, but the way they watch the women in the village. I don't like it."

At least it wasn't just her being paranoid.

"Their questions about you have been verging on strange," Baxter said. "It's like they know about your..." Papa flexed his hands and made a hissing noise.

"I haven't done it since the fishing trip. I think it may have been a reaction to the tonics I drank."

There was no other plausible explanation. Kate had tried and failed to make the heat happen in her hands many times. She never had any such ability before; why would one simply appear well into adulthood?

"Ah." Baxter readily accepted her theory. Maybe too quickly.

Frank, however, did not appear convinced. Either that, or he was still thinking about the Ever Faithful. It was hard to tell. In any case, she had already read the books she borrowed and had to return them. If she didn't, he might try to collect them after all.

"I'll be back this afternoon," she said, standing over her porridge, eating the last few bits before heading for the door.

"Please, please be safe," Frank implored.

"Always."

Strolling through the village, Kate found herself keenly aware of the doors that slammed shut as she passed. The tanner sneered from her porch, shaking her head as if she wanted Kate to be sure she didn't approve. Try as she might, Kate couldn't deny that it hurt.

Rounding the side of the castle, Kate begrudgingly met the Ghost King's mare and was welcomed with a frigid cold. She brought her suit but abandoned the tonics, suspecting they were the culprit behind her heat-conducting hands. She really hoped that she wouldn't have to use the suit if she could help it.

"I'm coming in!" she shouted.

Kate's voice echoed through the trees, stripped bare of their greenery. It would be at least three months before they shadowed the ground once more. The air smelled dry and fresh at the moment, but the clouds grew heavy with snow. It would be harder to trek up to the castle in those conditions. She would need to grab as much of the sand as she could for further study and as many books as she could carry. It was going to be a heavy trip.

"And I'm not wearing the fish suit, so please don't kill me!"

There was no response, but there was a noted uptick in the temperature as she traversed the hallway. She set her suit down in the courtyard. He had moved to a safe, unmoving distance.

The telltale blight was spooling from the tower window. Icy tendrils reached outward as if searching for their next victim. He had heard her and went to his designated spot. She swallowed the tight knot in her throat and went to the castle wall just beneath it.

"Back already?" he said, watching her from the tower.

Chills went down her spine, and the anger she once felt was smothered by a reactive fear. Her mind understood he wouldn't harm her, but her body responded instinctively to the threat that sent shockwaves through her system.

"I read the books you gave me," she said. "I was hoping to borrow more. The snows are coming soon, so I may not be able to return them for some time."

He waved her off, and too dismissively for her liking. "That is fine."

It might have been the last time she saw him for months, and he acted as though he couldn't be rid of her fast enough. The last thing she wanted to do was annoy him, but she had hoped he would be more sociable at the very least. "Do you want me to leave?"

Resting one hand on the ledge, he lowered his head. "Of course not, I…"

There it was again. He struggled to explain himself. Was he overwhelmed or perhaps conflicted? "I read words," he said slowly, "but speaking is hard. I like listening to you very much."

Sitting down, Kate opened one of the books she had borrowed. It was a book for women about how to conduct household affairs. Not the most exciting material, but so insightful on women in Paradise Lost.

She spent several hours reading to him. It was a fictional tale but read like poetry. It told the story of a pair of twin boys. One was much healthier than the other, so the royal parents decided to abandon the smaller, sicklier boy in a place called a jungle.

"What is a jungle?" Kate asked.

"Like the woods. Only hot and more beasts." He struggled with each word as though he knew a better one, but they couldn't find their way to his mouth. "Poison plants and lots of frogs."

Fascinating.

The parents were a king and queen who feared that the two boys would cause civil war since they had equal claim to the throne. While the healthy boy was given every advantage, the one left for dead was found and adopted by a panther.

"Panther?"

"Great big cat," the Ghost King explained. "As big as a deer."

She didn't know what that was either, but she kept reading.

The boy raised by the panther grew to be a strong warrior while his twin brother failed at every task appointed to him. The king and queen decided that the prince would not be crowned until he came back from the jungles with a trophy.

Kate could see where the story was going.

The Ghost King must have been sitting because she couldn't see him in the window. Still, his presence was dominating. An icy armor developed around the tower.

The moment she shut the book, he snapped upright and stared at her as if offended.

"It's going to be dark soon," she explained.

He looked to the sky and then nodded. She didn't want to leave him, but if she didn't, her fathers might try to come to the castle.

"The sand that comes from you. Would you mind if I collected it?"

"What?"

"The source of your blight," she clarified. "I can retrieve it from the stables if you like."

"What good could that possibly do anyone?"

The way he loathed his abilities made her sad. Perhaps her plan would bring him some solace. "I would like to study it," she said. "I think it might be of some use."

There was a plopping noise. If there was a chair in his tower, he must have fallen into it. She waited for his answer with the patience of a small child before their turn on the rope swing. Did he faint at the astounding logic and innovation she presented?

"My king?"

"I'm not a king," he said with enough gruffness to set her on her heels. "I'm just the fool who lost."

Kate's eyes narrowed as she pondered the meaning. Just because she came up with a brilliant idea did not mean he lost. What exactly did he lose? Perhaps the blight was finite.

"If you need to keep it reserved, we can return it when I'm done."

"What? Oh, take the sand wherever you can find it. I will leave sacks of it at the fork of the town tomorrow."

She felt as though she were a few unwanted hairs on his collar. One minute he was all but consumed by her, and the next, he was sullen and indifferent. It made no sense to her.

"Okay," Kate said. "Thank you. I will collect some books and leave."

He said nothing more, so she departed the wall with more than a few glances over her shoulder in case he changed his mind. He didn't.

In the library, Kate found herself struggling to make the encounter brief. While the Ghost King had lost his interest in a conversation, there were thousands of books ready to speak. Where to even begin? She shut the door behind her. If he decided to come down from his tower, there would be signs she was still occupying the room.

Overwhelmed by the options, the best course of action was to go in order. On her last visit, she took three books off the nearest row. Stalking the shelf, Kate noted those books were returned to the same location in the same order.

Rubbing at her chin, she realized he was arranging the books by the first letter of the title. A most logical arrangement if one had not read everything in the room. She would have put them in alphabetical order and subject matter, but it was not her library.

Kate took the next three books along the bottom shelf and lay on the chaise. There, she skimmed through an epic poem about the messiah of the Waters. It regaled in a tale of love and war before finally reaching a beautifully morbid ending.

So thus, the messiah of the Waters, the one who received the Accursed Gift of immortality, went mad. He marched into the ocean. Some say he's still marching to this day. No tide could alter his step, only delay it. The unsurmountable weight of the sea would never drown him, even if he pleaded on fallen knees for the salt water to fill his lungs...

Resting the open book over her chest, Kate sniffed back the unexpected tears. Was this how the Ghost King felt? She didn't want him to die. It was a selfish want, especially since he could never have a normal life. She wouldn't last a decade in his boots, and yet she expected him to endure just for her.

She realized there was so much context missing from the poem. For a person who knew the tale, it would have made for a fuller impact. When she was through with this library, the second read would no doubt spark in a totally different way.

The second book was little more than a cookbook. Skimming it was enough to get the idea. It wasn't that Kate disliked cooking so much that she was absolutely terrible at it. There was a reason her fathers still cooked for her—a grown woman—they feared for the safety of their only daughter and shop.

"*Accurate Prophecies*." She read the title, and the bile threatened to rise in her throat.

How did one decide a dream was a prophecy and not an act of self-importance? If Kate woke tomorrow and claimed the Water spoke to her, the villagers would jeer. It seemed to her that only people with power and no shortage of charisma could make such claims and get away with it.

Regardless, she opened the book to find that it was not what she expected.

Rows of dates and numbers with notation and page numbers lined the first five pages. She flipped past them to come across a name and biography of a man. After that, his actual prophecy about the messiah being born—one of a dozen listed. There was no way they were all accurate. They all conflicted with one another, and there was nothing about the Ghost King's bride. What an utter waste of time.

There were even drawings of the prophets. Kate noted their clothing was similar to that of the Ghost King. Clutching the book, she realized that if she wanted to, Kate could use this to prove her theory to the university. It was false, she knew that, but it would provide the same outcome.

If the university was forced to acknowledge her theory, it would force myth and provincial governing apart.

Tempting as it was, the Ghost King's words rang in her mind. *"If knowledge is what you truly seek..."*

And it was. It was just that preventing religion from sinking its claws into the continent would benefit mankind, wouldn't it? The last thing the warring provinces needed was another power wading into the fray.

It would also mean stealing one of his books.

Kate let out an exasperated sigh. She couldn't steal from him or use his kindness for her own ambitions. She'd never be able to face him again if she had, and that would be a worse punishment than any he could bestow.

Focusing on the room once more, she frowned at the sudden darkness. The day was fading fast. Kate replaced the books in their precise order and took six instead of three. The snows were going to fall any day now, and she would need something to tide her over until next time.

She was almost home when the frantic cries sounded across the street. The blacksmith's door was wide open. Baxter went over there to collect the window bars. She had never heard him scream before, and suddenly she was enveloped in horrid images of her fathers wounded or dying. They came all at once, and for a moment, she forgot how to breathe.

"What's happening?" she tried to say, but her voice was so quiet.

Frank and Baxter emerged from the smith's home. Supporting him on each side, they hurtled through the shop door while Kate heaved, thinking the worst had happened. Only after seeing them could she suck in a deep breath. They were okay. They were fine.

It was the blacksmith, covered in sweat, who was screaming.

"What happened?" she yelled over his wails.

"He lost control of the furnace," Baxter said as he forced the blacksmith down on the table.

A doctor made rounds from Flosses with the merchants a few times a year, but he was nowhere in sight, and it would take weeks to send for him. If they didn't act fast, the blacksmith would lose his arm or worse.

Shit.

Kate swiped a tonic off her shelf. "Drink this," she said.

The blacksmith was fraught with pain. He trembled with a tear-stricken face. His eyes were wide as he shook his head at her. This wasn't the time to allow prejudice to get in the way.

"It wasn't a request," she said, pouring the tonic into the man's mouth.

"Will that cure his burns?" Frank asked.

She frowned at him. Of all people, he should have known better. "I'm not a magician."

The blacksmith's cries became quieter until, all at once, he was silent. "Oh, that's better," she said. "I can hear myself think."

Baxter let go of the man's hand, and it fell with a thud on the table. "He's asleep?"

"Sedated," she corrected. "Yes, a deep sleep. He was going into shock, and I can't work on him like that."

Kate investigated the blacksmith's arms. They were burned all right. Blisters were rising from the skin. One spot on his forearm, in particular, was rippling as though it were on the verge of erupting. "We need cold river water, my sunburn treatment, antiseptic, and a fish."

"A fish?" Frank wiped his forehead and neck with his handkerchief.

"I just need the skin. I'll need a needle and thread as well."

While her fathers borrowed the more unusual things she needed from the villagers, Kate went to work washing the blacksmith's burns with the river water and antiseptic. Sea water would have been better, but they worked with what they had.

She applied the sunburn lotion everywhere, save for the worst part. There was no saving the delicate skin on the forearm. Most of the burns were superficial compared to that spot. That flesh must have made contact with the furnace itself.

Wiping the sweat from her brow, Kate shook off the tension that cramped her insides to bits. She didn't want him to die, nor did she want to try to amputate his arm. Her sights were hazy enough as it was—Kate didn't think she could manage it.

Stepping out, a cool blast of air revived her senses. She encountered a growing crowd outside her door. Pariah or not, the village was concerned for the blacksmith.

"Is he going to be okay?" the blacksmith's daughter asked.

"He's asleep now," she said loudly enough for everyone to hear.

She motioned for the daughter to come in and closed the door behind her. Kate was no doctor, and bedside manner was not her strength. The blacksmith's daughter saw her father's arm and burst into tears.

"Most of the burns will heal just fine," Kate explained. "Where the stove door fell is the worst of it."

"He can't lose his arm," she said. "We can't afford it."

Kate struggled to maintain her restraint. The man could have died, and her concern was financial? She reminded herself that the daughter, Emma, did not have a husband, and her younger brother was only fourteen. She would be expected to care for herself, her mother, her little brother, and her daughter. Such was the reality for most women.

"I'm going to try something," Kate said. "It's experimental, and there's no guarantee it will work, but if it does, he won't lose his arm."

Emma nodded her consent. They waited in a dredging silence until her fathers returned. Frank produced needle and thread from his pockets. "I haven't been able to find ours, so I borrowed from Bethany."

He hadn't been able to find them because they were in her bedroom. Baxter came up behind Frank, holding half a fish like a sacrificial offering. "Set it on my worktable."

Kate poured boiling water over the fileted fish and watched as the skin peeled from the corners. She removed it from the flesh and poured a gracious helping of her antiseptic on it before placing it over the burn.

All the while, Emma sat dutifully by her father and watched them work.

Did the woman think her so evil now? She was one of the women who shadowed Bethany's every step, but when removed from her mouthpiece, she had a voice of her own.

"You may want to look away," Kate warned.

She shook her head in defiance. If she wanted to watch, then Kate would allow it. Threading the needle with antiseptic-soaked thread, she sewed the fish skin over the blacksmith's burns. If it took, it would prevent infection and help him grow healthy new skin underneath.

If it didn't, the doctor would need to amputate the arm.

Emma craned her head, unfazed by what Kate was doing. "The Ever Faithful say that not all inventions are bad."

They had told Kate much the same, but the prickle along her neck whenever Faustus eyed her made her feel otherwise. "Necessity is difficult to argue with," Kate said.

The blacksmith's daughter nodded fervently, as if it had never occurred to her outside of what was possibly the worst moment of her life. Perhaps that was why Kate was as driven as she was. The slaughter of her village set off a chain of events that led her to live the most unorthodox life she could as a woman.

Emma was the perfect example of what it was to be a woman in the village. While her father worked night and day, she helped her mother with chores and looked after her little brother. She befriended women her own age and accepted myth as fact. She courted a few boys, but even Kate knew she eyed the young merchant that passed from Sundersong with his magnetic green eyes and smooth dark skin.

She often wondered what she would have been like had her village not been burned to rubble. Kate suspected she would have been a lot like Emma. Plain and simple, yet utterly courageous in the face of hardship.

It was in the early hours of the night by the time Kate finished. Frank and Baxter slept side by side, holding hands. Emma fought sleep until the very end when Kate tied the last knot and put down the needle. She went around the room, covering all parties with blankets before collapsing in bed.

The next morning, the blacksmith was not on the table, and her fathers were preparing breakfast.

"How is he?" she asked.

Baxter shrugged. "Fine, from what we could tell."

"He didn't have a fever and was able to walk home—" Frank was interrupted by an angry female voice from outside.

The three of them peeked out the window and watched. It was Emma swinging a skillet at her father, who was ducking and hiding behind a wooden barrel. "Don't you even think of going near that."

It was hilarious, but Kate wasn't certain it was appropriate to laugh. Emma was threatening her father with more injury, and head trauma was not something she could fix with a fish. She turned to find Frank biting his hand to keep from laughing. His eyes were watering profusely. Baxter was laughing, but he tended to go silent and wheeze when it came on too strong. So, she allowed herself to laugh at the strange display, knowing that it meant all would be well.

The blacksmith would be okay, provided his daughter didn't catch him back at work.

Chapter 14

K ATE WATCHED WITH AN amused smile as her fathers demonstrated their latest prototypes. Papa had created a simple shooting mechanism that could fire with enough strength to splinter the wall with a miniature crossbolt. It was small, easy to use, and quick to assemble. "That's far better than what I created," she said with approval.

Meanwhile, her dad held a roll-up ladder. She leaned forward, marveling at how neat and compact it was. It made a series of clickety-clacks when he tied it. Long enough to escape a second-story window if necessary. Kate clapped, and her fathers bowed.

Never in her life had her fathers appeared more childlike than they did in that moment. Their inventions were no longer for a rich man's game but rather a way to protect their village. She wished she could remind them that their other work also benefited people. The money they earned put shoes on her feet and food in her belly. But now wasn't the time.

"All right," she said, moving toward her workbench. "Since the two of you managed all of this, it's only fair that I demonstrate my contribution."

Her fathers were practically drooling. They had been hounding her ever since she announced her solution, but it wasn't until that morning that she found the sacks of sand as promised by the Ghost King.

She was dreaming of ice and sand when a sudden drop in the temperature woke her. Slipping on her shoes and blanket, she hovered by the frost-laden windows and waited until the cold broke. At the edge of the village, she came upon four flour bags full of sand. Laying her blanket on the ground, Kate rolled the sacks onto it before dragging it all back home in one trip.

There was no way she was taking it all upstairs, so she left the sacks near the outhouse and used her sample from upstairs to demonstrate.

If one stuck their tongue to the glass, they'd be stuck there forever.

"Put a pan on the table with a coal from the fire."

Her fathers set it up for her. The flame lingered on the red-hot coal. "A perfect specimen."

She took a small pinch of the sand and sprinkled it over the pan. In an instant, a plume of sooty smoke erupted, and all the heat had been dissolved. Baxter poked the coal with his finger before concluding, "It's cold."

Frank's face was one of utter amazement. "Do you have enough for the whole village?"

"I have four flour sacks full," she said.

So impressed, he took off his cap to wipe his brow, revealing his bald scalp. "If we sprinkle this on the thatching..."

Kate nodded. "No village will ever burn again."

Maybe she would never get justice for those she had lost, but preventing it from happening again would be just as good, if not better. The nods of approval from her fathers encouraged the sentiment. Yes, this is the right way forward.

"Now, if only the villagers didn't slam their doors in our faces," Kate said.

"The blacksmith is with us," Baxter said. "He and his family have not forgotten what you did for them."

"He was never a fan of the Ever Faithful to begin with," Frank added.

That was nice to hear. And though she had not spoken to Lori in some time, she imagined that the librarian wanted nothing to do with them either. Kate paced the shop as she thought of anyone else they could persuade. "What else do we know about those people? Where did they come from?"

"Bethany would know," Frank reasoned.

Yes, but would the seamstress tell them? She was never one to shy away from giving her opinion, and she prided herself on knowing everyone's business... "Can one of you speak with her?"

Baxter shrugged.

Frank sighed and said, "Yes, I'll take that one."

An outsider's opinion might be beneficial as well. From what little she knew of him, Shawn the Envoy was an honest enough man with a wider understanding of the world. "I'll speak with the envoy."

"Be careful with that one," Baxter warned. "Don't let yourself be alone with any of them, and don't get too familiar."

The sudden fury of Papa's voice gave her pause.

Frank's thin brows raised. "What did you see?"

"It's what I haven't seen," Papa said. "They have remains of their prince and their fallen soldiers, yet they won't leave. They ride off in small groups, returning at night. It's like they are scouting."

Steam was forming from her bawled fists. How could she be so stupid? All this time, she was so worried about the Ever Faithful that she overlooked the envoy's extended stay. Like the rest of the town, Kate took them at their words and congenial appearance, but she, of all people, should have known better.

She grabbed her coat and stormed out the door toward the house they occupied. Previously abandoned, the village decided it would be best to have them stay together. Mainly because there was no room to shelter nine soldiers anywhere else. Only three of their horses remained out of the nine. Papa was right; they were surveying the province.

She banged on the door, knuckles first.

Shawn answered. "Hello, miss," he said. "How can I assist you?"

Why won't you leave? Are you sending intelligence to your king so he can plan an invasion? What's hiding under that beard of yours?

"I wanted to ask you what you knew of the Ever Faithful."

His eyes scanned the village at her back before saying, "All I know is that our acolytes do not recognize their chapter."

"I do not understand what that means," Kate said. "We had no acolytes until they arrived."

He pressed his thin lips before an explanation came to him. "There are different groups, factions, if you will. They more or less believe the same things, but whichever one the king prefers becomes the standard chapter for his province."

"And this group, the Ever Faithful, are not among any familiar to your province?"

"That's right."

No wonder her parents found religion so tedious. The politics behind it all made her head hurt. "And these chapters, they're the same across all provinces or no?"

"I had always assumed that to be true," Shawn said, leaning in slightly. "I don't think they are what they say they are."

So, they were lying? That was just great. If being an outlandish cult with a ridiculous prophecy was the cover-up, she couldn't imagine what the truth was. Maybe they were wereshrews in disguise. That would explain a lot in Faustus's case.

"Thank you for telling me," she said. "Also, about how much longer does your company intend to stay?"

Shawn the Envoy's lip twitched at that. "Why?"

"Well, the winter snows will fall soon. Food will be scarcer. It's difficult for families to provide for others and themselves this time of year."

"Of course, I understand," he said with a short bow. "Once our king sends the word, we will begin our travels back home."

"I hope they are safe."

"Thank you, ma'am."

Kate tried not to cringe at ma'am. She was not so old, was she?

Shrugging off the unwarranted title, Kate eyed the library. She wanted so desperately to see her friend. Things had settled down since the projectiles were kept hidden. By all appearances, the village had gone back to ignoring her. Then again, she hadn't exactly interacted with anyone.

Anxiety coiled in her belly as her feet crunched on the cold ground. She knocked on the door, but no one answered.

Maybe it would be best if she didn't—

The bell rang, and Kate was dragged into the library. "What took you so long?" Lori railed.

"I...I didn't want them to think you were in league with me," she said.

Lori's hair was down instead of in its usual bun. Gray streaks flowed freely, shrouding the rest of her dark hair with silver. "I appreciate the sentiment," she said. "Things got a little out of hand, but it's been over a month."

"I'm sorry," she said. "I just didn't want you to hate me too."

"Psh," the librarian dismissed. "You have lots to catch me up on."

It was such a relief to spend an afternoon with Lori once again. The librarian placed a fourth pot of tea on the table just as Kate finished her story. "And then he just stopped talking out of nowhere."

"Kate, it's probably the longest conversation he has had in centuries."

Wouldn't that make him all the more eager to speak? She didn't understand Lori's point.

"You know how it's so exhausting to talk to certain people?"

She didn't like where this was going. The first person to come to mind was Jasper, following her around as a kid, speaking nonstop until Kate ran home and locked the door behind her. "Yes?"

"That's likely how he feels about all conversation. It must be overstimulating. Even if he did want to carry on the discussion, it must have been immensely draining."

It was something she hadn't even considered. Next time she went to the castle, she would try to be more considerate.

"Do you think the village is still mad at me?" she asked. While Lori didn't exactly have her finger on the pulse of the village, Harvey did. The merchant was always coming and going, delivering and picking up goods.

Lori contemplated the question with a frown. "I don't think it's you that they're afraid of, per se. It's the frequency of change that's occurring all at once. Most blame the Ghost King. It's not like they can lash out at him, so they go after the closest person."

"Me."

"And the envoy's soldiers," she added. "They have worn out their welcome, yet they insist on remaining."

"They told me they were waiting on orders."

"Do you believe them?"

It was an easy answer. "Not at all."

"I feared as much."

A much-needed swell of confidence gathered within her. If the village did not want the envoy, yet they remained, they would be more receptive to taking precautions against them or the Ever Faithful. She had no doubt one or the other would make their move soon, and they would be ready.

"We're trying to shore up defenses," Kate said. "Care to be a shining example?"

"It would be best to work under their noses. The less either group knows, the better. Install your inventions little by little and vary what you do as you go."

Leave it to Lori to be beyond clever.

"They won't see what comes next."

On her way home, two black-cloaked men watched Kate from between the grocer and the butcher's. They were a nosey lot, but her skin crawled when they made no attempt to look away when she pointedly stared at them.

"Good afternoon."

The voice startled her, and she jumped. Though when she turned around, she was not at all surprised to see Faustus, the nasty creature. "How long have you been standing behind me, Faustus?"

He gave an apologetic tilt of his head. "You were so focused. I didn't want you to turn around and bump into me."

"Well, you are on my porch," she said, shaking off the fear nipping at her fingertips. "What can I do for you?"

"I saw the blacksmith today," he said. "The thing you did to his arm, it was amazing. He says he will go back to work next week."

She was glad to hear it, even if it came from a serpent's mouth. "That's good to hear."

"What gave you the inspiration, I wonder?"

There it was. Dominion was whispering evil devices in her ear, prompting a revolution of innovation that would bring on the end times. Doomy and gloomy. "It's not my idea at all," she said. "It's nature's."

"Oh?" Faustus's expression felt patronizing.

"The blacksmith had no skin left in one spot. He needed skin to cover that exposed wound and—"

"Fish skin was the best option."

"Precisely," Kate said, though she chafed at being interrupted. "Fish are less susceptible to skin infections like we are, and we have it in abundance. Otherwise, I'd have to amputate, and I did not want to do that."

Faustus shook his head in agreement and took her hand into his. "No, that would be terrible indeed. You are a treasure to this village, Kate."

The way he said it made her toes curl. It was greasier than the bacon fat Frank used to season the pots and pans. Slipping her hand out of his grasp, Kate forced herself to smile. "Thank you. I should be going now."

Faustus bowed and spun away. His cloak made a dramatic twirl as if it acted on his behalf.

Kate fumbled with the door. She couldn't get inside quick enough. She shut the door with both hands and pulled the bar down to lock herself inside.

Frank looked up from his blueprint. "Is he still there?" he whispered.

"You mean he's been waiting for me?"

Baxter nodded.

Why did she get the feeling she was a wounded mouse hiding from a multitude of owls lurking in the trees? She shook off the thought. "Okay, Lori is going to help as well. Here's what we're going to do."

Drawing a mockup of the village, Kate wrote what defenses would be implemented first. There were nine homes that would need ladders. All would need the sand and crossbows. The blacksmith was their secret weapon. He could go around and set up bars for those who couldn't install them while Lori and Harvey gave out the sand with instructions.

"If we can instruct people to have accidents that need repairing, we can install emergency exits. As for the bars, just talk them up. Soon everyone in town will want them."

"Like a fashion trend," Frank offered.

"Exactly. It will be all too easy for Harvey to sneak a bag of sand and a crossbow to each house."

"Lori said that the villagers are pressuring the envoy to leave, so it's only a matter of time before they're gone."

Glancing up from her plan, she looked outside, and her heart slumped. The first snow was falling.

Chapter 15

THERE WAS NO USE in hiding.

Every time Kate stepped foot out of the shop, men in black cloaks were watching. She emerged from the grocer's with a half dozen eggs while a cloaked figure lingered between the buildings. Clutching her basket tight, she pretended not to notice, but others did.

"Oy, you there," a petite woman with a pixie cut shouted. "You're scaring off the business."

In a move that could only be described as brazen, the Ever Faithful continued to stare at Kate. Every nerve in her body screamed at her to run, but this was her home, and if she had to run from anyone, it would be from pitchfork-wielding villagers. Though, it hadn't come to that.

"You deaf?" the woman, who could be no one other than the butcher, asked. It didn't take a scientist to determine the bloodied apron and the meat cleaver were trademarks of a butcher. "I said," raising her voice until everyone paused in the street, "push off!"

Half the village was outside.

The snow was falling, and it would keep falling until people were forced to shovel their way out of their homes. Just like her, they were readying themselves for the coming months.

"Is there a problem?" the grocer asked, brushing the snow off his vest.

The butcher pointed at the cloaked man with her cleaver. "This one is scaring off customers. Orders for cured ham are being taken today, but not a one has been made. And I wonder why."

His wax-curled mustache twitched. "Bob, it's far too cold to be out here. You should come inside."

"I was instructed to patrol the village," Bob answered from under his hood.

The tension on the grocer's face was so taut that Kate expected his facial hair to tick in different directions. He clearly expected Bob to do as he bid. It must have been embarrassing for the grocer to have his guest openly deny such a simple request.

As fun as the scene was, the cold was bearing down on Kate's coat, and her tremble was no longer from being stalked around the village. "I need to place an order," she offered quietly.

"Right," the butcher said. "Come in before those eggs freeze."

Kate followed her in, but not before giving one last scowl to the cloaked Bob, who turned his back on the grocer to watch her leave.

The scent of blood and meat hit her so hard that Kate had to put a hand over her nose. It made no difference. Metallic vapors filled her mouth as she tried to breathe. Sausage links and cuts of meat hung from the ceiling like some bloody massacre had taken place.

Meat was a seldom treat before the butcher came. Kate told herself it was only because she was unaccustomed to eating it, but the shop put her off from ever wanting to eat animals again.

"What in the infernal devices was that about?" the butcher raged. "I have half a mind to throw that bucket of pig's blood on him."

"At least he'd be warm for a few moments," Kate said, her voice nasally from plugging her nose.

For what it was worth, the butcher was apologetic for the smell. "Eh, I just butchered a few pigs. I only do it in the winter. Keeps the smell down. In a few days, the salt will take over, and it won't be nearly so bad."

Kate hoped for the butcher's sake that was true. How could she sleep in a place like that? She must have been so used to the smell that she didn't notice anymore. "My fathers would like a ham when they're ready."

"Right." The butcher went behind her counter, knocking a dangling goat's foot out of the way. She opened a book and asked, "Do you want the one year, the eighteen months, or the three years?"

She had no idea what any of that meant. Her fathers never told her how they ordered cured ham. "I...don't know."

The butcher looked at her with bright blue eyes. Her hair was unusually light for someone from Flosses. "So, the longer they're cured, the better and more expensive they are."

"The first year," Kate said, knowing full well that meat was already a luxury for their family as it was.

"What name do I put the order under?"

"Frank and Baxter."

At this, the butcher looked up and smiled with recognition. "Oh, you're their daughter! They're nice chaps. They were the first to welcome me and even helped me build my counter."

Kate smiled. "That sounds like them."

She frowned then, as if something else had occurred to her. "Is it true then? What they say about you?"

Kate imagined the villagers said a great many things about her. "What do they say?"

"That you talk to the Ghost King," she said. "You go up there as you please and take his books."

There was a reverence in her voice that Kate found surprising. She had always assumed everyone feared her for going to him, but in hindsight, the village didn't hate the Ghost King; they only feared him. But fear was a knife's edge for most people. When they were cut with the blade they wielded, it often led to hatred for the tool.

"He's not what people think," Kate said, shifting her weight from one leg to another.

"Not what those cloaked men think, you mean."

She regarded the butcher then. Her twinkling, mischievous face revealed that she said what she meant and was fearless of any repercussions. Then again, Kate imagined few were willing to challenge a woman with a meat cleaver.

The butcher escorted Kate across the street. Turning to scowl every so often at Bob, who was still lingering where they had left him. "You didn't have to walk with me," Kate said. "I would have been fine."

"That's not how I see it," the butcher said. "Apparently, those men have been talking an awful lot about you. Trying to gather a town meeting to discuss you."

A wave of dizziness came over Kate. So desperate to fulfill their prophecy—no—that wasn't it. The Ever Faithful were not as they seemed.

Kate faced the butcher. "I need you to do something, not for me, but for the village. Tell them to ask the envoys about the Ever Faithful. They are not what they claim to be."

The butcher nodded. "Everyone who comes to my store."

Kate closed the door behind her, leaned against it, and steadied her breath.

Her parents looked up from their plans.

"They want to hold a meeting with the town," she said.

"We need to get you out of here," Baxter said. "They can't hurt you at the castle."

In any other circumstance, Kate would have laughed. Papa was willingly sending her to the Ghost King. She shook her head. "I won't make it. They're watching."

"Then we'll go with you," Frank said, rising to his feet.

She regarded her fathers. So brave but so old. Cataracts glazed over her dad's eyes, and soon he'd be entirely blind. Papa's dark hair was thinning and growing in a faded shade of brown. As strong as he was, she did not think they could defend themselves alone against a dozen young men.

She imagined the cloaked men beating her aging fathers to death before dragging their bodies into the forest, where no one entered but her. No bodies, no crime. The Ever Faithful would claim the three of them went to the castle and never came back.

"No, I need to stay. It would look suspicious if I went to him now."

That, and if the villagers even considered handing her over, she wanted to look them in the eyes when they did it. She wanted to see their guilt when they threw her to the wolves.

"Eh, Kate?" Baxter said.

She looked up. A faint smell of wood burning curled under her nose.

"You're doing it again."

Moving away from the door, she groaned. She had burned a patch of the door.

"I wondered what that smell was," Frank said.

What was once her sanctuary had become her cage. The old pine walls closed in on Kate. It wasn't any different from last winter or any winter before that. This was typically the time of year when they bundled up in blankets and drank tea. She would work the days away and help her parents with whatever tasks they had.

The only difference was that a bunch of possibly murderous cultists would watch her venture out to buy bread and cheese.

Right. Gulping large breaths like she expected to be plunged underwater, Kate joined her fathers at the table. The work would distract her worried mind and trembling hands. Each crossbolt she made would ensure the safety of herself and her fathers. She dared not touch the projectile devices hidden under the floorboards.

Come spring, she would watch them melt in the blacksmith's forge.

The blacksmith who forged them in Flosses sent her blueprints back with the crate. It was a professional courtesy to do so, but Kate wondered if she should follow up and make certain he did not replicate her design. Their world had no need for such a thing.

An alternative would be made, of course. Perhaps a similar design involving a fuse that sent a shaft with the force of a bullet, only effective at close range. Useful only to a farmer or the butcher.

Notes of citrus lingered in the air. Frank set down a cup of tea before her. "Is this what I think it is?" she asked, inhaling the scent with her eyes closed.

"I saved some for days like this," he said with a knowing smile.

"You're a treasure," she said, taking hold of the tea.

There was a timid knock at the door then. Kate turned around, but she didn't get up from the table. She left that to Baxter, who still had a carving tool in his hand when he opened the door. Craning her neck to see around Papa's big frame, Kate recognized the frilly dress.

"I am notifying everyone of current events in the village," Bethany said with an air of formality. "The envoy and his soldiers claim they are unable to travel through the snows and will be staying the winter."

It wasn't the most thrilling news, but their stay might deter the Ever Faithful from doing anything too outrageous. She didn't trust soldiers any more than she trusted a fox that stalked a henhouse, but the real enemy was the Ever Faithful. Soldiers loved nothing more than stomping on necks to prove their prowess. Just so long as those necks were cultists' necks.

"They're Noranger soldiers!" Baxter said. "It snows year-round up north. You'd think they would be used to it."

"Just as well, they refuse to leave." Bethany's voice was stiff, almost forced. "Also, there is a town meeting tomorrow at the library."

"What about?"

"The Ever Faithful have a request."

"What does this request involve?" Baxter pressed.

"I don't know," Bethany stammered.

She was afraid, Kate realized.

Here Kate was, crying about being trapped in the house like she was every winter while her neighbors were trapped by the very guests in their homes. Kate flexed her hands to free the tension and stood. "Would you like some tea, Bethany?"

Baxter shifted slightly, allowing the seamstress entrance.

"No, I'm afraid I can't," she said. "I am needed back home."

Scooping up a bag of sand and the tea container, Kate went to the door. "For the road then," she said, placing the tea canister in Bethany's hands. "Frank's special brew," she said. "Best to be used by a roaring fire."

Bethany's hands clutched the container. Her eyes widened as a little piece of the blight nipped at her fingers. "Thank you."

A cold gust blasted her face as Baxter shut the door. He gave Kate a nod of approval.

"Where's the Ghost King when you need him?" Frank lamented.

"He can't control his blight," she explained. "It constrains him as it does empower him. He won't risk innocent lives getting caught in the fray. I'm afraid it's just us."

Chapter 16

A LOW RUMBLE SOUNDED from the road. Kate stood and watched as a wagon carried charred bits of wood. They went outside to investigate like everyone else in the village. It was the Noranger envoys, and they were carting remains of a village.

Kate gasped and feared the worst. Had another village burned? Did the people who killed her parents also kill these people? Her throat went dry as she peered into the wagon. Charred bones and half-melted boots. There was a black cloak like the Ever Faithful wore. It was draped over the top to conceal the ghastly contents.

"Where did this come from?" Baxter hailed the troops.

"Fear not," the soldier said. "These are remains from a village burned long ago. We only collect remains from the soldiers we had stationed there."

Her entire world fell away in that moment. There were soldiers there, and yet they still died. What was the point of soldiers if they couldn't protect anyone? In a way, they were no different from the projectile device. They were made for protection but seemed to do anything but.

"Do you know what happened?" Her voice was so distant.

As if he realized it was personal for her, the soldier took off his cap. "That village had many people," he explained. "Being on the border of Sundersong, we knew there was a good chance it would be attacked by our enemy, so we stationed there. We lost."

Where was he in all this? Where was the Ghost King? A single pass through her village could have put out the fires, yet he didn't come. Why didn't he come?

"Then it was Sundersong troops who burned the village."

"They deny it, miss, but I wouldn't be so sure. I'm sorry."

The wagon rolled away, and with it, the faith she once held in the Ghost King.

Pulling away from her fathers, Kate gathered the books and marched to the castle.

Frank was shouting at her in the distance.

She whirled around, poised for a fight, only to find he was chasing after her with the suit, coat, and travel bag in his hands. "You're going to need these."

Her anger broke in the wake of their enduring support. "Thank you."

This time, she did not sneak or hide her intent from the village. "Where are you going, Kate?" the blacksmith called.

"I'm going to give that king a piece of my mind!"

"Waters preserve him," he said with a laugh.

Her fathers told her she needed all the facts. That vengeance was poison. But what about justice? Those people deserved to live and had done nothing wrong apart from being close to another province. If Noranger troops had come to their aid, the Ghost King must have realized they were vulnerable. Why did he not act?

Anger set her blood on fire, and she ran to the castle faster than the rivers rushing to the ocean. So absolute in his authority only for the fact that no one could approach him to say otherwise. Kate would hold him accountable.

Kate barged through the front doors of the castle. Her belongings fell away as she stormed her way to the library, still holding the books in her hand. Kate walked in on him. The room was wall-to-wall ice, and the carpet was crusted in frost. It was only a passing thought that she could not feel the blight.

"How are you...?" His eyes were wide, and the book fell away from his hands. "How is this possible?"

"My village," she said. "The other day, you sent me home at the mention of it. I thought you were just bored of my conversation, but that's not the truth, is it?"

"Kate," he said. "You need to get out of here before whatever spell you've cast wears off."

Then her death would be on his conscience, along with the rest of her family and village. She hoped he choked on his grief. "Why didn't you stop it from happening? How is it that a king in the most remote part of the continent came to help, but you did not bother to leave your castle?"

"Is that what they told you?" he asked with infuriating calm. "That they were there to help?"

Doubt seeped into her skin, and the cold came along with it. *No. Hang on to this anger. It's what keeps you alive.*

"Where were you?" she flared, the heat redoubling once more. The puddle at her feet sizzled and steamed.

He stepped away then. Like he was afraid. Good. She wanted him to feel scared. Even if it was just a fragment of terror that village felt in the end, he would learn.

He kneeled then. Kate craned her head with surprise.

Looking up at her with his inky eyes and illuminant skin, he pleaded through sharpened teeth. "I didn't know you dwelled there. Had I known—"

She couldn't deny the pull at her heart when he said that, but how could she ever want him after learning his choices could fall to a single whim?

"You'd what?" she scoffed. "Save hundreds of people? You should have wanted to save them!"

"I made a choice," his voice raised with a sternness that suggested he was done pleading. "Two villages were under attack. I had to choose between your village and the village with all the wheat mills."

The rage that burned within her was no longer a red-hot fire. It had burned white like the coals in the blacksmith's forge.

Deceptively calm and seemingly expired, but hot enough to melt gold. She was shaking all over, rigid and tense.

"You saved buildings over the lives of that many people?"

The Ghost King shook his head as if she misunderstood, but it was clear to her.

"If the mills and wheat fields burned, the entire province would starve. Kate, so many more would have died. Monster that I am, I'm only one being and cannot be in two places at once."

His logic was cold, just like his frozen heart. She was so stupid to have ever fawned over him the way she had. The Ghost King was everything she wanted to be. Cold, factual, and immovable except in the face of new evidence. Her heart and her mind seldom got along, but in that moment, they aligned.

Kate struck the Ghost King across the jaw.

Her burning flesh connected with his frozen tissue and revealed an unclear winner. The angry red handprint across his face was beginning to welt. He closed his eyes and gasped. His mouth went slack as his chin lifted, exposing the veins of his neck and Adam's apple.

The reaction set her on her heels. He enjoyed the pain. It had been an eternity since he felt the touch of another. It made sense that any touch induced a positive response. She didn't know how to explain the emotion that came next. Something like heat, but it stirred in a different direction than anger.

The cold was falling over her like fresh snow. Kate was losing her fire and fast. "Here are your books," she said, dropping them in the puddle at her feet.

She headed for the door, but not before grabbing the stack of books she had meant to take the last time she was there but couldn't carry in her already full arms. "I'm taking these!"

Stupid, stupid... Of all the parting words, she'd said that.

Fleeing the castle, she outran the blight as it nipped at her heels. The anger slowly fumed away as Kate treaded down the hill. She had a face-to-face encounter with the Ghost King and did not freeze to death. She had touched him. Well, slapped him, but still. It was an amazing self-discovery, though she wished she understood what it meant.

It wasn't the most practical method of interaction. Not that she intended to ever interact with him again. If he wanted the rest of the books back, he'd need to come and ask for them. No amount of groveling would be enough.

Though, the more she thought about it, the quicker her anger evaporated. The Ghost King was forced to decide between protecting the entire province or a single village. He made a choice that was right in theory but wrong in practice. Yes, the primary food source would burn, but Flosses and Taus would have traded with them.

They would have been forced to rely more on their gardens and their farmers, but she did not believe anyone would have perished.

Then again, the Ghost King had seen more of the province than she. If there were villages as small as hers, there were likely many pockets of people unable to pool their resources. Kate shook her head and sighed.

As much as she hated to admit it, he was not to blame. Only the people who perpetrated the crime were responsible. Even if the Ghost King claimed that responsibility for his own. Still, she couldn't bring herself to face him. Not after knowing he smelled the blood and the flames and turned away from their suffering.

Branches snapped in the forest. Kate reared her head in that direction. Her eyes locked with a massive brown animal foraging in the clearing. It had a set of sharp protrusions from his head, thick and knuckled. There was an unfathomable depth to its brown eyes as it regarded her. She had seen them before and knew that if she left it alone, it would leave her alone.

"Hello," she said to the creature.

"The woods are haunted, you know," a voice said to her right. One of the lumberyard workers. Probably the same one that tattled to her parents and gossiped to half the village, the rat.

"Are they now?"

He was a short, squat man with overdeveloped arms. He wore a cap that reminded her of Frank's and a pair of worn overalls. "That's why no one ever goes into those parts. Why we don't chop down the trees past the marble steps."

There was no point to be made, but despite the cold, Kate indulged in the conversation. She often wondered why they called him the Ghost King and not the Blight King or even the Asshole King.

Tilting her head, she asked, "Have you ever seen the ghosts?"

He shook his head.

"Then how do you know it's haunted?"

The lumberman frowned at her as if it were obvious. "You talk to them all the time."

She didn't have time for whatever this was. The villagers could believe in ghosts, gods, and even wereshrews for all she cared. That did not mean she needed to indulge in it.

"I must go now."

Turning to give the animal one final glance, Kate was startled to find it had disappeared. She looked back to the lumberman, who shrugged and went back to chopping. It was the queerest feeling. As if those around her understood elements about her that she did not.

Of all the times she had seen that species of animal, not once did a hunter bring home anything remotely like it.

Home had a way of releasing a person of all the burdens they carried throughout the day. When her little shop came into view, her step became lighter, and her shoulders less slumped. The soft breeze of winter was pushing around the dry leaves, and the air smelled of rain. All good things as far as she was concerned.

Wordlessly, she entered the shop and sagged into the only chair with a back.

The ability she wrongly assumed to be a side effect had fully weaned, leaving her feeling hollow. Like the very marrow of her bones had been liquidated by the heat that kept her alive in the face of the blight.

"Oh, Lemonberry," Frank said when he emerged from their bedroom. "Are you okay?"

It was a closet before they gave her the attic. When she became old enough to need her own space, her fathers emptied out all the tools they kept within the room and put a door up. It was barely enough to fit their bed. Kate had offered to switch rooms with them many times, but her parents refused, stating they wanted to be closer to their work.

"I slapped him," she said. "I slapped him and did not die from the blight."

Frank sat at the table and called, "Baxter, we need you."

She waited with a weary calm. Frank's demeanor assured her that the truth and full circumstances of that day would be given.

"Show her," Frank said as he looked over his shoulder at Baxter.

Papa's upper lip sputtered, and his mustache flapped with protest.

"She slapped him with her bare hand, Baxter."

Her father's eyes widened. "Truly?"

Kate nodded. "The two of you never seemed all that surprised by my ability. What am I?"

"Our daughter," Baxter said with eye-watering earnestness.

She smiled, never growing tired of hearing that one, especially amid so much uncertainty. "And what else?"

Frank lowered his head. "We don't know, to be honest. Do you remember anything from that day?"

Kate shrugged. Not a solid sequence of events. More like a patchwork of sights and smells. Physical pain never remained in one's mind, but her mother shielded her from the worst of it, she suspected.

"My mother held me while scratching at the dirt floor, trying to dig an escape route. Even if it was only large enough for me. Then you broke through the wall, and Papa pulled me out."

Frank looked at Baxter, and Papa rolled up his long sleeves revealing arms covered in burn scars. Her stomach tossed so hard she feared she'd vomit right then and there.

"Your mother was burning over the top of you. When Baxter tried to pull her off, you held fast. The flames—it was like they didn't touch you. You were totally unaffected by the smoke that killed your mother and the fire that burned the work gloves clean off his hands."

It was a good thing she was sitting because, in that moment, Kate's knees went all soggy. "I...consumed the fire?"

Frank shook his head. "No, it was like it just didn't touch you. It burned away all your clothes and hair, but you were fine otherwise."

It was a lot. Her newfound power wasn't a side effect or a re-action to the blight. The one thing she feared so wholeheartedly, with such irrationality, couldn't actually harm her. Even in a burning building, engulfed by flames that burned away her hair and clothes, it could not kill her. The suffocating smoke that stung her eyes and took the air from her lungs had no effect.

"That's one of the many reasons we don't want you to speak with the Ever Faithful," Baxter added. "If you are this bride, and they strongly suspect you are, your life is in danger."

The Ghost King had never heard of it, so it wasn't a real thing, but the Ever Faithful wouldn't see it that way. The village wouldn't protect her any more than they were willing to protect the Ghost King. And she couldn't rely on her power. Flames were unpredictable, just like her emotions.

Kate frowned. A thought suddenly occurred to her. "Wait," she said, sitting up in her chair. "If I'm the so-called bride, a source of strength to the Ghost King...doesn't that mean I shouldn't be able to hurt him?"

"Your slap hurt him?" Frank asked. A faint smile tickled his lips. He was impressed.

"Oh yeah. I burned a handprint on his cheek." She still wasn't certain hurt was the effect. His moan was not one of pain. But she'd leave that out of her parents' version of the story. There were some things parents did not want to hear, even hers.

"Good girl," Baxter said.

Of course Papa would approve of her physically assaulting a man. They didn't even care about why or if he deserved it. The farther she was from the event, the less she felt it was warranted.

"The province was attacked on several fronts," she said. "He could only save one."

Her fathers nodded with an understanding that victory would have been impossible given the circumstances.

"A lot of things do not add up," Frank said. "Not about the Ever Faithful or the envoy."

"We should focus on getting the village's defenses up," Kate said, dragging her body out of the chair, wishing that her parents had traded rooms with her. "Winter will be busy."

Chapter 17

S TANDING IN THE FROST-COVERED courtyard of the Ghost King's castle, the cold no longer touched her. Kate outstretched her hand and grasped a single bloom on the cherry blossom tree. He was somewhere in the castle. There was a sense he was waiting for her, though not a single word was spoken. It was her home, and the tree belonged to her as well.

The sound of wood smacking wood. Unintentional and seemingly outside the world. *I'm dreaming. Of course I'm dreaming.*

But it was such a nice dream she wanted to remain for just a few more moments.

The loose plank groaned. It was coming from the shop downstairs. Bolting upright, Kate held her breath to listen. Was someone downstairs? There was nothing for several moments, and she began to think it a dream.

A squeak sounded from below. Kate's body went rigid. Someone unfamiliar with each creak and groan of the shop was fumbling around downstairs.

The fire in the oven had long died down. The morning chill descended upon her. The woolen winter nightgown served well enough when she slept but not when she was sneaking around her own room, feeling for anything that would serve as a weapon.

So, they were going to kill her in the night and flee the village before dawn. She winced. All the crossbows were on the table for anyone, welcome or otherwise. Shit. She doubted they would figure out how to use such things in the dark without knowledge, but her stomach hardened at the thought.

If there was ever a time for her powers to work, it would have been now. She needed to be angry, but it was hard to be angry when she was knee-knocking scared.

As much as she wanted to run and hide, Kate inhaled and called, "Who's there?"

Her eyes were adjusting to the darkness, but the stairway would be pitch black. What if someone was lurking there, waiting for her?

"Papa? Dad?"

There were signs of life in the stillness. Not a noise, but a warmth reignited. Almost as her fathers' presence awoke. "Kate?"

A frantic bump was followed by scuffling from downstairs.

Kate rushed down the steps and found Baxter wrestling a dark-cloaked figure. "Papa!"

He was tall, whoever he was, but he was no match for Baxter's strength. They grappled, a mass of black, ever-shifting in the night. Crossbolts went clattering to the floor, and wood scrapped against wood amid the grunts and Papa's curses.

"I'm looking for a light!" Frank called from the bedroom.

A heavy thump landed on the workbench. The stranger had Papa pressed against the table, and she could hear him struggling for breath. Something molten hot was bubbling to the surface. How dare they come into her house and attack her family!

Kate grabbed the man to pull him off her papa. Her hands burned through his cloak, and the room stunk of burning fabric and flesh. He screamed and hurtled out the back door faster than a wraith fleeing the daylight.

She pinched the wick on the nearest lantern and the shop appeared in her stinging eyes.

Baxter was soaked in sweat. He was still leaning against the table, rubbing his neck. "What was that?"

"A who, not a what, and I think we know the answer."

Investigating the back door, Baxter traced the hinges. "They undid the pins."

"I told you we needed a lock on the back," Frank said.

Baxter glowered at him. "You said we didn't need locks at all!"

Frank's hands danced in the air, knowing he had lost the argument.

"Was he armed?" Kate asked. "Did you get a look at his face?"

"No, but I woke when he came in. I watched him for a time to see what he would do."

Something in that was a relief. She wasn't in nearly as much danger as she thought. Her mind, of course, jumped to the worst conclusions. "What was he doing?"

"He was rummaging through the chests and in the cupboards. At first, I thought he was just a beggar searching for food, but the moonlight reflected off a pair of shiny boots. He was looking for something specific."

There was no doubt in her mind of what he sought. The projectile devices. If they fell into the hands of the Ever Faithful, the whole town would be at their mercy. Hardly any of the homes in the village were prepared for an attack that was becoming more certain by the moment. The Ever Faithful were making all the moves while they stumbled to catch up.

"We need to get rid of those devices," Kate said, though she didn't trust the blacksmith to destroy them in secret. He was a good man, but he coveted the horrid things just as much as the next man. She would have no way of making sure he destroyed them without raising suspicion.

"What's the plan, Kate?" Frank asked.

"We attend that meeting."

The snows had covered any trails of their nightly visitor.

After lacing up her snowshoes, her fathers helped her into a flouncy skirt that Bethany had made her for her birthday one year. It was a pointed attempt to pretty her up after too many afternoons of encountering Kate covered in dirt with leaves in her hair.

Since there was no sleeping after the home invasion. She worked through the night sewing pockets on the inside of the skirt. Its numerous ruffles and bows would hide half the tools of the shop. She twirled, letting the shirt fan out. "You know, I think Bethany always wished she had a daughter."

"She almost did," Frank said. "When we brought you home, she petitioned the village to make us give you to her."

"What?" Kate hissed.

Frank eyed her like she was a box of combustible powder. "You were her last chance at a daughter."

The reasoning quelled the audacity. It explained why Bethany was so unnaturally invested in her upbringing. She didn't dislike Bethany, but she didn't like her all that much either. The seamstress was more like an obnoxious aunt one learned to love.

"I'm grateful that didn't happen."

"I know the last few months haven't been the easiest," Frank said. "But this is your home, and the people here are your family."

Kate nodded. Sure, they may have criticized her or disliked the things she created, but they had a right to do so. She did create dangerous things. Her heart soured at the thought. It wasn't her intention. All she wanted to do was help people, but they turned everything into pain and terror.

Still, it was hard to put her life in the hands of others. Not when she had always walked her own path. It wasn't that she questioned their morality but rather the indignity of having others decide on her behalf. She wasn't livestock to be traded at auction.

Taus may have arranged marriages to discard their difficult daughters. Sundersong held meetings to discuss the future of their women with their village elders. She overheard Noranger troops attempting to flirt with Emma. Describing how they simply stole away a beautiful girl and it was perfectly lawful!

Fully dressed, Kate staggered under the new weight. "Woo, this is heavy. I hope my shoes hold out."

"You're really going to wear those?" Frank asked.

She didn't need to glance down at her shoes, knowing full well what was on her feet. A pair of ratty winter boots. Strapped to them was a series of wood and leathers woven into a sort of reverse halo underfoot.

"Not stylish enough?"

He raised one eyebrow. "Those scare the children, and you know it."

"If my skirt gets wet, it will be apparent that I'm hiding things in it."

The dance hands waved, and Kate followed Baxter out the door. Snow was piled up two feet higher than the porch. Tentatively placing one foot on the snow, Kate slowly added more weight until she was standing directly on it. Despite the additional burden, her snowshoes allowed her to walk on top of the snow rather than fight through it.

It also garnered a lot of stares from the villagers making their way to the library. Scratching at her sleeve, she remained by her fathers' sides as they dug a path with a wide, flat shovel.

They were halfway to Lori's when a small voice said, "Excuse me?"

Kate lowered her head to find one of the blacksmith's grandchildren staring up at her. Emma's daughter, though she couldn't recall her name. "Hello," Kate said with a smile.

The smile felt forced and awkward. She hoped it didn't frighten the child because Kate was trying her best to be friendly. Sometimes children cried at the sight of her. Dad said it was a natural response young children had to strangers and that she did the same. Somehow she doubted her fear of strangers was the same as what Dad called "stranger danger."

"How are you walking on top of the snow?"

"I have special shoes that help me."

"Are you going to the library? I would like to see them." In the little girl's eyes was a curiosity that Kate recognized.

"Of course."

The porch outside the library was already shoveled clear of snow, and a multitude of soggy shoes and boots lined the wooden platform. Her little friend watched as Kate untied the lacings. The child's fingers wiggled while she stared intently at the snowshoes.

She held it up for the child to touch. "See, just leather, wood, and string."

The child held one and turned it over to investigate every lace and curve. Children were the most brilliant scientists, even if she found them unpredictable.

"Can I put them on?"

Kate hesitated, unsure of what to do. Of course she wanted to put them on. She found herself unable to say no, and before she knew it, the girl set off running in the opposite direction. The child was awkward at first, learning the gait required. What took Kate days to learn, the child picked up straight away. The child faded from her fuzzy eyesight.

"Ah shit," the blacksmith complained. "There's no catching her now."

Kate giggled. "Indeed not."

The shoes were easy enough to make, and besides, her parents had just arrived, leaving a trail she could use to walk home.

Faustus and three of his followers were at the door, greeting everyone that came. When Kate walked in, he welcomed her no differently. "Waters preserve you."

She saw it for what it was. He acted as though nothing was amiss. That was how Roy comforted a chicken before he chopped its head off. Scaring the animal only made the kill harder, and he truly only did so because he must. She imagined Faustus felt the same in his own twisted way.

The rest of his minions stood in a row in the back like some tacky curtain. They watched her from under their low-hanging hoods. She wondered which one of them had burns in the shape of handprints on their ass.

She spotted Lori on the stairway. Making her way to her friend, she said, "Excuse me, Lori? Could I use your outhouse?"

The librarian caught on. While the villagers knew the two of them had been friends for years, the Ever Faithful would know far less. She had been seen carrying books around the village several hundred times, so it was a reasonable conclusion to make that Kate frequented the library for books, not to socialize.

"Just out that door." Lori pointed to her back door.

Stepping into the outhouse, Kate reached into her skirt and began removing the projectile devices. Silently laughing at the audacity of her appearance. She was grateful for the lock on the door. If someone accidentally walked in, they would think she was doing...well, something else.

The device fell into the hole with a wet sploosh. One by one, she dropped them into the shit. She never imagined she'd find so much glee in ridding herself of a modern marvel, but it was for the good of all that she did this. In time—and sewage—the devices would rust to disrepair, but it wouldn't be too long before the hole was filled with dirt and the outhouse was relocated.

Stepping out, Kate adjusted her skirt. She felt approximately seven pounds lighter.

Chuckling at her own toilet humor, she stepped into the shed and unburdened herself of the sand. In the freezing little tool shed, the sand appeared perfectly ordinary.

Inside, Kate made a final deposit in the tin box Lori used for outgoing mail. While most people did not have such things, a librarian with a merchant for a boyfriend kept a letterbox by the door.

Letters addressed to the envoys of Taus, Sundersong, and Flosses. She had already confirmed that Noranger did not recognize the Ever Faithful as a religious chapter. Perhaps the other provinces would have more insight.

Faustus was already talking to the crowd. It was mostly welcoming and reminding everyone who they were and what they did as if everyone did not already know. She scanned the faces of the villagers as she took her place beside her fathers. Some appeared to be intently listening. Others, like the blacksmith falling asleep in a chair or the butcher picking her nose, were less than enthused to be there.

"My friends," Faustus boomed, waking the blacksmith with a startle. "It has been a pleasure to stay in your village. We have been honored by your warm welcome."

She hoped the sentence that followed was the announcement they were leaving.

"As you all know, our chapter seeks out the Ghost King's bride, but prophecy is a tricky thing. When our father had this vision, we had no way of knowing whether he saw the past, present, or the future."

Of course not. Leave it to cultists to determine that if a prophecy wasn't real, that didn't mean they couldn't find evidence wherever it pleased them.

"We suspect there is a wolf among your flock," Faustus said, looking directly at Kate.

Nerves high and prickly and at full alert, she struggled to remain calm when Faustus called her out in front of the whole village.

"With your permission, we would like to conduct tests on one of your own. If she proves that she is not the bride that will bolster Dominion's right hand, we will trouble her no further. But if she is indeed the bride, we humbly request you relinquish her to us in the name of the righteous."

She kept her hands at her sides and took extra care to touch nothing. The last thing she needed was to display her powers for all to see. Rage and adrenaline pumped through her veins, allowing all the blood in her body to rush to her head. Too enraged to speak, Kate startled when the village broke out into shouts and questions.

"You're not touching my girls!"

"For the Waters!"

"What kind of tests?"

"Breathe," Frank whispered in her ear, breaking the spell long enough for her to gasp for air.

Faustus motioned with his hands, silencing the crowd. "There is only one person in question, and I think we all know who that is. Our test consists of a few questions and the Trial of Waters."

What was that? Kate had never heard of such a thing. She looked to her papa, who was now leaning against the wall for support. His skin was the color of snow. Her fires went out all at once, like a lantern that had been turned off. If Papa was frightened, the Trial of Waters must have been very bad.

"For those of you unfamiliar with this barbaric torture," Shawn the Envoy emerged from the crowd with his hand on the hilt of his sword, "the prisoner is strapped down to a board and their face covered with a cloth. Then water is poured on their face. When the cloth is wet, it makes it nearly impossible to breathe."

Frightened murmurs and concerned exchanges wafted about the room.

"If she passes the trial, she will be absolved of all accusations," Faustus said.

"That's just it, though," Shawn interrupted. "The trial would frighten and half drown the woman into saying anything for it to stop. Don't you see? They would coerce her into pleading guilty just for the torture to end!"

So fixated on the image of what the Ever Faithful intended to do with her, she was unaware of the tears rolling down her face.

"Over my dead body," Baxter boomed. Most flinched at the sudden burst of noise, including Kate.

"Aye," the blacksmith said. "Kate is a weird one, I'll not lie, but she's not afraid of the Ghost King. Just last month, I watched her storm up there, giving him what for. Seems to me that we need someone who can stand up to him!"

"What has the Ghost King ever done to us?" Roy stood. "Other than protecting our lands? Seems to me that a safe land without taxes is a good one!"

Bethany stood next. "We've gotten along just fine without torturing our own. I don't see the need for it now."

One by one, the villagers refused Faustus.

Their reasons spanned a spectrum from morally wrong to self-preservation. Not a one saw a legitimate reason to give in to Faustus's request. Exhausted from the influx of emotions, Kate leaned against the wall and dried her tears.

"We don't even know if what they say is true," Lori added. "What if there is no bride? I've never heard of such a thing in all my years."

It was as if all the resentment she harbored for the Ever Faithful had transferred to the villagers. Not only did they dislike the proposal, but they were also accusing the cult of taking advantage of their food and goodwill. Of wasting their time and of obscuring the true message of the Waters, which would have never condoned torture.

Kate watched with smug pride as Faustus backed against the wall. It was their turn to be afraid. His followers shuffled around the room to stand at his back in case things got out of hand. There was an invisible line between the villagers and the Ever Faithful. The envoy and his soldiers were siding with the villagers.

Kate sniffed back the tears, her heart full by the unanimous decision. Never had she been prouder to live in a nameless village in an unruled province than she was in that moment.

Faustus was either unaccustomed to being told no or incapable of reading the room.

"Your permission is an act of courtesy, not a requirement!" he raged, sucking all the joy out of the moment for Kate.

Shawn drew his sword with a hiss, and his soldiers responded in turn. "This village is under Noranger's protection. Their law stands."

It was an incredible sight. She wanted to hug every single person in the village and thank them for everything. They were afraid, but they never rejected her. Not truly.

Their jeers and mockery became too much for the Ever Faithful. If they had pitchforks, Kate would have feared for the cultists' lives. She watched in total astonishment as the Ever Faithful fled the library. They had won!

Chapter 18

THE SNOW HAD CEASED the week following the village meeting. As if the winter itself was with them, allowing little excuse for the Ever Faithful to remain where they were not wanted. Kate looked up from her book to note the trail of cloaked figures with bags made of burlap departing the village.

By the end of the week, most, if not all, the villagers turned out the cultists until there was nothing but stragglers. Guards patrolling the street had become commonplace after Faustus threatened to imprison and torture her. She imagined they, too, would leave before too long.

This did not slow her plans, however.

Without the watchful eye of the Ever Faithful, Kate and her parents were free to install bars on the windows and escape ladders for those who needed them.

"You want me to put sand in the thatching?" the butcher asked.

"It's not just any sand," she explained, holding out a frosty glass jar. "It's the Ghost King's sand. I think it's the source of his blight. Even just a pinch will put out a fire."

The butcher took the jar and touched it. "Shit, it's like winter in a jar."

"Precisely."

"This will make the house colder, though."

It was a worry among many. Fuel for the fires was rationed out for the winter. People feared the cold more than an impending fire because freezing to death was a more immediate and tangible threat that reminded them every morning.

"If you scatter it thin enough along the thatching, it won't be noticeable," Kate explained. "A grain here or there isn't strong enough on its own. Only in multitudes can the sand alter the climate."

"Same goes for people."

It was an insightful comment. One she'd remember.

Ignoring the dull ache in her heart, Kate kept busy. It was the only thing that provided her with any solace. At night, she read until her eyes closed against her will. When sleep came, so did the mare, snorting and kicking at the frozen earth as if urging her to climb into the saddle.

Sometimes she did. Knowing full well it was only a dream, she rode through the winter snows at a speed that gave the snow the appearance of falling stars as she rode through time and space to be with him.

Only to wake, gasping with tears rolling down her face.

Her traitorous heart was split in two. One half wanted nothing more than to scale snow and icy hillsides to be by his side. The other half wanted to put a torch to his crumbling castle. Fire and ice. So contradictory that no matter what she wanted, they could never coexist together.

More and more, she found her mind drifting to what would come with the spring. Her fire starters sold quickly at the grocery store. In full swing of winter, they sold faster than they could make them. She imagined it would slow in the spring and summer months, but the Noranger soldiers were so taken with the device that they asked to make a bulk order to take back with them. It was an easy, steady income her fathers could rely on.

She had the books she needed to gain access to the university. She wouldn't need a theory, all Kate had to do was wave one in front of those snooty bastards at the door, and they would lick their lips at the prospect of seeing a book from the Ghost King's library.

They would probably think her a thief that ransacked his castle while he was away, but Kate didn't care. She was a thief due to the simple fact that she could never return them.

The stack was half-finished. Absently reaching for the next, she frowned at the foreigner in her hand. Kate didn't remember taking it.

Double checking, she counted seven books, including the one in her hand. Kate could have sworn she only took six.

The priority was medical advancements and aqueducts, the things she deemed most important to study over the winter.

They were arranged well in advance and carefully curated, yet the book in her hand was a compilation of...love poems?

Did he slip this into her stack? No. Kate laughed at the notion. The Ghost King, the bane of distant kings, Dominion's creature, the rider of the night, blight bringer, and painfully introverted beast, would never have dreamed of slipping love poems into her books.

It was small and thin and probably got stuck to a book by accident.

And yet...

She opened the leather cover and gasped. Etched in a dry, chunky ink that faded at the end of each hard-pressed stroke was a letter addressed to her.

Dear Kate of the nameless village,

I have endured this world well beyond my time and have waited centuries for an end to my misery. Day after day, I welcomed any who would challenge the blight and survive. You can imagine my surprise when it was a girl in a hideous suit whose only weapons were unceasing questions.

You trespassed my castle. Frightened me and Gertrude with your inventions. Worst of all, you've interrupted the grand schemes of the gods themselves. Yet, I look forward to your intrusions. You have taken my resolve and replaced it with something I cannot abide. Hope.

Yours eternal,

Elijah

She did not know how much time had passed since she opened the book. Pages unturned, Kate read the letter over and over until she felt a hand on her shoulder. It was Dad, leaning over to read the thing that had left her stunned.

"Oh," Frank managed before walking away. "Oh."

Baxter made an inquiring grunt. When Frank didn't answer, he, too, read the first page of the book still clutched in her hand.

He had feelings for her. The Ghost King—Elijah—had feelings for her. He wrote them down in a book of love poems like a schoolboy slipping a note into her bag when she wasn't looking.

"What is that supposed to mean?" Baxter asked. Whispers of astonishment softened each word.

"I don't know. What does it mean to you, Kate?" Frank asked.

Still holding the book, her entire being was rocked with confliction. From the first moment she saw him, Kate longed for this. It was a harbored desire covered with excuses of logic and self-preservation. She never needed him to protect the village. They could clearly manage on their own.

Knowledge was something she always desired, but the yearning for him superseded the flat and dull explanation of logic. What she felt for Elijah surpassed explanation. To deny her feelings for him was to deny her true self—whatever that may be.

Turning to her parents, she spoke through trembling lips. "What should I do?"

There was a knock at the door. She let out a growl of frustration. "What now?"

Flinging open the door, Kate found herself face-to-face with Harvey. He was panting with a fury in his eyes she had never seen before. He was holding a letter. "You need to see this."

She wanted nothing more than to go back to staring at the letter the Ghost King had written her, but that would have to wait. He had forever, after all.

While the villagers accumulated outside, Kate read the letter.

Greetings on behalf of His Majesty, the one true king of the continent, King Carver the First,

The Ever Faithful is known to us. They were driven out of our providence last year for the crime of worshipping Dominion, the scourge of the Waters. Only on pain of death may they return.

It is His Majesty's suggestion that they be considered highly dangerous fanatics and to use the utmost caution.

The day was full of mind-warping letters.

If the Ever Faithful were, in fact, Dominion worshippers, why did they want to make the Ghost King less powerful? They must have known, she realized. The Ever Faithful was aware that he was not Dominion's ally.

Huddled in their furs and blankets, villagers were gathering in the street despite the winter cold. She could overhear Bethany muttering, "I knew they weren't real acolytes."

Lori probably opened the letters first, only to have Harvey snatch them out of her hands so he could tell everyone. Kate didn't mind, but she wished she were first to learn of it and not last. In her heavy petticoat and fur-lined hat, Lori came running up to her. "Wolf among us indeed!"

"They mean to undermine the Ghost King," she said loud enough for everyone to hear. "They know he is no friend of Dominion's; that's the real reason they were here."

"Those bastards," the blacksmith said. "I say we go have a talk with those so-called faithful!"

United in their stance, Kate had more than her father's support; she had the entire village standing behind her. She searched the crowd but did not find any of the soldiers or Shawn. Had they finally left? It seemed unlikely.

A roar of consensus responded in kind. Caught up in the moment, the exhilaration was contagious. It satiated a thirst she always bottled up inside with nowhere to go. Others were grabbing their shovels. Kate reached for their own when Frank stopped her.

She looked at him. Dad's disappointment was palpable. It was worse than when she went to see the Ghost King without telling them. Guilt wilted all the excitement, and for a moment, she understood why he stopped her.

"You think they mean to kill them?"

"There's no telling what people are capable of in groups," Baxter said.

She flinched away from the shovel then. There was so much she didn't know or understand, even as an adult. Not that adulthood came with a blueprint, but Kate imagined she would have a lot more of the right answers as she neared her thirties. It seemed she didn't. Her fathers were beacons of wisdom that she followed as they trailed behind the angry mob.

Anxiety foamed and frothed underneath her stern expression. They didn't have to walk too far. The crowd descended upon a series of black tents cropped around a smoking fire. Where did they get black tents? Black fabrics were hard to come by in the village. They must have hidden their belongings somewhere as if they had planned a quick escape.

The Ever Faithful gathered from their fire or from their tents and lined themselves behind Faustus. Suddenly, she was very glad the villagers brought tools. The group had doubled in size.

They must have had half their group waiting at another location. There was no other town nearby apart from the one she… No. Kate had never visited the remains of her old village. The memories were too painful to face. She had no idea what remained, but perhaps there was some semblance of a shelter.

"You trespassed the burned village," Kate said, pushing through the crowd to face the cultists. Her tempered rage threatened to break. "How dare you dwell where so many lives were taken!"

As if they sensed the pain in her words, the villagers went silent. They lowered their shovels.

"You are far too clever," Faustus admitted. "They couldn't very well stay with me. It would have caused so much alarm."

Something in Kate's brain clicked then. Like an air bubble surfacing a murky pond. She understood what had never occurred to her before. "That town was erased from most maps," she said, stepping right up to Faustus. "Few would sell a map outdated by twenty years. That town was already known to you."

If there was a shred of remorse within Faustus, it was not in his eyes. They were two glassy orbs staring with a crazed sense of purpose she did not understand. How could they? She had longed to stare into the eyes of the people responsible for burning her village. To demand answers and exact pain and judgment. But when the moment finally arrived, she wanted nothing more than for them to simply go away.

She didn't want their answers, but she needed the rest of the village to know.

"Why?" Her voice cracked as a myriad of awful memories danced around in her mind.

"You were born earlier than our prophet predicted," Faustus said, his pitch high with agitation. "When we arrived, there were no visibly pregnant women, and we realized we were too late. We had no way of knowing which child was you, so we took...precautions."

Kate shook uncontrollably. It was because of her. They killed everyone because of her. A numbness took her heart to shield her from the pain too great to bear. How could they do such a thing?

"You heard the screams I heard," she uttered. "And yet you kept burning."

A glimmer of guilt crossed Faustus's face. "All we needed was you."

"Because I'm the Ghost King's bride?" Kate said in a bitter, mocking tone. "We know you worship Dominion. Why not make him stronger?"

Faustus shook his head. "You really don't know, do you?"

She turned to regard the villagers then. They came for violence, but they would have carried that sin to the ground, and their ashes would never be scattered to the winds. What remained on their faces was heartbreak. Lori clapped a hand over her mouth as Harvey pulled her in close. Bethany was clutching her stomach as if she were going to vomit. Void stares and pallid skin.

Whatever their intentions, she did not believe it was murder.

Facing Faustus again, Kate pushed her hands toward him. She didn't touch him, but a surge of heat blasted him and his minions backward. Black robes littered with powdery snow. Kate stood over them and raised the fire so high that the melted snow turned to steam. Those who were too close to the fire screamed and rolled away as their tacky robes caught fire.

He was flat on his back, thrusting a dagger in her direction. "The kingdom of Dominion will not be thwarted! The messiah will not be suffered."

Kate grabbed his hand. Flesh sizzled like fatty bacon, and Faustus screamed. "This is but a taste of the suffering you bestowed onto others," she said before slicing the palm of her hand with his knife.

In the black and whites of the world, Kate's red blood broke from her hand and dripped onto the snow and all over Faustus. His eyes went wide as if he had just put it together.

"You're summoning him?"

She would not take their lives, but they would not hurt anyone else ever again. If they scattered to the winds, defunct and broken, it would be enough. It had to be. She had no more room for pain in her heart. Their demise would be their own doing, not hers.

"He will come soon," Kate said to the village. "Go home."

The villagers wanted no part of the blight, and some had already departed before she had said anything. Frank and Baxter remained just a few steps away in case she needed them. She smiled at them, especially Dad, who was on the verge of sobs.

"I'm okay," she mouthed to them, and her parents nodded.

Lori and Harvey also remained. The librarian lunged at her for a hug. "What was that?"

"I'm not entirely certain, but at least I can control it now."

What was once brought about by anger could now be called upon if she willed it. When Frank stopped her from grabbing the shovel, it occurred to her that she had almost lost control with the crowd in the same way she had lost control of the fires within her. By focusing on the outcome she wanted, Kate was able to control her anger and, thus, her power.

Their future was too important to be swallowed up by the past. When she let go of that need for revenge, a new sense of self took its place.

"You guys should go before he comes," she warned.

Lori and Harvey made their way back to the village. She turned to her parents and said, "You should go too."

Frank shook his head, and Baxter folded his arms in a stance that suggested he would not be persuaded to leave. Not without his daughter. They were so stubborn, her fathers.

Faustus was still nursing his blistered hand.

Kate knelt and packed snow over his burns.

He shook his head in disbelief. "I killed them all, yet you tend to my burns?"

"I thought that's what messiahs did."

"You don't understand," he said. "Dominion is progress. He is industry. If you, the messiah of the Waters, stop that...humanity will never ascend to its rightful place beside the gods."

"That is far more logical than all that bride nonsense."

His eyes widened. "But it's true! Our prophet foresaw your union with the Ghost King. If you marry him, balance will be restored. Dominion's hold on man will lessen."

There was an irony in all this. The Water's messiah, the voice of nature, was an inventor. She wondered if that was by accident or design. All of Kate's best devices were the ones that used nature to help man.

"Not all devices of man are Dominion's work," she said softly.

As if years of folly had undone him all at once, Faustus released his grip on the dagger as he sunk deeper into the snow. Most of his minions were running away, but some chose to remain and cower with their leader. Ready to accept the fate riding toward them. "But we do need to go now," Kate warned as an invisible force pushed against her fires.

The three of them left the cultists in the snow. She needed to get her parents out of the cold and somewhere safe and warm.

"I'm so proud of you," Frank said as he kissed her temple.

"You were right all along," she said as they walked. "Both of you."

"Of course we were," Baxter said. "But...what were we right about this time?"

She laughed and said, "I'll explain everything at home."

The mirth of the moment fell away at the echoes of an all too familiar popping noise coming from the village.

Chapter 19

IT COULDN'T BE. THERE was no way the Ever Faithful had anyone else lurking around the village. Another crack resounded in the night air, making the three of them flinch. How did they find the projectile devices?

As if he was thinking the same, Frank whispered, "I thought you threw them into an outhouse latrine."

"I did!"

Baxter grunted with disgust, and rightly so. Someone had to have climbed into the shit-filled hole and fished the devices out. Was humanity so desperate for violence and power? Of course they were. If an actual god and not just a metaphor could be born of human greed, it could tolerate a swim in raw sewage.

When the rooftops of the village came into view, the three of them crouched and snuck glimpses among snow piles and frozen barrels. The town appeared deserted, but in the second story of the butcher's shop, she spotted the grocer and the butcher in the window. They were waiting for something. Kate's heart was pounding, and her breath was so hot it melted any snow in its wake. She had a terrible feeling that she had forgotten something important.

They moved behind the houses, amid the chicken coops and the outhouses, but there was no sign of anyone. It wasn't until they were almost home that she spotted a soldier tucked between two barrels.

He was kneeling behind the seamstress's house, taking quick glimpses at the road.

Kate snuck over to his side. Frank and Baxter whispered and grabbed at her as if to stop her, but she needed to know what was going on.

"What's the situation?" she asked the soldier. He was no more than a boy around nineteen. He had no beard like most of the troops, and he was shivering so hard she feared his teeth would break.

He stared at her wide-eyed and said, "You're not supposed to be here."

A lifetime dwelled within the moments before Kate truly understood his meaning. The Ever Faithful were not the threat. The envoys were not protecting the villagers. They were the ones attacking. She had sent the villagers home amid an invasion.

Kate followed his downward glance to the abomination in his hand. Her creation. Her device. He was using it to shoot her people. Hotter than the blacksmith's forge, the snow steamed all around them, and the boy pressed himself into the wall as hard as he could.

"I'm sorry, miss," he stuttered. "I'm just following orders."

As if that excused everything! Shooting innocent, unarmed people because a man with a bigger beard told him to. "I was supposed to be burned alive as a child," she said through gritted teeth. "By men who were just following orders."

He fell back, kicking at her as he fumbled with the device. She could smell the explosive powder on him and warm, salty perspiration running down his temples. He was trying to light the fuse with a bit of flint and a pocket knife, but his hands fumbled as he attempted to juggle the device.

"Stay away," he said. "Please don't make me hurt you."

Kate rolled her eyes and yanked the device from his hand. "What do your people want?"

"Orders came in from the king," he spoke freely as if he wanted nothing more than to confess. "When he read the reports of all the wheat and the unused farmlands, he ordered us to invade the province again."

Papa was right. The envoy had been scouting and sending information back to Noranger. It made sense they wanted to expand southward. To inhabit warmer, fertile lands that would nearly triple their current size would make Noranger the strongest nation on the continent.

"And you thought you could defeat the Ghost King with this?" she asked, holding up the device.

The boy soldier nodded. "It can hurt him from far away. We're not supposed to shoot any of the villagers if we can help it. We're ordered to only shoot him."

He said that as though it were good news. Oh, we're just going to invade your lands, but don't worry, we only want to kill your king. Then we will impose our laws and taxes and conscript your men and boys. There's no reason to be upset.

She thought about how she burned Faustus's hand and reeled those fires back before she did the same to the boy. He was young and stupid, and if she was honest with herself, the only person Kate was truly mad at was herself.

The devices should never have been made. She could have spent more time considering the consequences rather than allowing herself to be cowed by the fear of foreigners. In the end, she was right but also wrong about them. She feared them for the wrong reasons, and it clouded her judgment. If she had taken the time to learn about them, perhaps the boy in front of her would have come to her for help rather than clinging to his superiors and their agendas.

She doubted that boy asked to be conscripted. He clearly did not want to harm anyone. Kate inhaled a breath to cool the fires raging inside. She wasn't angry at the boy so much as she was herself for not seeing the obvious.

The Ghost King was getting closer. She could feel it. Like a beacon in the night. He was coming, and for once, she wished he wouldn't.

"Go to my parents," she said, pointing in their direction. "They won't hurt you."

He didn't move at first. She imagined he feared a trap. "Go, you stupid boy, and tell them the Ghost King is on his way."

He said something earlier that was important. Something she missed.

"Wait—" Kate said, grabbing his arm. "Have your people been here before?"

"The commander came here once a long time ago, but they failed."

It was a kick to the belly, but suddenly everything made sense. "Before you were born, I imagine."

"Yes, ma'am."

Kate sneered at the title. "Leave before I change my mind."

The boy scampered in the direction of her fathers, leaving her to think in peace and assess the situation. Heaps of muddied snow lined the homes, giving way to the empty street. The houses were dark; no one had lit their lanterns. It appeared vacant, but tension coiled in her gut. They were waiting for something...or rather, someone.

Damn it all! If she hadn't summoned the Ghost King, they would have been forced to wait it out in the cold all night. Getting outmaneuvered by a bunch of bearded soldiers from the north might have been as big of a fumble as creating the projectile devices.

Amid cursing herself, the temperature in the air plummeted. There was a series of fanatical screams severed with an abrupt end.

Kate squeezed her eyes shut.

Go away. It's a trap. Can't you feel it?

The pressure of the situation was bearing down on her. For all she knew, the villagers were killed or held hostage. She had to do something. Standing on shaky legs, Kate raised her hands and slowly walked down the road.

The hair prickled on the back of her neck. She was being watched. With no sign of the villagers, Kate could only conclude that it was the enemy trailing her with their eyes.

"I wish to speak with Shawn the Envoy." Her voice broke slightly as she spoke.

"They didn't do away with you?" the envoy said, emerging from behind the grocery. "They begged us to let them have you. Why did they let you go?"

Right. The Ever Faithful's outlandish beliefs were a large spoonful to swallow. The envoy did not think for one moment that she was a bride or messiah or anything other than a peasant girl who made trinkets to please their king. Kate sniffed with indignation. The fires within begged and pleaded for her to show him otherwise, but that was pride and ego. She would hold her only advantage for as long as she could.

"You knew what they were all along? Fiends of Dominion."

"Useful idiots," Shawn said, coming a few steps closer. "Faustus was much more decisive than his predecessor. If Ignatius hadn't delayed all those years ago, you would have been born into Noranger, and you would have been safe."

She squeezed her fists so tight that her tendons ached. Kate wanted nothing more than to turn him to ash. Not yet. Not at all if she could help it.

"You mean to tell me that you were responsible for the attacks on the grain mills over twenty years ago? It's hard to tell how old you are with the beard."

He chuckled with surprise and absently touched his beard. "It must be, indeed. I was a young man then. The Ghost King was supposed to be preoccupied with the fires, but their leader had delayed their plans for some reason."

"So, your attack got the Ghost King's attention."

The Ever Faithful didn't start burning her village until well after the Ghost King was clear on the other side of the province. Immortal or not, he couldn't get to her village in time. He didn't choose grain over lives, but he assumed responsibility because that's what kings do.

He wasn't some infallible god high up on the pedestal she placed him; he wasn't even a king. It would be nice if she could stop being wrong about everything. She didn't expect to be right all the time, but if life could throw her a line occasionally, it would help.

"Who dug the projectile devices out of the latrine?" she asked, raising a brow.

"The same one who failed to steal them from your house," Shawn said evenly. "What did you use to burn him with? Cattle prods?"

In the corner of her eye, she spotted a glint of light from the second-story window of the library. Lori was sending a signal, letting her know the villagers were safe and waiting for the next move. They waited on her signal.

Focusing all her pain, all her rage, all the lives lost on her account, Kate's hands burst into flames. She pushed against the blighted air, shoving in Shawn's direction. The envoy went flying and landed on his back several feet away.

Shouts broke out throughout the town. Soldiers waiting for commands and villagers peering out their windows. The envoy sat up, looking twenty years younger. "They were right!" he said, crawling away. "You can shoot fire out of your hands!"

It wasn't quite accurate. She sent a hot gust. The beard was the only casualty of her fire. Playing on the dramatics wasn't exactly Kate's style, but if it helped her walk away from the encounter, she would do it. All that mattered was keeping the villagers safe.

And perhaps mending things with the Ghost King.

Glass shattered from above in all directions. The villagers had grouped together in the houses with upper stories, and they were aiming their crossbows at Shawn the Envoy.

Kate grinned. They were so clever! With the right tools, they could defend themselves just fine.

Her glee only lasted for a moment. A group emerged between the shop and Bethany's home. Frank and Baxter were walking deliberately toward her. A shiny, silver tube gleaned in the snow's reflection, and it was pointed at their heads. Kate's stomach plummeted like a stone in the sea. Clamping a hand over her mouth was all she could do to keep from screaming.

"I'd stop unless you want them dead," the soldier said.

He wasn't the boy. "Where is the boy soldier?" she asked. "The one without a beard."

The soldier frowned. "Traitors are not welcome in Noranger, and neither are witches."

Already claiming the province as their own, making it a place where women like her were not abided. The insult stung more than it should have.

"Please don't hurt them," she begged.

There was a whooshing noise followed by a dull splat. The soldier said nothing, did nothing for a long, painful moment before falling over. A crossbolt was firmly lodged in his back.

"Run!" Kate screamed at her parents.

Frank and Baxter bolted for the shop. In a blur, a firefight broke out all around her. Bolts flew and pelted the muddy frozen ground. Popping noises responded in kind. She ran for cover, diving behind the blacksmith's water barrel. There were groans and cries of pain, but it was impossible to tell who was injuring who.

Kate watched as the envoy crawled out of sight. She started to pursue, but a bolt landed just inches from her face. She scowled and looked up in the direction it was fired. "Sorry, Kate!" Lane called from the tanner's window.

They had little to no training, she reminded herself as she crawled after the envoy. It wasn't intentional. Even though there were no soldiers near her! Judging by the bolts lodged all over the buildings, the kickback was too great. Adjustments would be needed.

"Kate!" Papa's voice was panicked.

He was holding Dad in his arms and dragging him inside. No, no, no...

She was running then.

The night sky was showered in bolts and smoke. Sulfur filled the air, and she could hear screams as soldiers tried to kick in the tanner's door. None of it mattered. She barreled into Baxter. With a free arm, he grabbed her and pulled them into the shop.

Frank was groaning in pain and covered in blood. She searched him for the wound, praying it wasn't fatal. Kate had designed the device to kill, not to wound, and treating it wasn't something she had prepared for. The integrity of the bullet wasn't required. If it splintered, there would be an infection. There was no way she could get all the fragments out.

"Get him on the table," she said.

Baxter lifted his husband like a straw scarecrow and placed him gently on the table and lit a lantern. The light would no doubt attract the soldiers, but she needed to see to save Frank's life. Papa was already barring the doors and nailing wood over the windows.

Ripping his sleeve away, Kate located the wound. It had hit his forearm. From what she could tell, it was a graze. A deep one that burned an awful gash, severing muscle, but at least there wasn't a bullet lodged in his body.

"This is going to hurt," she warned him.

Before Frank could respond, Kate cauterized the wound with her fingers.

Flesh burned, and she cried as her dad screamed until he suddenly went silent.

"Is he dead?"

"No," Kate said, checking his pulse for the third time to be sure. "He just fainted from the pain."

Papa took Dad's hand and kissed it.

With the boards over the windows, it was impossible to see what was happening. The silence could have meant anything. The soldiers had rounded up the villagers; a cease fire, maybe? The villagers had frightened off the soldiers without their commander? That was unlikely.

Ice crackled along the frame of the doors and spread across the boards on the window. "Papa, start the oven."

While she covered Frank with several blankets, Baxter used a fire starter. Within moments the flames were burning, but it would be a while before the fire would be hot enough. Kate closed her eyes and let the heat radiate from her body.

The villagers must have recognized his coming and started making fires of their own, leaving the soldiers to perish in the blight. Longing pulled at her. She wanted to see him again. She wanted to tell him that it wasn't his fault, but most of all, that she was sorry.

She stood at the closed door and fretted. What if he didn't want to see her after their last encounter? She did slap him. It wasn't her proudest moment.

"Kate…" Papa said.

She turned to her father.

He was nodding. "Go to him."

Unbarring the door, Kate stepped outside. The blight railed against her with all the fury it could muster, but it was nothing more than a light breeze on a summer day. The Ghost King—Elijah—was on his horse. He saw her and pulled the reins, rearing the horse toward her.

There was so much unspoken between them. Once, she had been the spring that trickled a stream of hope into his heart, but did he still feel that way? He was all the answers she had sought in the world, even if she came with the wrong questions.

"Elijah," she whispered.

His chin lifted with recognition.

I know your name. I read your poems and letter a thousand times over.

A pop in the night startled them both. Smoke enveloped the Ghost King as Shawn the Envoy limped away from the tanner's second-story window.

Kate waved the smoke away as she got closer. "Elijah?"

She let out a gasp. He was slumped in the saddle. The horse stood there as if nothing had happened, or perhaps the mare was waiting for an order.

Kate rushed to him and shook the Ghost King. He let out a groan.

Was he dying? He couldn't die. The whole point of being immortal is that you can't die. Icy smoke curled out from the hole in his back. Her device had grievously harmed the Ghost King. That was what those cultists feared. Messiah or not, Kate had managed to create a device that could kill him. She didn't mean for it to happen, but she hadn't meant for a lot of things.

Climbing into the saddle behind him, she grabbed hold of the reins. The Ghost King was muttering for her to get away. Even in his state, he feared the blight would consume her. They needed to get back to the castle. If there was anything that could save him, it would be there.

"You won't hurt me," she said, urging the horse into a full gallop toward the castle.

Chapter 20

S HE RODE AS HARD as she dared through the forest. Sand spilled from his wound and fell away in the wind, creating a snowstorm behind them. The moonlight was slight, but the mare knew the way even if her riders could not see it.

"Elijah," Kate said, "stay with me."

A weak growl came from his throat. "The cellar. I need to get to the cellar."

She recalled cellar doors alongside the stable. Was the secret to his longevity somewhere below the castle? It went against everything she had ever learned, but Kate had to put faith in the myths. Suspending logic for a moment, she thought about the myth itself. Dominion was a god born of the evils of man and their inventions. If he created the Ghost King out of Elijah, it meant Dominion was an inventor himself.

And all inventors had tools.

The castle tower steadily rose above the horizon. "We're almost there."

"I can feel you," he said. "I can hear your heartbeat and smell your hair..."

Kate closed her eyes and allowed herself to take in the moment. She held him close. Whatever came next, she would cherish this moment in case they didn't have another. "Just hang on a little bit longer."

His armor was warm against her hands, and his hair now sagged around his shoulders. The very fabric of his clothing had gone slack against his body. Her warmth combated the blight, but it was thawing the Ghost King. He couldn't fight his injury and her warmth at the same time. She was killing him faster than the wound itself.

Reeling in her power as much as she could afford, the blight bloomed around them once more, and he gasped. "That's better," he said, taking hold of the reins.

She was cold but not painfully so. At her decreased temperature, Kate could sense the blight was significantly weaker than before. She was barely using any of her fires. *Hang on, Elijah. We have too much to talk about.*

Hooves and shouting were thundering from behind. Kate turned to see the envoy and his soldiers hurtling toward them on charging horses. A few were aiming her own devices at them. Two lit fuses burned in the night like a pair of evil eyes watching them as if it were Dominion himself.

"We need to go faster," she said. "They're gaining on us."

With his blight weakening, the soldiers could attack them with ease.

"Gertrude's smart, not fast," he said.

She supposed it was up to her then. With an outstretched hand, Kate formed a ball of fire in her palm. Straining with the focus, she unleashed the ball. It hurtled downward several feet before shattering into a shower of tiny flames.

It wasn't quite what she had in mind, but the horses screamed and reared, breaking up the regiment. Kate roared with triumph, but her victory was short-lived.

Charging from the shower of sparks, Shawn and a few others remained undaunted and racing ever quicker up the hill.

"We're almost there," Elijah said, urging the horse on.

Once over the highest point of the hill, the terrain flattened, renewing the horse's pace as she trotted to the side of the castle and into the stable as if she was more done with the night than they were.

Kate slid off the horse—who was still trying to get into her stall even with the rider on her back—and helped Elijah down. Half leaning against her, he braced the wall of the castle. His face was racked with pain. In his arms, her fingers traced the hole in his armor as he labored for breath.

"It's all my fault," she said. "I did this to you. The power that keeps me alive is killing you."

The corners of his mouth turned up several times. As if he were trying to smile after long forgetting how. "This final day has been the best day of my immortal life."

That was not what Kate wanted to hear.

Pulling open the heavy cellar door, she pulled at him. "It's not over yet."

He made it down the steps. There were several swooshing noises behind her. As she went to close the door behind them, Kate turned to find the envoy and his soldiers with empty crossbows. They stared at her with wide eyes as if they were waiting for something.

Her back burst into pain. Dropping to her knees, blinded by agony, she found no words to speak. They had shot her in the back with her own crossbolts. Panting on the ground, she never knew such pain in her life.

Elijah roared. In his fury, he released what was probably the last reserves of his blight. Pulling the cellar doors shut, he engrossed them both in total darkness.

Dragged to her feet, Kate burst into a wet coughing fit. Hot liquid spilled down her chin.

Elijah was half yelling, half moaning. Like a wounded animal trapped in his den.

She hurt so badly. Every movement, every breath pushed the tips of the bolts deeper. She needed to see what was happening. Where they were going.

Using what little power she could muster, a pale-yellow flame rose from her hand.

"Save your strength," Elijah said, pulling her deeper into the labyrinth under his castle. "Creatures like me have no need of the light."

Be that as it may, she needed it. Besides, Kate noticed that the fire soothed the excruciating pain that was existence. "It's helping."

He didn't argue the point any further.

It would take some time for their pursuers to find them. Stone slabs melded with perfect symmetry, creating a dizzying series of pathways. It may have been the blood loss that left her disoriented. There was a pattern carved along the upper corners of the walls. Kate recognized it from her books.

"Paradise Lost?"

"They're supposed to be wards," he said, leaning against the wall to steady them. Elijah was glossy wet, as if he were melting from the inside out. "To keep me in."

Keep him in where? She didn't have the breath to ask. One of the bolts had made its way to her lung, and each breath burned with violence. Urging him on, they came to the center. It was a chasm with a massive open grave.

He helped her sit down at the edge before sliding in. "I need to bury you," he said.

The world was fading fast. Kate had so many questions, but if she didn't do as he said, she might not live long enough to hear the answer.

As if the proximity to the grave alone restored his strength, Elijah, the Ghost King, pulled her into his arms. The bolts were embedded too deeply to be pulled out, so he didn't try. Laying her gently on her side in his grave, Elijah covered her in the blight sand. She resisted when he poured handfuls on her face.

"It's the only way," he coaxed.

She nodded. Already numb with death, Kate let the cold seep from the ground and into her dying body. In the darkness, she felt herself sinking in the ever-shifting sands beneath her. As if it were consuming her and eating away at the life she once knew.

"I'm going to close the tomb doors," a soft voice said. "Stay here."

He didn't want her to be afraid. As if she could be. The sands were telling her a story. It filled her ears with whispering in long-dead voices. She opened her eyes, and the sand showed her visions of a forgotten time. She opened her mouth, and the sands filled her throat and aching lungs. It was there that Kate found her answers.

Where she found Paradise Lost.

Chapter 21

THERE WAS A BLINDING white light. Her first suspicion was the obvious one, but her eyes adjusted, revealing a world unknown to her. She wasn't dead. At least, she didn't think so.

She was standing on a paved road beside a magnificent water fountain. In the center was a giant woman with a jar of water constantly pouring into the fountain. It must have been using a gravity siphon like the ones she read about.

The buildings were also somewhat familiar. Stone pillars cropped up porches. Some with red tiles on the rooftops, and others were too tall for Kate to see the tops. She gasped at the magnitude of the city. From where she stood, it expanded down to the ocean, where giant boats swayed in the blue waters.

She was standing in a city of Paradise Lost.

The people were wearing robes that wrapped around one shoulder. Drapey things with brightly colored sashes. Kate wondered if the sashes signified their status within the city. She was just about to ask an old man when he walked right through her.

It felt like...nothing.

How could someone walk through her? It was like she didn't actually exist. She waved her hand a few inches from a woman's face to receive the same response. After attempting to take a bite out of a man's loaf of bread that he held in his hands, Kate concluded she was not truly there. This was a memory, but whose?

Men marched around wearing costumes strikingly similar to Elijah's. The only difference was that they wore pleated skirts that cut at the knee, whereas he wore leather pants. She had long suspected he took them off a victim or found them. Kate didn't blame him. The skirts were uncomfortably exposing. She had never seen so many half-naked men in her life, and she lived with two.

She questioned the rationale behind exposing so much of their legs but wearing heavy helmets. While she could not feel the sun beating down on her, the people around her were panting and wiping their brows. They splashed their faces with water from a man-made river snaking through the city. Those must have been aqueducts of some sort. Despite her efforts, Kate could smell nothing, but if she could, she imagined the city did not smell as bad as Flosses did.

There were blacksmiths and pottery makers, things she recognized, but there were also great wagon-type things drawn by horses, and the sheer scale of everything felt overwhelmingly impossible. Men preached principles and theories on the streets, not religion. She wanted to listen but couldn't seem to focus on anything for too long. It was like her brain was overloaded, and she could only absorb her surroundings at face value.

That was when she saw him.

A man standing on a makeshift platform. His hair was a shiny black, and his eyes were blue, but it was Elijah. His skin was pale but healthy and without veins. Even from where she stood, she could see his teeth were not sharp. They were perfectly normal.

He was talking to the crowd, and young men were lining up to sign on a piece of parchment.

It was a recruitment of sorts. Elijah was recruiting soldiers. Was he a king? She didn't think so. He wore clothing similar to the philosophers. His sash was purple, like few she had seen on the streets. Elijah might have been nobility or a person of great wealth, but he was not royalty. The scene before Kate shifted and dissolved into countless grains of sand. She stumbled as she tried to back away.

Turning around, Kate found herself within a new memory.

There was grass beneath her feet, but not like the lush, healthy lands she knew. This was brown and patchy, as though the ground itself was poison. Kate turned in a complete circle. There were no trees. As far as her eyes could see, life did not exist. There were no birds in the sky or bugs crawling on the ground. There was nothing but rubble. Broken and muddied chunks of stone lay scattered. Kate approached a pile, and in it, the face of the woman from the fountain emerged from her camouflage. A raindrop plopped on her cheek and rolled down the way a tear would.

The white city was no more. She was standing in a wasteland. No light or life, only the aftermath of something terrible.

A massive, black metal boot came from the sky. It stomped on the pile. Kate fell back and crawled away as another foot sailed through the sky and shook the ground as it stomped half a mile away. Kate tried to see what it was, but the rest of the monster was obscured by blackened clouds.

It was Dominion. There was no other conclusion. Kate scrambled to her feet and rushed to the pile of rubble. The statue was no more. All that remained was a pile of sand. The winds were whipping her hair around her face, making it hard to see.

There was a roaring, rushing noise. In the distance, a wall of water was hovering, threatening to fall on her at any moment. She couldn't outrun such a thing, but there was no stopping her from trying.

Running from a memory did as much good as denying the future, and Kate was swept up in the current. Only, it wasn't water that crashed into her; it was countless armies. Rushing through and all around her. They drove carriages powered by steam as explosives erupted from tubes in their hands. Not unlike her projectile device.

She didn't want to know anymore.

"Elijah!" Kate shouted, hoping he was somewhere. That he could pull her from the nightmare that was his past.

Amid the countless legions of the monstrous army, one fully armored man shot at the metal giant. Pulling off his helmet, he revealed himself to be Elijah, back when he was just a mortal man.

The giant crushed the metal army underfoot. There was a droning mechanical noise that took the shape of laughter from the skies. Elijah reloaded his large-scale projectile device and took aim at Dominion once more.

A massive, metal hand with sharpened fingernails came down from the smoke-filled clouds. It was aiming for the front of his carriage. She cried out a warning, but Elijah couldn't hear her. In his hand was a torch, but he saw the creature coming, dropped the flame, and drew his sword.

"Get out!" he yelled, slashing at the workings of the carriage. Two horses fled from under the hood.

She gasped as the animals bolted. One of them was a beige mare. Kate shouted a cheer to the unhearing masses. He was trying to fight Dominion with his own instruments. It was folly, but solutions always appeared easy in the aftermath.

Abandoned on his unmoving carriage, Elijah whipped his sword into a striking position and charged at the feet of Dominion. Kate cringed. The attack was doomed to fail. Why would he risk himself in such a way? She looked around and understood his reasoning.

Elijah was not charging to defeat Dominion. He did so because there was nothing left.

All around her was devastation and wreckage. Nothing remained of the city nor the army that swept the lands. All their modernization and industry had taken the shape of a monster they could no longer control.

The man once called Elijah stabbed his sword into a space in the armored foot. It lodged deep in the toe. Elijah didn't even attempt to retrieve the sword. Dominion's mechanical laugh echoed in the skies before a thunderous voice said, "Do you really think that could kill me, boy?"

Elijah whistled, and out of the smoke, his horse came running. Kate cried out with relief at the sight of her. Oh, she was a smart girl indeed! He got on the horse and began to ride away, but not before calling back to Dominion, "But what was on my blade, monster?"

What indeed? Kate watched him ride away like she had so many times before. She wanted to run after him, but the future could not run toward the past. She watched as the giant hand scratched at the boot. He was trying to find the sword, but his metal fingers were too large and bulky. It reminded her of Baxter trying to pull a splinter from his heel with his stubby fingers.

A growl that sounded like grinding gears boomed from the sky as Dominion itched and scratched at the foot. In what was most certainly to be an error, Elijah reared his horse around and watched in the distance. *Keep running, you fool! Ride as far as you can, and even then, never stop.*

A knee hurtled to the ground, cracking the very foundations of the earth. It split open, and a rush of water came flooding from the gap. Waters splashed, and a hissing noise erupted from the knee so loud that Kate was forced to cover her ears.

The wet joint strained and refused to budge. Dominion was trapped, and the waters were rising. "The Waters come for you, monster!" Elijah taunted. "The promised messiah has come!"

Kate rolled her eyes. Of course he thought he was the messiah.

All but Dominion's head was revealed. He was shrinking and lessening by the moment. A second knee fell into the waters, sending another eruption of steam into Kate's face. Waving away the smoke, she watched as prickly vines sprouted from the wound in his foot. She laughed. He stabbed a sword laced with prickly blackberry seeds into Dominion. Everyone knew those vines were the bane of every gardener's existence. The only way one could grow them was to keep them in a pot. Otherwise, they would take over every inch of soil.

The only way to remove them was to burn every leaf, stem, and berry. Yanking them out, even at the root, did not stop the invasive species. As Dominion hacked away at the vines, they fell to the ground. They would root themselves in the earth, as barren and poisoned as it was, and continue to thrive.

Elijah was gloating. He was laughing and taunting the immobile giant. She could understand the urge to laugh at the triumph of defeating the destruction of everything one loved, but even still, it was not an attractive look.

"Messiah?" Dominion asked. "So, humans want someone to save them from themselves? She has not delivered, but I will because I am a generous god."

His hand lunged then. Kate's heart felt as though it were rupturing as Dominion grabbed Elijah, horse and all. The poor animal screamed in unison with the man as they were whisked out of Kate's sight.

The second hand clawed into the ground, where the rubble was crushed into what remained of Paradise Lost. Elijah and his horse were cast into the massive grave and swallowed up by the sand. "You can be my messiah. My final parting gift to humankind. A reminder of all that I have done for this world. A reminder to your goddess of what her creatures are capable of."

Kate fell to her knees and watched as time lapsed before her eyes.

Countless dawns rose and fell as the rains extinguished his flames and the vines covered every inch of metal. The Ghost King and his horse emerged from the grave each night. She watched as he threw the remains of his beloved city into the grave. Remnants dissolved into more sands until all that remained was an open grave of a desperate creature that could not die.

Kate approached him. She knew he couldn't see her, but she knelt beside him all the same. His hair was white, and his eyes were black, but it was still Elijah and not the Ghost King she had first met in the castle. With his head buried in his hands, he was the image of pure despair. His horse nuzzled his neck, and he rubbed her face, but his expression remained unchanged for what must have been decades.

There was shouting in the distance. She saw a group of men coming from a field of emerging saplings. They were shouting at him. Rather than face them, the Ghost King got on his horse and rode away. After all he had done for mankind, they hated and feared him. She wanted to shout at them, to berate the ignorant ghosts, but they were long gone.

The corpse of Dominion had been entirely devoured by nature. What was once metals and gears had been broken down and reshaped as part of the landscape. No more than a large hill in the countryside. Kate sat on that hill and watched the men in the distance as they built a tomb around the open grave.

They chiseled and carved the maze. It must have taken several years, but it was no more than a few minutes to her eyes. She was unable to determine whether it was in memory of Elijah and his defeat of Dominion or if it was peasant superstition to keep the Ghost King from escaping his grave. She suspected Elijah was right. It was the latter.

As time hurtled forward, Kate remained unchanged on her hill. She was beginning to wonder if she had died and was watching time repeat itself. Was this what came after death? Just a series of memories carried by the elements she was buried in.

There was a newfound respect for the funeral rites of her people. If this was indeed death, it meant that those burned in the pyres were never burdened by the past like those buried in the ground. As if people instinctively knew the sins of their past awaited them in the earth.

One day, the Ghost King returned to the tomb. His horse pulled a cart of stone. Together, over the course of decades, then centuries, she watched him build what she knew to be his castle. It wasn't crumbling like she had always assumed, but rather unfinished. He built wall after wall with his tireless hands as if he were ensuring that no one could approach his tomb by mistake.

A bird landed on her hillside beside her. The first she had seen since the memories began. It dropped a seed before fluttering off. Fully expecting the seed to remain unmoved, she tried to pick it up anyway.

Except, she could.

All at once, the world became tangible. The air held moisture and lingering notes from the forest. The winds swept her hair, and between her fingers, the seed was hard. It was scratched by the bird's beak and cold as a pebble. A surprised giggle came from her as she held it. She could feel the cold. She could feel and touch once more!

She pushed the seed into the hilltop with utter glee and watched as it rose from a sprouting to a full-grown tree, and the world around her grew into a familiar shape. Kate found herself at the place where her story started, and she laughed.

Chapter 22

"Only you would laugh in a grave," he whispered in her ear.

As if she had woken from a dream, Kate was conscious and in her still body. Partially covered in the sand that was cold no longer. There was a dawning realization that Elijah's arms were wrapped around her. The arrows had been removed, but she didn't know if that was his doing or the sand's.

"I saw..."

She couldn't explain it all. Centuries had flown by within what might have been minutes. Her hands sought the wound in his chest, but it was no more. "How long?"

"Time is not easy to grasp within the sands," Elijah said. "I know what you saw, for I see it every time I sleep. We've been here less than an hour."

Kate sat up and touched her torso. There was no pain. She also noted—with a major concern—that she did not need to draw breath. She turned to Elijah, who nodded. "You are something like me now. I'm afraid you'll never be able to see your people again."

So, she was now enveloped in a deadly blight for all eternity?

Yet when she raised her hands to her face, Kate could still sense something. It was not the fires she once knew, but the blight that surrounded them shifted and focused on the tips of her fingers. Elijah sat up as he took notice. "How are you doing that?"

"I controlled my fires in this way," she said. "It stands to reason that I can control the blight the same way."

Swaying her hand left and right, the cold shifted. She pushed against it, and the blight expanded. Kate pulled, and the blight contracted before extinguishing it almost completely. They needed the blight in the same way she once needed her fire. She couldn't snuff it out entirely, but it wouldn't be a danger unless she willed it.

"Amazing," Elijah said as he cupped her face in his hands. "You are the Water's mercy, made flesh."

She kissed him then. His lips parted, and a soft groan escaped his throat. Pulling her closer by the waist, his mouth sought hers with an urgency that only existed in her most private of thoughts. His sharpened teeth cut her lips. Blood dripped down her chin and fell in frozen droplets into the sand.

They would make new memories in the sand. Happy ones that would allow them to sleep in gentle bliss.

"Knock them down!" a muffled voice sounded from the tomb doors.

Breaking from their kiss, she let out a frustrated sigh. Just when things were getting good. "I suppose we must deal with them."

Unfazed by the ruckus at the door, Elijah was wiping blood from her lips with his thumb. Staring so intently at them as if nothing else mattered. In the grand scheme of things, she supposed he was right. The lives of those behind the doors were as brief as the fleeting days and nights that she saw in the memories.

But if they did not deal with the soldiers, they might decide to take their frustrations out on the village, and that could not happen.

Rising to her feet, she extended a hand to Elijah. "The sooner we eliminate our enemies, the sooner we can move on to more pleasant things."

He was on his feet and leaping out of the grave. "Let's not waste any time. For now, I have reason to cherish it."

It was a gorgeous way of saying, "Hurry up and jump into bed with me." Kate giggled as he pulled her out of the grave.

Behind the door, the men were counting before they threw themselves at the entrance. Elijah moved to open the door, but she stayed his hand. "Do that, and they will run headlong into the grave. Then we'd have blighted soldiers to contend with."

He smiled a ruthless smile. The soldiers smashed against the door, and it gave a few inches. With clawed hands, Elijah gripped the door and pulled it open. The blight was still suppressed, so they didn't turn to ice straight away. Rather, the soldiers stared at them wide-eyed in a heap on the ground.

"Run," she said, forming a mass of concentrated blight in her hand. It didn't work so well when she attempted a ball of fire, but perhaps the blight would perform better.

Elijah watched the soldiers run away with fascination. She raised an eyebrow, and he said, "I'm not used to them running away. Just screaming and then...you know."

Mercy was a choice for most.

One of the cruelest aspects of Dominion's curse was that he took that away from Elijah. "It will be okay now," Kate promised him as she took his hand. "People will be able to enter your halls and stay in your guest rooms if you wish."

He hesitated at that. She imagined he built that dining hall not because it was secretly something he wished for but perhaps because he did not know what else to do with his time.

"We are not like them, Kate," he said. "We cannot live among them, and there can be no others."

She nodded. "I know."

Stepping forward, Kate followed the stench of body odor and the distinctly warm trail that smelled of ammonia. She kept the blight contained to a small radius around them just in case they encountered a lost soldier, but there were none. Content to follow, they scurried like rats toward safety.

The light of the dawn was brighter than it once was. It didn't hurt, but it was annoying. Perhaps this was why he preferred to ride at night. Her eyes couldn't dilate anymore. Were they as black as his, or was it a slower progression?

"Their leader abandoned them?" Elijah asked when they stood alone in the falling snow.

It seemed that way. Shawn must not have anticipated their return or assumed she and Elijah were dead. "He must have returned to the village to rally the remaining soldiers."

Elijah whistled, and the horse came trotting from around the corner. Mounting Gertrude, he helped Kate up, and together, they returned to the village to finish what Noranger had started over twenty years ago.

The horse lulled to a stop at the fork in the road.

Villagers were being rounded up from their homes and lined up along the freshly fallen snow. Shawn the Envoy was walking along them, twirling a crossbow in his hand. Elijah's hands squeezed the reins. He was resisting the urge to charge them for the sake of the villagers.

She exhaled, more out of habit than anything, and dismounted the horse.

Elijah remained in the saddle until Kate turned and said, "You can walk among them now."

He blinked. "Right," he said, dismounting the horse.

Soldiers shouted and clumsily lined up to protect the envoy, who motioned for them to sheathe their swords. "What is this?" he asked, strolling toward her.

She found her fathers and Lori in the line. They stared at her, horror-stricken. She hadn't exactly had time to look in a mirror, but she imagined she appeared different. More like the Ghost King.

"I'm okay," she assured them, but they didn't respond.

"Look at me when I'm talking to you," Shawn demanded.

Elijah growled and confronted the envoy, as if daring him to speak again.

Shawn stumbled back.

Looming over the envoy, Elijah had every intention of smashing his face in.

Kate grabbed him around the waist and pulled him away. "Don't! Your touch would still kill him."

That clearly wasn't an issue in his mind. It would take time for him to relearn the humanity he lost to the centuries of isolation. She only hoped she would be strong enough to help him.

"Look at what he's done," Elijah said, motioning to the lifeless body on the ground. "Why does he deserve to live?"

Kate knelt beside the body, careful not to touch it. She recognized the flat brown hair. He was one of Bethany's sons. She looked up at the seamstress. One of her eyes was black, and her once beautiful dress had been torn. Her eyes were red, and tears streaked across her dirty face.

Bethany broke into mournful sobs.

They killed her sons. Her heart broke for the seamstress. The pain she must have felt was unfathomable. "I'm so sorry," Kate whispered.

She turned to face Shawn the Envoy and said, "Go back to your king. Tell him what happened here. Tell him that the Ghost King lives and rules over this province. If you step foot on these lands again, you will be killed on sight."

The envoy lowered his head and nodded. He turned and motioned for a retreat with a circular motion of his hand. She gave Elijah a reassuring smile when the envoy suddenly turned back. There was a meaty noise, and something was plunged into her stomach.

There were cries of fear and panic, but she felt no pain. Shawn's grin fell into the utmost terror that one has when they seal their own fate.

She looked at her stomach then. The sword was still embedded in her belly, and Shawn's hand was still on the hilt. It was an odd sensation. She felt the sword puncture her flesh, but that was it. There was confusion...a great deal of it. One never knew how to react to being stabbed, she supposed.

Lori screamed, and her fathers were held back. Elijah hissed between pointed teeth, but Shawn was determined to finish what he had started. Emboldened by her new death-defying ability, Kate stepped forward.

She took another step, but the envoy was too horrified to let go or step away. His hand was within inches of her. His hand turned black. It seemed she didn't have total control of the blight. Such a shame.

The envoy shrieked and tried to pull away, but his hand broke off instead. Kate gave an exaggerated sigh as she pulled the sword from her belly. She tossed the sword, hand and all, at the feet of the kneeling envoy. It hit the ground with a dull thump.

"If all six projectile devices and blueprints are not dropped at my feet within ten minutes, I'm going to take a hand from each and every one of you."

And six devices were dropped into the snow.

"I burned the blueprint in the fire before they broke in," Papa said through trembling lips.

She winced. His reaction hurt more than the sword wound that was knitting itself shut.

Was he just cold, or did he fear her? She hated the idea of her fathers being afraid of her. Perhaps they would come to accept her in time. Then again, maybe that was why Elijah said they must remain alone.

"Thank you, Papa."

There was a glimmer of recognition in his eyes, and Kate smiled, suspecting it would take far more than a ghastly new appearance to keep her fathers away.

The soldiers helped their fallen leader to his feet and got him on his horse. She watched as they rode off without food or supplies. Elijah tilted his head as he watched them run away as though it were a magical thing. She supposed mercy was a type of magic.

Frank and Baxter approached, but Kate stopped them short of her blight. "You can't touch me anymore."

Dad was already sobbing, and Papa held him close. "You're like him now."

"More or less," she confirmed. "But I can control our blight."

Elijah joined her side, and there was a moment where she forgot they were immortal divine creations. She was no longer a blighted messiah, and he was not the creation of Dominion. She was just a daughter, introducing a boyfriend to her parents.

"Dad, Papa," Kate said, gesturing to the Ghost King, "this is Elijah."

Their heads bobbed in nods, but she suspected it was more like shock.

"It's nice to meet you," Elijah said with a formal bow.

She had never introduced a man to her parents before, but she was pretty sure bowing was awkward. They would need time to adjust, including Elijah.

"The village is safe once more," she said, loud enough for everyone to hear. "Each of you had a part in that, and I am so grateful for everything you have done. You sheltered me when I had no one. Protected me even when you feared me. Tried to avenge my village when their attackers returned. I owe you everything." Kate's eyes were on her fathers as she said that last bit.

"You are going back to the castle," Baxter said.

Kate nodded. She couldn't exist in the village no more than they could endure the castle. She turned around, allowing Elijah to escort her back to the horse. Not knowing whether she'd see her parents ever again.

"But you'll still visit, right?" Frank shouted from a distance.

She grinned at Elijah, who only stared at her blankly. Looking over her shoulder, Kate said, "As often as you like."

Chapter 23

T HE STRANGE WINTER HAD concluded its business, allowing for a spring full of blooms and new developments. Wooden stakes marked freshly leveled ground for the foundation of a town hall. In no small part thanks to the inventors who had struck a small fortune selling their fire starters.

Jasper brushed out his colt before double-checking the connection to the merchant's wagon. "We should set off soon," he said to the merchant, who was preoccupied with the librarian.

"Yeah," Harvey said before returning his gaze to Lori. "Hey, when I come back, there's something I'd like to talk to you about."

Lori's eyes narrowed from under her glasses. "If you're referring to that ring I found in the drawer..."

Choking on his own surprise, Harvey was silent for once in his life.

Lori grinned and nodded. "We'll talk about it."

Beside the library, the empty house was being unlocked by a newcomer to the village. An older man with far too many young children. He opened the door and hung up a sign in the window that said, "Barnum's Printing Press."

Nothing had changed for the blacksmith as he worked the forge on his porch. Each hit with his hammer clanked a constant, familiar rhythm that the village went by. The tanner tanned alongside their home, and the grocer haggled with a merchant over exorbitant prices.

The butcher's shop was fully set up and no longer smelled like a slaughterhouse. Mostly because her new bride refused to be carried over the threshold otherwise. She and Roy worked out a deal and built a shack to conduct the necessary aspects of her work.

"Psst," she yelled out the window, forcing the grocer's attention. "I heard a bakery is coming to town. Watch your britches, grocer!"

Straightening his vest like she had touched it with her bloody hands, he said, "Good! I'm a grocer, not a baker. We'd be better off for it."

The butcher cackled before going back inside.

Roy, the farmer, had many new additions.

"Too many," his wife complained as she rubbed her full belly. "We have far too many animals and not enough hands."

"I asked Jasper to hire some farmhands for us on his first merchant trip."

Nearly every female sheep on his farm was as pregnant as his wife. By his count, there were sixteen babies due in the summer months. "Waters preserve us," he said, rubbing his brow. The farmer hoped his son was better at selling wool than he was at herding sheep.

Bethany, the seamstress, had gone to Flosses for an embroidery competition. That left her remaining sons free to receive tips from the old inventor on how to brew beer. The two of them had been conspiring together on a copper still that the boys kept hidden in Baxter's woodshed.

"That is a good still," Baxter said, rubbing the belly of the contraption. "You read all the books Lori gave you?"

They eagerly nodded.

"Be sure to follow the directions. Bad alcohol can make you go blind," he warned.

One blanched at that, but the other son was self-assured, as most young men were prone to be.

The inventor eyed them skeptically. "On second thought, I'll help you with the first few runs."

"Baxter," his husband called from inside the shop.

The big man's eyes went wide. "Got to go."

Inside the shop, there were some changes. Kate's worktable was moved out, and what was once their bedroom served as a tool room and pantry. Neither was prepared for their daughter's abrupt departure, but when they received word that she was visiting, they hurried to make it appear otherwise.

Frank was flittering around, picking things up, arranging, and rearranging the plates on the table. Baxter was getting motion sickness just watching his partner. "We haven't seen her in months," he said. "Do you think she's happy?"

"She better be," Frank said. "I'm not moving that bed."

Kate sounded happy in her letters. With the blight under control, they could send letters that were deposited into a letterbox a safe distance from the castle. Frank had asked her to come several times, but she was always busy.

"She spends all day in that castle. What could possibly be keeping her so busy?"

Baxter had a few suspicions. They were young once too, and it surprised him that the obvious hadn't occurred to Frank. "Well," Baxter started. "They are like newlyweds, I imagine."

Frank turned to stare at him, his face fixed in horror. "Oh..."

Baxter nodded, but his husband kept going.

"Why didn't I think of that? He's been alone for centuries, after all."

He was going to make this dinner awkward, wasn't he?

The sun had finally settled on the horizon, and so had Frank, who was draped in a chair, staring at the door. Not that Baxter wasn't doing the same. Life was just so different without their Kate. This was the natural progression as a parent. A child should grow up and move out. It was a sign that the parents had done well.

But that didn't mean they had to like it.

The last thing either of them wanted was for Kate to feel like they were lost without her. So, they did their best to make it appear as though life had moved on. It wasn't as though they were unhappy. There was so much more room, and they could do as they pleased; it was just different. And different was hard for old men.

A soft knock came from the door.

Invigorated by the fact that she was there at last, both men sprang to their feet and welcomed their daughter home.

Over the last few months, she had been testing the limits of her powers and the extent to which she could control the blight.

Mainly, she practiced when the children of the village came to the top of the hill and dared one another to touch the castle. It was an ideal exercise for her, and Elijah found the children amusing. As the children cursed and fell over one another, he let out something that was almost a chuckle.

Some things happened faster than others.

She could touch things without them turning to ice, and she was even able to plant a new tree in the courtyard without killing it. The cherry blossom tree had ended its season, but she found several seeds waiting for germination. The sapling grew from the dead stump with a rapidness that suggested magic was involved.

"It's growing so fast," she told Elijah.

"Too fast," he said. "This is not our magic."

She sensed much of the same. Somewhere in the world, something had awoken, and their little sapling could feel it.

"Come," Elijah said, with a gentle brush against her arm. "Your fathers await."

The thought made her nervous, but she had promised to visit and had been coaching Elijah on table manners and suitable conversations. It would be fine. Everything would be fine. She just hoped her parents would love him as much as she did.

Riding into town, they received a wave from Lori and the blacksmith from the windows. People were still too afraid of the blight to come out, but there was progress and growing trust. Elijah would need to learn to trust as well.

"The lanterns are still lit," he said as he stared at the flames. His black eyes reflected the light. She gave his hand a squeeze.

Such little things, but they meant everything to him.

Kate gave Elijah another glance before knocking on the door that was once hers. It was strange to knock, but it wasn't safe for her to just barge in as she once did. What if she ran into one of them and hurt them?

She had control of her power, but she wanted to be cautious. She had more fathers than most, but she wasn't willing to part with either.

Elijah was reluctant to go. The last thing he wanted was to accidentally kill her fathers, but Kate insisted she could handle it.

"But what if something happens?" he asked as they dismounted Gertrude. "I don't want you blaming yourself."

She knew his fears were not entirely about the blight. He was the Ghost King. Lone rider and death incarnate. Not exactly the parent-approved possible future son-in-law most had in mind. Pulling him into an embrace, she kissed him, and Elijah went silent. "They will love and accept you."

The door opened, and her fathers greeted them. Frank moved to hug her but jumped away as if remembering. Kate hugged him instead. He was ridiculously warm, but then again, she might have been on the cold side.

"You can control it?"

"Almost entirely," she said, letting Frank go. She hugged Baxter for a long moment as well. "Frank, Baxter, this is Elijah."

"And Gertrude," Elijah said, motioning to the porch where the mare stood unmoving.

Frank's brows went over the rim of his glasses. "Gertrude."

Kate cringed. Of all the things they practiced, he opted to introduce his horse. Interacting with people had been a challenge for the last several centuries. He spent many years conversing with the horse. It made sense; she just wished he went in with a "nice to meet you."

"Come in," Baxter said. "Have a seat."

They sat, and Kate glanced at the space that was once her work area. Of course, it was empty. It was good to see they were adjusting to her sudden departure. What was once their bedroom had been reverted to a storage area. It was good. She imagined they put all her stuff away and perhaps sold the things she wouldn't have wanted to keep.

It was like her time with her parents was a dream or something that happened ages ago. Elijah told her time worked differently for them. This must have been what he meant. She knew things would change but didn't expect the surreal detachment to the place she once called home.

She forced a smile and said, "I see the town hall is coming along."

"Yeah!" Frank said, pouring tea for everyone. "We're thinking it will be a sort of community center too. A learning place for kids during the day and, of course, more official stuff."

Easing into her chair, Kate's smile became earnest. "That's a wonderful idea."

"Are there a lot of children in the village?" Elijah asked.

Baxter raised his brows. "Roy and his wife are expecting twins. The butcher got married too."

"And don't forget all those orphan boys Mr. Barnum employs for the printing press."

Kate's eyes lit at that. Of all the changes in the village, she was most eager for the printing press. "He could print the books in the library," she said, looking at Elijah.

"Or you could write one of your very own," Elijah said.

She knew what he was doing. Dragging her parents into it wasn't fair!

"You're thinking of writing a book?" Frank asked.

"Elijah wants me to publish my thoughts and ideas," she said. It was sweet, but she worried it was too much of a vanity project. She thought the Ghost King was a work of a fallen civilization and not the gods, but she was wrong, as it turned out.

It's true he was born during that time, but they certainly did not make him. She still wanted to modernize medicine, but she was only just beginning her research. As it turned out, the scholars in Taus were much more receptive to the queen of the nameless province than they were to Kate of the nameless village. She held ongoing correspondence with their scholars, and she was even consulted on a variety of topics.

"I'm not ready to write a book yet," she said. "But I recently was asked to hold a lecture at the university."

Elijah was glowing with pride. Frank nearly dropped the serving spoon in his hand.

"That's amazing!" Baxter said. "I was worried you would give up on your dreams after getting married. Too many women do that."

"I wouldn't allow it," Elijah said. "She's too important to mankind to keep all to myself."

"He's...exaggerating," she said through her clenched smile. It was one thing to be loved by a man who thought she did no wrong; it was another when he thought she was literally a messiah.

Over the last few months, he had brought up the idea. There were many conversations and debates that ended with a frustrated Elijah as he struggled to speak his mind in an articulate way.

Kate found this to be true for herself as well. When it came to matters that she understood in her heart but had no logical basis for. She had a theory that the sands held so many memories of the past that their minds struggled to comprehend it all.

This led to knowing with the heart. Memories took shape in their hearts in the form of feelings and not tangible words and knowledge the mind could explain with words.

It was fascinating. When Kate went about testing this theory, poor Elijah started hiding from her. At some point, he took to locking himself in the tower just to get a break from her. She was beginning to understand so many behaviors her parents exhibited, including the one where Baxter went fishing alone.

Frank served them buttered bread with fresh green beans and parts of a roasted chicken. She felt bad they went through the expense. "I'm sorry, I should have said something sooner, but we don't eat."

She glanced at Elijah, who was inspecting a green bean like he had never seen one before. "This," he said. "It's not indigenous to our lands."

Kate and her fathers exchanged surprised glances. "What do you mean?" she asked.

"Precisely what I said. Someone would have had to bring this form of bean from another continent. It did not occur naturally on these lands."

Frank's bottom fell into his chair as her fathers stared at Elijah as he casually revealed something all of them thought impossible.

"But that would mean they had boats big enough to cross seas," Baxter said. His interest was more in the boats than anything. Being from a port town, constructing larger boats was always a point of debate.

"They're called ships," Elijah said, setting the green bean back on the plate. "When Dominion began enslaving humankind, many people decided the best course of action was to flee the continent. I always liked to think they found other lands."

Baxter was nodding with approval. "I bet those ships could bring in massive fish."

"Oh yes, in the ocean, there are fish several times larger than a man."

The conversation was drifting to an odd kind of normalcy. Elijah knew a great deal about fish and boats, and Baxter wanted to know all about it.

"Kate, can you help me with the plates?" Frank asked while they carried on.

What her father really wanted was to get her alone to ask the questions that kept him up at night. She picked up the plates, and they put the leftovers in a pot. She noted that the pantry was full of food. Perhaps the chicken was just a part of their regular diet. "You guys have been doing well for yourselves," she said.

"Well, those fire starters sell faster than we can put them out. We even have competitors in other provinces."

Kate was impressed. "Baxter streamlined them and removed the device inside?"

"He did." Frank scraped the last of the chicken into the copper stock pot. Another new addition.

"How are you," he whispered. "Really?"

She smiled. "Excruciatingly happy."

Her father's cheeks flushed when he smiled. "And him?"

How could she explain it? A year ago, she nearly blighted herself to death to get to him, and now, he was talking about fish with Papa. She never imagined it would turn out this way, but she was so happy it had.

"He is the part of me I did not know I was missing. It just works," she said, washing the plates in the sink. "I can't explain it, but it's like I'm learning things about myself through him."

Frank shrugged. "It sounds like everything a father wants to hear," he said. "Though, I imagine children are not going to happen."

Kate shook her head. "We are essentially dead. We cannot die, but we also cannot create life. And if I am honest...I'm glad. I never wanted children."

She expected her dad to argue or be unhappy about her confession. Having children was the natural progression in life. It wasn't expected so much as it was simply an outcome between two married people.

"We didn't think we'd have children," Frank said, glancing back at Baxter. "Given that we're both men. But when we pulled you from that fire, everything changed. The village was hesitant to let us keep you. Bethany said a girl belonged with a mother, but they realized they would need to pry you from our dead arms and that it wasn't worth it."

"I don't imagine we'll come across a child in the castle," she said, omitting the children who often visited. The conversation was chartering uneasy waters that left her feeling nauseated.

"I'm just saying. Things change, even when you didn't think they could."

The hour was late, and Baxter was slumping over the table, trying his best to keep up with Elijah, who never tired.

"We should go," she said. "But you can continue this conversation later... Maybe next week?"

The visit went well. Her parents had all their fingers and toes still intact, and her rein on the blight remained in utmost control. And the best part was that Elijah appeared to enjoy himself. She saw no reason why they couldn't make these visits a regular thing. Perhaps she'd visit Lori soon as well.

They said their temporary goodbyes to her fathers. Elijah was about to get back on Gertrude, but Kate stopped him.

"I want to show you something."

She led Elijah through the woods to the hilltop. There, she took his hand, and together, they walked the rest of the way up. It wasn't that the mare couldn't handle the incline, but Kate wanted to be alone with Elijah. The horse always stared at them without blinking. It gave her the creeps, but she didn't have the heart to tell him.

Who knew what went on in the mind of an immortal horse?

"I came here often," she explained as they ascended.

"Ironic," Elijah mused.

The cherry blossoms were in full bloom and were beginning to shed their petals. "This is the tree I planted in your courtyard."

"Our courtyard."

She only said it because she enjoyed it when he corrected her. "I used to sit here and look at your castle. I had always hoped I'd see you walking the walls, but I never did. I guess I should have been out here during the night."

Elijah gave his castle a hard stare. "I used to feel it was my prison. With you, it feels like a home."

Wrapping his arms around her waist, he pulled her close. She draped her arms around his neck as he kissed her forehead. "Will you not consider making our relationship more formal?"

"We're bound in eternity," she said with a giggle. "How much more formal can it get?"

He looked to the sky and sighed. "I felt like a liar when I referred to you as my wife to your papa."

Kate understood. She, too, felt as though she had taken some liberties when she declared herself the queen of the nameless province. By all accounts, she was his bride. They shared a grave and bed alike. The only difference was that they had said no vows.

"I, Kate of the nameless village, take you, Elijah of Paradise Lost, to be my husband," she said with a grin. "For all eternity, come flood or famine, our love shall endure."

He frowned. "Is that the vow your people make?"

Was it not good enough for him? They were simple people with large problems. She had thought she gave it a nice touch with "all eternity" rather than using the phrase "By the Waters."

"More or less," she said.

"In my time, marriage was a ceremony that lasted for days."

She hadn't gotten to the books detailing marriage and family life yet. "Sounds overwhelming and a bit impractical."

"Hm... I suppose your fathers would be confused if I sent goats wearing jewelry."

The image of goats covered in gold chains and gem-encrusted rings on their horns sent Kate into a fit of laughter that probably echoed throughout the lands. Her fathers' faces... It would be priceless.

Elijah didn't quite laugh, but he was smiling. No doubt pleased with himself for making her eyes well with tears in a good way. He had yet to learn how to cry himself.

"Maybe we should," she said. If the confusion of decorated goats roaming through town didn't get him laughing, nothing would.

His face softened as he regarded her.

In the safety of their solitude, Kate had released the blight, allowing it to form around them like a globe. The petals of the cherry blossom tree froze and blew away from the tree. Snow and petals flurried around them in the moonlight.

"Wherever you go, there also go I, your husband and protector."

Lost in the moment and the ages, they remained steadfast in their vows.

The Ghost King and the messiah ushered in a new age of prosperity for the continent. The wars of distant kings meant nothing in the face of their united power. The children's children of the self-declared kings laid down their swords and bowed at the Ghost King's feet. There would be no more war and no more villages burned.

In lands without borders, Kate could learn and share knowledge freely. When the time came, the Ghost King built a special bookshelf in the library (despite his wife's protests). There he set his most cherished books, a series titled *Devices of Man*.

About Author

A proud Washingtonian, S.M Fox lives in the Seattle area with her husband and children, and might be obsessed with her Great Pyrenees dogs, Teddy Brosevelt and Stevie Nicks. She was the first person in Washington State to obtain a small business license for selling Vanilla Extract, and can be found at the Farmer's Markets every summer.

Devices of Man is her full length debut novel.

Follow her on Twitter at:

https://twitter.com/SMFoxAuthor
and

Http://www.SMFoxAuthor.com

Flowers of Cardhon Nimloth

The oldest of their clan was dead.

Nesterin finally croaked at the age of one-hundred and sixty-five. It was a long life by clan's standards. But with her passing came a thrashing uncertainty within the hearts of the Runda Nor. The old, grumpy female might have been the last of their clan to be blessed with prolong life as her people would say. Radelia always thought it their god's way of punishing the clan for their ineptitude. Whatever the case, with Nesterin's passing was a reminder that the clan's former glory was never coming back.

Radelia stepped out of her hut and was greeted by the dewy forest air. Her hut, like all the others was little more than a child's treehouse with a nice circular balcony. The growing murmurs from the accumulating crowd could be heard even from several trees away.

Whatever was going on, it wasn't typical. The Runda Nor avoided the dead at all costs. Perhaps the old woman hadn't kicked it after all and gave the healers a few whacks with her cane to prove the point.

Grabbing hold of a rope, Radelia unfurled it from the post. The zipping of rope against wood was the only warning she had before her feet left the bridge. Hurtling upward, the wind pelted her face and whipped her hair. Closing her eyes, she smiled.

Letting go of the rope, she landed on a bridge three levels higher with a woody thud. The onlookers paid no mind. The Runda Nor wasn't the clan that bowed or fawned over their future empress. They'd leave that to the High Elves.

"Nesterin was found this morning," she said as the crowd gave way. "Why are you all standing around?"

"The healers won't touch her," Jonik said, motioning to the exposed doorway "It's their job, but they won't do it."

That was strange. Radelia didn't know why the healers would suddenly refuse to do their job. She tilted her head and made light of the situation. "Nesterin and that resin cane are Elpharae's problem now."

In the sprawling treetop village, only the healers were permitted to touch the dead. Everyone knew that except the healers, evidently.

Mutters of curses trickled from ear to pointed ear. Radelia shook her head. Few things frightened the Runda Nor. They would face charging boars and scale mountains, but when it came to the dead, they were paralyzed by terror.

Her father said it was because death wasn't natural to elves. They lived and endured the ages with grace and wisdom, and...well, she sort of stopped listening by then. But point was, her clan were descendants of a race that didn't typically die, so it was scary.

It wasn't that she couldn't relate. Death scared the shit out of her too, but someone had to deal with the body, or it would stink up the whole village. Nesterin's final petty senior revenge.

"Is there a healer here?" Radelia asked, her eyes scanned the crowd.

One emerged from the hut, wiping her hands on her apron as she whispered a prayer. Radelia smiled. Katar may have been a healer, but her best friend wasn't the holier than thou type that caused scenes like the one Radelia was currently dealing with.

Katar nodded for Radelia to join in her inside. She hesitated for a moment. Hanging out in a hut with a dead body gave her the creepy crawlies, but she entered the hut anyway. "Why are they refusing to do their job this time?"

"Many of the healers claim they can hear Elpharae no longer," Katar said. Her brown, chin length hair was poking out of her healer's cap. "They think our god has forsaken us and they won't be protected if they touch the body."

"Is that it? I thought perhaps she left a curse on the hut."

"She did," Katar said with a mischievous grin. "I burned it before anyone saw it."

The healers weren't protesting because Nesterin threatened to haunt them from the grave for giving her daughters her cups or something, at least, not to their knowledge. They found some other reason to shirk their duties.

"It's always something with the healers," Radelia grumbled, glancing at the lump still in the bed. She looked so small in her bed despite the piles of fur she had accumulated over her multiple marriages. The hag outlived all six of her husbands and had the furs to prove it.

"Yes, but this time I fear they're right. Another babe was born last night..."

Radelia put a finger to her mouth and shushed her. She glanced at the doorway to make sure none of the others had heard. Her father had been trying to keep the problem under wraps. The last thing she or her father needed was for the clan to learn that babies were born without their elf characteristics.

"Rounded ears?" she whispered.

Katar nodded. Moisture accumulated along her lash line. When Katar was scared—which wasn't often—her eyes instantly teared up. Maybe it was true. If Elpharae had forsaken the Runda Nor, what would become of her clan? After everything they sacrificed to worship them, just for them to abandon the clan was, well, it was unbelievably fucked up.

"Maybe it's not their fault," Radelia offered, hoping it would ease Katar's fears. "Something might be blocking their voice, their power."

Katar cracked a smile and brushed Radelia's cheek with a warm hand. "How is it your skin never dries, even in the winter air?"

Any conversation that veered away from the things Radelia could not control were welcome. The future empress wanted to be a strong leader for her people. To be a graceful and otherworldly elf like in the stories her father regaled them with as children. She wanted to lead with the wisdom of ages and the spirit of Elpharae.

But in truth, refinement was not a trait used to describe Radelia Bellas.

"A good beauty regimen," Radelia teased. "One that involves fresh air, lack of food, the occasional bath, and no small amount of dirt."

"Ah ha," Katar said in a mocking tone. "Well, I don't suppose you'd take a break from such a rigorous schedule to help me with the remains."

Something inside Radelia squirmed. She didn't want to be anywhere near the body, but she wasn't about to let Katar do everything herself. Her father helped the clan in any way he could and so would she. High Elf kings sat on thrones while their people did the dirty work. It was why her people left Cardhon Nimloth in the first place. Among other things...

"I didn't come to watch," she said, reaching for the apron hanging on an uncut branch. "How can I help?"

Using an old cart delegated to the task of ferrying the dead to the mountain, Katar and Radelia each grabbed a railing and pulled it through the forest. When her mother had died, there was scarcely a trail. But in the twenty years since her mother's death, the way to the mountain was trampled, and the dirt underfoot was smooth and hard.

"Would you rather deal with a latrine blockage or eat snails alive?" Katar asked. It was a game they played when tasked with mundane work.

Straining to pull the cart through a wet patch, Radelia grunted and cursed something crude enough that even Katar's brows raised. The cart finally gave, but the sudden lack of tension caused her to trip. If she wasn't an elf, she'd be ass over face in the mud.

She considered her friend's question. Radelia had done both things at one point or another and she wasn't sure that she had a preference either way. They were both shitty options that left her cringing on the inside. The hollowed bamboo pipes that carried sewage from the treetop huts to the latrine pits below were notoriously unreliable. But it was either that or countless elf asses hanging over windows.

When shit hit the ground from that height, did it splatter into nothing? Game was the clan's food staple, so she imagined the hunters would still need to watch their step.

Her lips twisted around on her face before Radelia said, "Live snails, I guess."

Katar's mouth opened as if she were about to heave the dried meat they had for breakfast. "But they are wriggling and slimy..."

"And so is the shit."

Too far?

As a healer, Katar seldom did manual labor. She had a trade and apprenticed for years with some of the most skilled healers they had. They joined the apprenticeship together, but it wasn't long until her father sat her down and explained that she wasn't suited for the work.

In other words, the healers ran to her father and complained so much that she was kicked out.

After a brief stint in the military, and a traumatizing afternoon in the nursery, it was decided that Radelia was best suited for tasks that required a strong arm and problem-solving skills. Unburdened by others.

Katar's eyes screwed shut. "Ah! I wish you didn't tell me that!"

Radelia grinned. Her friend's reaction was worth it. "They're not so bad once you get used to them."

The healer gave her an incredulous look and cried out, "Why?"

"If I'm hunting, I don't always have time to stop and set up a fire. I'd rather eat raw snails than lose the beast and have a village of hungry elves to contend with."

Katar was quiet then. As if Radelia said something thoughtful for once.

The forest air was sweet and piney. Birds called to one another across the canopy and the ferns rustled with the occasional breeze that shifted through the woody maze. The forest was home. It was where Radelia's soul drank from a well of fortifying peace.

Her pointed ears pricked. She let go of the splintery rail.

Katar said nothing, but she too stopped. It wasn't that they heard something, it was the opposite that gave them pause.

Searching the clusters of branches and leaves in the canopy, she noted the birds had gone quiet. The air was stifled by a silent threat, yet the trees themselves said nothing of the trespasser. Radelia's mind instantly went to the worst-case scenario; High Elves.

If it was a hunter from the Runda Nor, the birds wouldn't notice. Only an elf unfamiliar with the forest could alarm the birds. Trees were never the most observant beings. To them, all elves looked the same, and if they didn't hold axes, the trees didn't care what they did.

Daggers materialized in Katar's hands, and she was poised for an attack. Radelia almost felt sorry for the High Elf, except she didn't. Not a stone's throw away from where they stood, her mother had been found. Her leg had been badly broken, and her throat slit. Radelia had no intention of turning it into a family tradition.

Her mother had broken her leg on a hunt when she was found by High Elves. Rather than waste their magic on healing her, they killed her the way one puts down a lame horse. Such a typical High Elf move. Just because they still had magic didn't mean they got to decide who was or wasn't worthy of it. Her mother deserved it. Damn them for thinking otherwise.

The only warning they got was a break of an errant breeze. Someone was behind them. Radelia and Katar spun around at the same time. Notching her arrows, Radelia followed the movement, ready to strike. Daggers flew from the healer's hands in a rapid succession. Where did she keep them all?

There was a cry of surprise from a recognizable voice.

In a blur of movement that even Radelia struggled to register, Katar had pinned someone to a tree with her daggers. It was General Kieran, and he was scowling at the healer as if she had pissed in his shoes.

Radelia folded her arms and laughed. "High and mighty General Kieran," she said with a mocking bow. "What are you doing out here?"

The general had the dark brown skin of his mother but the most unusual hair color. It was a burnished red. Not like her bright, copper color, his reminded her of wood stain. No one else had hair like it. Some said he used henna dye, but if that was true, he had been using it since they were children.

His voice was slow and deliberate as if it took every bit of willpower to keep from throttling the healer. "I came to help."

"If that were true, why not actually help rather than trail behind us for half the journey?" Katar asked, her grip did not lessen in the slightest.

Radelia's eyes shifted between the two. Had he really been following them the entire time? General Kieran was a busy elf. For him to take time out of his day for anyone was unusual. Her cheeks went flush. Out of the three, she knew the forest far better, yet the general was able to trail them without her detection. Katar had somehow known all along. So much for being good at something.

"Couldn't live without me?" Radelia asked with a grin and a wink.

Kieran sighed and rolled his eyes. "Just get me down from here."

Once the general was freed from the staggering number of blades, Radelia watched as Katar put each of them back. If was captivating! There were hidden pockets in the healer's flowing sleeves, in her apron pockets, inside the apron, she even had a few in her cap.

At some point the small blades were being tucked into a garter. Radelia leaned over and said, "I didn't even see you lift your skirt."

Katar laughed. "I'll never give away my secrets."

"No," Kieran said, his back was turned to them. "But you give everything else away."

Radelia turned to give him a piece of her mind, but Katar was always quicker.

"Remind me to visit your first lieutenant tonight, I haven't gotten her yet."

They always bickered like that. It was probably why Kieran didn't want to make himself known and why Katar was happy to ignore him for a time.

"What is it with you too?" Radelia asked.

"You keep poor friends," Kieran said. "She will lead you astray from duty."

"Says the elf who is shirking his duties to stalk us doing ours!" Katar flared back at him like a child who was unjustly scolded.

"No, *we* are all friends. At least we used to be," Radelia said. Her throat was raw and tight. The air was too muggy. She needed to be free.

Radelia took off. Running into the forest while Kieran and Katar called and pleaded for her to come back. They could push that cart up the mountains and feed the beast birds themselves.

Slowing only when she came to the edge of the forest, she scaled up a branchy tree and perched at the top. The horizon was something they seldom saw living among the trees, so Radelia squinted against the unrelenting light.

The world was so big from up there.

She felt so overwhelmingly small in that moment. The lands of man were green rolling hills and planted in the middle of it all was a ginormous living castle. The birthplace of all elf-kind and the source of their magic, dwindling as it may be. The only hope for the Runda Nor was to reclaim it just as her father said, but they still had to convince General Kieran.

Also By S.M Fox

Next in the series...

Flowers of Cardhon Nimloth